# BLIND

## ALLEGIANCE

# BLIND
## ALLEGIANCE

MIKE KENNEDY

Book design copyright © 2019.
*Cover design by Jim Villaflores*
*Interior design by Vanz Edmar Mariano*

Published in the United States of America

ISBN: 978-1-7339772-1-0
Fiction / Thrillers / Espionage
April 24, 2019

# Dedication

To my wife, Andrea.
Thank you for 30+ years of love and friendship.

# Acknowledgement

I would like to thank my wife Andrea and our children Shawn, Cameron, Shannon, and my daughter-in-law, Veronica. You have always supported me as I continue to write my Mark Springfield novels.

To my readers, Mark Salvatore, Danny Ricci, and Brian Jones, your input and encouragement is treasured. Thank you for your continued support.

To everyone who has read THE HUUT and Red Fortress ob der Tauber, your enthusiasm keeps me writing. I truly hope you find Blind Allegiance as intriguing as the previous two. Thank you!

# THE HUUT

T HE HUUT is book 1 in the Mark Springfield trilogy. It revolves around the Huntsville Unit, a unique satellite system that has the ability to image deep beneath the surface of the earth. When China reveals its knowledge of the HUUT's existence, the CIA plants operative, Mark Springfield to work as a double agent. Unknown to the CIA, Russia has their own spy working within their very midst.

It is an intriguing espionage novel that examines the high stakes involved when both China and Russia attempt to steal American satellite technology and the extent to which a country's agent will go in order to return to his homeland as a hero.

# RED FORTRESS
# OB DER TAUBER

Red Fortress ob der Tauber is book 2 in the Mark Springfield trilogy.

Ramous Bohdan, one of the CIAs top operatives, has a decision to make. Wait and leave Russia with the information he has been sent for or leave with a secret he has just received from a long-retired KGB agent. The new information is so powerful that it will shatter the already fragile relationship between Russia and the United States. Unbeknownst to Ramous, he is being stalked by a beautiful Russian agent.

Mark Springfield races his Ducati Monster 821 hard across Europe and into Russia. The freezing cold finds every small opening in his black leathers. His premonition about his fellow agent has forced him to become relentless in getting to Ramous. If he is still alive, Mark will need to use every trick in the book to save him.

Learn the special tie the KGB agent had with President John F. Kennedy and how it could have changed the course of American history.

# BLIND ALLEGIANCE

# Prologue

*January 24th 2003*
*Scientific drilling ship, the Resolution research vessel*
*Anchored, 7900 feet above the Atlantis Bank*
*Far off the Southeast Coast of South Africa*

"Doctor, the instruments indicate we are close to your suggested depth."

Doctor Stanton laughed. He turned to his young protégé who had just entered his office and jovially said, "It's not *my* depth, James. It's where the aquifer is." With a big smile, he added, "And where our microbes live." He turned back towards the map that hung on the wall of his small office, and with his middle finger, he pushed his round, silver glasses up the bridge of his nose. His bushy white hair covered the temples of the glasses making it look as if his spectacles were balancing on the bridge of his nose.

Picking up a pencil, he circled a spot seven thousand, nine hundred feet beneath the surface of the ocean. At the bottom of the ocean floor sediment, he had drawn another circle. Next to the map, the CORKs (Circulation Obviation Retrofit Kit) digital depth gaugeread out displayed 825 which gave them a total of eight thousand seven hundred twenty-five feet.

Doctor Damon Stanton, scientist from the Oregon State University has been after the allusive microbes for years. A grant had sent him after the bacteria that live at one thousand feet beneath the bottom of the ocean floor, within the Earth's three and a half million-year-old crust. To be able to explore these depths and retrieve the life forms that live in it gave Doctor Stanton and his colleagues a unique opportunity to understand the life that thrive in the seemingly hostile environment. "James, what is the temperature of the crevice next to our collection point?"

James pulled a small notepad from the back pocket of his blue jeans, flipped it open, and ran his forefinger over several entries. Stopping halfway down his list, he flicked the paper with his fingers. "It's hot, sir. We are approaching one hundred forty-nine degrees Fahrenheit."

Stanton nodded his head. "Very good. It's what I expected." He continued to study his map and after several long seconds, he said, "Yes, the last of our one thousand feet below the sea floor. One hundred and seventy-five feet through the basalt, and we will be there. The CORK will be set." He turned and smiled at his associate. Then he walked to his desk and picked up a small light-brown wooden picture frame, which was adorned with pink ribbons and several small blue beads and held the picture of his wife and two teenage daughters. He said, "I'll be home soon, my loves."

"Doctor, shall we join the team on deck?" Still smiling, he jerked his head up and said,

"Yes, yes. Please, James, lead the way."

*February 3rd 2003*
*(Ten days later)*

Raymond Wesley, captain of the Resolution Research Vessel, studied the horizon. Below him on the decks his crew and the scientist he had ferried to the drilling site months ago were passing around bottles of champagne.

"Captain! The last of the microbe samples are being sent to the surface." There was champagne to drink and the call from the crewman over the radio had been rushed.

Nine samples had been collected and preserved in solution. Seven of the samples had been carefully secured in a safe. The eighth and ninth sample, SAAB-2003-105 and SAAB-2003-106 had been stashed in one of the crew's lockers. The sample that would be marked as SAAB-2003-107 was on its way to the surface.

On the bridge was an array of instrumentation for not only the ship's operation and navigation but, copied for the captain to monitor were gauges for the drilling process. This included the Blowout Preventer (BOP), a safety feature used to monitor and trap well bore pressure, especially in the event of a natural gas build-up in the casing.

The captain again looked out at the horizon. The ocean was calm and the sky took on a deep blue he had rarely seen. The lower half of his windshield had been swung open and a much-needed cool salty breeze filled the bridge. He reached over and tapped the BOP's digital readout. He bunched his eyebrows together wondering why none of them seemed concerned about the rising pressure. He glanced again at the party going on around the lower decks. He spotted some of the crew laughing with the scientist.

Suddenly, there was a chirp, followed by another. Three seconds later, alarms blared from around the ship.

The captain watched the BOP's pressure race quickly up the scale, turning from green to yellow. He knew it would soon turn red.

Seconds after the alarms started to blare, the Remote Operated Vehicle broke the surface in a white froth of foam. It turned in small circles and then ran itself into the side of the ship. Fifteen seconds after surfacing, while in its uncontrolled course, it had shut itself off. Its two operatorswere hunched over the control console. Both had been shot in the base of their skull with a 22-caliber handgun.

Larry Boshart tucked the handgun in his waistband and quickly left the dark control room and ascended the ladder from the lower deck of the research vessel. He glanced at his watch. *Five minutes.* He pursed his lips wishing he would have given himself more time.

When he opened the hatch to the main deck, the alarms that seemed subdued below appeared to suddenly screech an earsplitting tone that made him wince. He quickly ran through the opening and was almost knocked over by a crew member running to his station. The alarms continued to shriek from around the ship.

The killer ran through another hatch and hurriedly descended the ladder to the berthing area and straight to his locker. He quickly worked the lock's combination. When it failed to open, he smashed it with his fist. "Damn it!" On the second try, it snapped open. He threw the lock on the deck and violently swung open the door. He reached into the locker and pulled a small blue backpack that had been stuffed into the corner. Inside were the samples he had stolen earlier. Another quick check of his watch brought a heavy groan. "God damn it. Two minutes." He bolted towards the ladder and ascended it with three long strides. The yelling and piercing squeal of the alarms from around the ship was disorientating. He sprinted towards the port side of the boat.

Captain Wesley screamed into his microphone. "It's the well bore pressure!" No one else knew what had been causing the alarms. All of the gauges in the drilling control room had been altered and indicated normal as they monitored a sabotaged Blowout Preventer. Meanwhile, the BOP gauge on the bridge was running out of control.

Wesley stopped suddenly and looked at his crewman. The shudder that coursed through the superstructure of his enormous ship drained the blood from the captains weathered face.

The killer both heard and felt the ship groan as he slid down the shaking ladder towards the ocean. He abruptly stopped on a corrugated metal landing, ten feet above the water. Instead of taking the time to extend it, he jumped into the ocean and swam over to one of the two Avon Rigid Hull Inflatable Boats (RIB) that had been tied to the ship's lower rail. Boshart tossed the pack into the closest boat, grabbed the rope that had been threaded around the outside of the boat, and then pulled himself up and over the side.

From the upper deck, a sudden explosion tore the valves from the base of the drilling platform. Three seconds later, the C4 that he had placed earlier, using the cover of darkness, detonated. It caused a secondary explosion that sent an orange fireball miles into the sky. The blast ripped through the scientist and crew standing near the platform, and the blast wave propagated across the deck and shattered the windows on the bridge. It shredded everything and everyone inside.

The killer felt the right side of his face burn when the heat from the blast spread out across the ocean. He felt the ship shudder and push itself into the water. It rocked back and forth so violently that it caused the inflatables to smash into each other.

Boshart stumbled and then fell across the deck, ramming his head into the side of the steering console. Reaching the Avon's helm, he turned the key. Without hesitation the, twin 120 horsepower, Mercuries roared to life.

As the ship jerked around, it pulled the inflatable's mooring lines too tight for him to untie. Fishing a knife out of his pocket, he cut the boat free. Then he glanced at the Remotely Operated Vehicle that was bobbing in the ocean and cursed himself for setting the charges too soon. There was no time left to retrieve the additional deep-water sample. He pulled the throttle aft and shifted into reverse, quickly backing his RIB away from the doomed vessel. When the boat was clear, he jammed the throttles all the way forward to their stops.

The two Mercury outboards growled, their rotary teeth bit violently into the ocean and the Avon instantly climbed out of the water and up on a plane. Another violent explosion caused Boshart to instinctively duck his head. The blast pressure hit him across the back but he held tightly onto the steering wheel. Blood ran freely down his face from the two-inch gash left by his fall.

As a rock skips across a calm pond, the inflatable rocketed away from the ship. The killer hunched low and turned his craft west.

# 1

The hard crack of thunder mixed with the raw energy in the air stirred something inside and it made him smile. The flash from the distant lightning cast an eerie shadow around their small cabin.

Mark Springfield sat low in an old black leather chair. He stared through the rain-streaked, floor-to-ceiling windows and watched the lake appear with each flash of light, catching glimpses of his ramp and his eighteen-foot sail boat, which he was relieved he had covered earlier in the day. A sudden intense flash of light made Mark wince.

His five-foot, ten-inch, thick frame combined with his sharp wits had served him well as an agent for the CIA. However, he knew it was time to drive a desk after his sister, Mary had been kidnapped two years earlier. He had been working as a double agent trying to root out a mole spying for a foreign power. China was getting close to stealing The Huntsville Unit. The HUUT, a one-of-a-kind satellite, able to image deep below the surface of the earth and the U. S. pulled out all the stops to protect its existence. Once it had been discovered that China was trying to steal the technology, Mark had been planted as a double agent and it almost cost his sister her life. He thanked God everyday he had been lucky enough to have saved her. Mark looked up into the loft of the cabin and visualized his sister, Mary and her husband Cole asleep in the four-posted bed he had bought just for them.

Mark had acquired the cabin a year and a half ago through an estate sale. It had sat in disrepair for years. He had used a local contractor to strengthen the foundation and reroof, what he called, his lodge. However, most of the work had been completed by him. He had used all of his vacation time to renovate the eighty-year-old cabin. When he and Cole had set the last of the four floor-to-ceiling windows, it had given him a sense of accomplishment he seldom felt.

Another intense flash of light blinded him. He smiled, feeling an inner peace from the storm

"Uncle Mark, are you scared?" The question came from his niece Ashley. She had been sharing an air mattress with her older sister, Christina, who had been lightly snoring and unfazed by the storm going on around them. Another loud crack of thunder brought a slight screech from Ashley.

"Ashley." Mark chuckled. "What are you doing up?" He flipped his wrist to get a look at his watch. "Do you know it's three-thirty?" Mark looked over his left shoulder. He saw a lump buried deep beneath the doubled-up sleeping bags. He pushed himself up from his chair and reached over to the hide-a-bed he had been using and pulled off a blanket. "Come here before you wake your sister." Mark didn't have to ask twice, his niece bound from her bed and into his lap, her long black hair slapped across his face. She wrapped her arms around his thick neck and buried her face in his chest. Mark laughed as he brushed her hair away from his nose. "You're getting too old for this," he said, slapping her on the side of her leg.

"Never!" She yelped. "And I'm only eleven."

Mark pulled the blanket up and draped it over the both of them. He reached under the blanket and tickled her. When she yelped again, he shushed her and they both laughed. "If you wake your sister, it'll be curtains for you."

"Curtains?" she asked after a few long seconds. "What does that mean?"

"Shhh, I'll tell you in the morning. Now close your eyes!" Mark lightly rubbed her back. Five minutes later, he felt her arms relax and her body go limp as she fell into a deep sleep. A secret that Mark would never share was that Ashley was his favorite. The fact that he had been there for her birth may have had something to do with it. Another crack of thunder had drawn Marks' attention away from his niece. In his periphery, he caught the faint glow on his cell phone. If it hadn't been for the sudden darkening of the room, he would have missed the call.

\*　　\*　　\*

Cameron Butler, a twenty-year veteran of the California Highway Patrol, had met Mark Springfield two years earlier when Mark had enlisted his help. Cameron had responded to a call that had claimed the life of who appeared to have been, Mark and Mary Springfield. But a wild change of events had sent Cameron on a night with one of the CIA's top operatives. Cameron had made a snap decision. He had helped Mark on a dark night and it was a decision that had changed his life. The biggest change was his friendship with Mark. It started when he had committed to help a complete stranger and grew over their love of firearms. Now the six foot, two hundred and fifteen-pound redhead needed to make a call.

Mark held Ashley tight to his chest. He pushed himself out of his chair and reached for his phone. He picked it up from the end table and slowly worked himself back into his chair. He glanced at the incoming number and instantly recognized it. He pressed the green button and said, "Doesn't anybody know what time it is?"

"Mark?" Cameron said, sounding surprised. "I hope I didn't wake you. I expected to leave you a message."

"Well, we have quite the storm going on here. I'm kind of surprised I have reception."

There was silence on the other line for so long that Mark finally asked, "Cameron, are you there?" Still nothing. However, Mark could hear breathing on the other end. "Spit it out, young man."

"Mark, if I ask you a question off the record, will it really be off the record?"

"Depends" Mark answered. He liked Cameron. He had always been straightforward. Mark had described him to others as 'solid'. Now, at three-forty in the morning, Mark could feel there was a problem. "Cameron, you do remember who I work for?"

After several long seconds, Cameron asked, "So, where does the 'depends' come in?"

"What's wrong, Cameron?"

Cameron let out a long sigh and then slowly continued. "Two days ago, we were investigating salvaged titles. I really can't go into the why."

"Is this payback for our outing a couple years ago?" Mark kidded. When Cameron agreed to help Mark two years earlier, he had known two things: Mark's sister had been kidnapped and there was satellite technology worth dying for. But Mark had never told Cameron what the satellite was capable of.

"Mark, saving Mary was enough," Cameron retorted.

"I'm joking, Cameron!"

*　　*　　*

Cameron sat back in his chair and scanned the walls of the office in his home. Several awards and pictures had been hung neatly. In the center of them was the commendation he had received from the director of the CIA. To the left was a photo of him and Mark shaking hands while they both held the award. To its right was a picture of Mark's sister Mary, her husband Cole and their two girls Christina and Ashley. He felt a lump in his throat almost everytime he looked at it. Cameron rubbed his hand over his short red hair. Then he leaned in and said. "Two nights ago, I was working with two other investigators. We were running the VINs (Vehicle Identification Number) on a few cars we were looking at. At roughly seven thirty, I punched in a series of numbers." Cameron paused. He started to have second thoughts about telling Mark. Once he turned this page there would be no going back.

# 2

*August 2012*
*Mono Lake*
*California*

Cameron's boots and the lower half of his black BDUs were covered in mud. He stood on the side of the embankment while the tow truck had pulled the last of the two cars from Mono Lake. He and his partner were from one of several law enforcement agencies that had been called to investigate what two scuba divers had found after clearing the lake's drainage grates. After swapping out their dive tanks and completing the work, they checked their pressure gauges. The two avid divers decided that they had had enough left over for an extended swim into the lake. It was pure chance that they had stumbled onto the submerged cars. The visibility in the lake was low, but the divers had easily seen skeletal remains sitting in the driver's seat of the car closest to the embankment. Thick mud had covered everything from its waist down. With the exception of being full of mud and sediment, the car farthest out appeared empty.

Cameron watched the cars being pulled from the lake as water spilled out from the open windows. The forensic team moved in and started taking pictures. Cameron moved around the cars, working his own camera. "There doesn't seem to be any license plates on this one," he said, nodding at the car that had been farthest out. When forensics had finished snapping pictures, they removed what was left of the body. Then they checked the cars for additional remains. Not finding any, they turned the vehicles over to Cameron and his partner.

Cameron started with the car that had been furthest out in the lake. He forced the driver's door open and when he wiped the mud from the cars' data plate inside the doorjamb, the plate's top rivet broke loose. "This is in bad shape." He said, looking at the severely corroded plate.

Veronica, one of the forensic examiners, looked at Cameron and said. "Yup, Mono Lake has a high salt content." Shaking her head, she added. "It wouldn't take long for that plate to corrode."

Cameron nodded his head. He walked over to his cruiser and grabbed a small green tool bag. He fished around until he found a punch and a small hammer. He walked back to the car, crouched down in front of the plate and centered the punch on the remaining lower rivet. Two strikes with the hammer and he was holding it in his hand. He stood, looked at both cars and asked. "How long do you think?" He walked over to Veronica and handed her the data plate. "How long do you think it would take to get this eaten-up?"

Veronica flipped the plate over and looked at both sides. She handed it back to Cameron and answered with a snicker. "Sorry, detective, not my swim lane."

A thin smile grew across Cameron's lips. He shook his head while he walked back to the cars. He was stuck with not one, but two nicknames. Because of his hair, he had picked up Red in the academy years ago. Two years earlier, when he was still a Highway Patrolman, he had met Mark Springfield. Cameron was ready to start with their investigative unit, so Mark referred to him as detective. Cameron tried to explain that they weren't detectives. But Mark insisted and the name stuck. However, it was an exclusive group of his peers that would refer to him as detective. Only the ones who had been involved in the aftermath of Cameron's encounter with Mark had picked up on the name. Veronica had been one of the technicians called in to work the crime scene. She and Cameron had started a relationship that had been short-lived. It ended when Cameron became too involved with his new position.

Cameron retrieved an evidence bag and identified it with the make, model, and color of the car the identification plate had been removed from. But, before he dropped it inside, he studied the Vehicle Identification Number. Most of the alphanumeric numbers were still legible. A few had been eaten away by the corrosive properties of the lake. He guessed four of them and wrote down what he thought was the number down in his notebook. When he was finished, he drew a line under the number and walked over to the second car and repeated his actions. Only this time, he only had to guess two of the numbers.

After spending the remainder of the day searching the lake where the two cars had been found, the divers game up empty handed.

Tired and hungry and with a nice sunburn on the back of his neck, Cameron finally sat in his patrol car. He opened a bottle of water and took a long drink. He watched the cursor blink on his car's computer monitor. "I think we're done here." The comment from his partner had taken him by surprise.

"Yeah, give me a minute. I may run these numbers." Cameron turned the monitor so it faced him. He pulled his note book from his shirt pocket and opened it to the VINs that he had written down. Flicking the page with his fingers, Cameron looked at the underlined numbers that he had guessed at. He hesitated, then quickly typed them in and pressed enter. He turned from the car and looked out over the water. The air had a comfortable feel to it with a slight breeze blowing across the valley from the east. He had never been to Mono Lake but found it fascinating. The Tufa towers that had risen up from the water had intrigued him. Earlier he had been told they had been made of Limestone. The computer's monitor beeped and Cameron returned his attention to the screen. He furrowed his brow, pursed his lips and slowly shook his head when he read what had been returned on the display. "What...?" He said quietly. "Hmmm..." He grabbed the evidence bag and removed the data plate. Matching the numbers to his notes he ran the plate again. He shook his head. "So much for guessing." He grabbed the evidence bag and dropped the plate back inside. *I'll look at this later*, he thought.

"Whatcha find?" Cameron's partner asked as he walked up to the car knocking dried mud from his pants. Cameron reached over to the keyboard, pausing over the Delete key and said.

"I got a hit, but...it can't be right. I'll run the data plates through the lab and we'll get the right numbers. Then I'll give'r another go." Cameron took one more look at the address displayed on the monitor - Jack W. Springfield, 2600 Lord Baltimore Drive, Baltimore, MD 21244 - before he pressed the key.

# 3

*January 29, 1774*
*Palace of Westminster*
*Meeting of the Privy Council*
*Great Britain*

Benjamin Franklin stood stoic on a round elevated platform in the center of a packed room. Decorative wooden posts connected a marble railing that had been fashioned three quarters of the way around the dais. He stood in a full-dress suite of spotted Manchester velvet. Long gray hair jetted from under his white wig and fell onto his shoulders, both hands gripped the railing. Slowly, he scanned the large hall. It seemed as if the room would burst open as he watched people being pushed into the railings on the upper balcony. The chamber was called the Cockpit, and just as the building that had once stood in its place was used by Henry the VIII and his friends to fight their prized birds, each wagering which would tear the others to shreds, he felt the atmosphere was the same. Franklin knew the crowd had gathered like sharks around a bloody carcass, waiting for the man that sat across the room to take bites out of him.

For an hour, Alexander Wedderburn, the solicitor general, demoralized, insulted, vilified and slashed the character of one of the best-known men in the world. His attack on Franklin brought hoots, jeers, and laughter from the audience.

Franklin was brought before the council for admitting that he had forwarded the confidential letters of Thomas Hutchinson, the English appointed governor of Massachusetts. They were published and interpreted as part of a British plot to enslave the colonies. They were treating the Americans as subjects, not subjects of simply King George but of Parliament. These letters fueled anger that inspired the Boston riot which had led to forty-five tons of tea being dumped into the Boston harbor by colonials loosely dressed as Indians. It was an assault against the British crown and Parliament.

He remembered how, on this very spot, he had successfully argued against the stamp act in 1766. But he knew then that unless Britain changed their designs for the colonies, the burning tax ember would be fanned into a raging fire.

Benjamin Franklin stood silent throughout the ordeal. When the 68-year-old was instructed to submit to questions, he refused. Outrage, not humiliation, coursed through his veins. Franklin glared at his accusers and thought if those smug lords and corrupt ministers would treat the colonies better, they would not have to go down the path that was becoming clearer.

At the conclusion of the hearing, Franklin left the great hall and within forty-eight hours, he learned that he had been stripped of his assistant post master general position in the colonies.

Feeling like he had outgrown Philadelphia, Franklin had spent most of the last eighteen years in London. He knew London better than he had known Philadelphia. But this London was not the London he had known just a few years earlier. Corruption now overwhelmed parliament and as time went by, he knew his real home was the land of his birth, America, and lingering almost a year after the hearing had made it painfully clear... London had changed. He left by coach and caught the Pennsylvania packet at Portsmouth and sailed for home.

While underway, Franklin held tight the railing of the ship. The thunderous boom the bow made when it crashed into the sea mirrored how he felt inside. He still burned with anger and disgust. Franklin knew himself to be the most reluctant of revolutionaries. But he knew what had to happen. He knew what he must do. He would use his influence and drive the rebellion to a genuine revolution.

However, a chance meeting in France with a few bankers and friends, whom he would call the group of five, would seal the fate of the emerging American nation.

# 4

*October 2012*
*Altadena, California*

An early dusting of snow had covered the hills of the Angeles Crest Highway. Inside the Altadena California Highway Patrol office, Cameron sat with his partner, Lee Thomas, and the office's salvage investigator, Dave Ford. Cameron slowly brought a cup of coffee up to lips, it had been his fourth cup since noon. He sat in front of a computer terminal tapping his pen on a sheet of paper. In his left hand, he held a small notebook that he had flipped open to the set of numbers he had retrieved from the identification plates on the two cars that had been pulled from Mono Lake. He sat quietly going over the sheets that contained numbers of missing or stolen vehicles. The numbers he had written down were not listed anywhere.

"Red, what do you say we take Mr. Ford out to get something to eat?" Lee stood and grabbed his jacket from the chair.

Cameron looked up from his notes and over to Dave Ford and then his partner. He shook his head. "No, I'm going to stick around and look at a few things. But, if you want to bring me whatever you're having, I won't turn it down."

"OK. But it wouldn't hurt you to take a break every once in a while." Lee quipped, when Lee passed by Cameron, he lightly slapped him on his shoulder and said. "Be right back."

Cameron called over his shoulder, "take your time. This stuffs' not going anywhere." Cameron looked up and watched Dave close the door. He waited a few minutes then stood and walked over and peered through the window. He watched the two men drive away. Cameron stepped over to the coffee pot and poured himself another cup. He had no idea why he was drinking so much except that his nerves where on edge. When he sat back down at the table, he pulled all the sheets of paper in front of him. He studied the forensics lab report for the fifth time. Cameron was familiar with the type of testing that had been performed on the data plates. The top layer of metal had been chemically removed and in doing so exposed a perfect set of alphanumeric numbers. He guessed correctly. Both numbers from the data plates matched what he had originally written down. He wanted to run the numbers again. Just not when anyone else was around.

He typed the number in the station's computer. When he was finished, he moved his hand over to the enter key and paused while thinking. *How could a car registered to Marks' dad end up in a lake? More importantly, how do I tell him?* Several long seconds later, he pressed the key. While he waited for the computers return, he picked up his coffee cup and brought it to his lips. The smell repulsed him. He crunched up his nose and set it back down. "Yup, I had enough."

Eight seconds later, he received the same message as before while sitting in his cruiser at Mono Lake. Across the screen scrolled the address - Jack W. Springfield, 2600 Lord Baltimore Drive, Baltimore, MD 21244.

Cameron sat back in his chair and stared at the monitor. Over the past two years, he had gotten to know Mark Springfield. Last year he had spent a few days at their place in Kitty Hawk, North Carolina. Mark had explained that his mom and dad had been killed in a traffic accident in 2003 and had left the beach house to him and his sister, Mary. During the conversation, Cameron had learned that Marks' dad's name was Jack. And that Mary had named her oldest daughter, Christina, after their mom.

Cameron slid his chair over to the adjacent monitor. He pulled up their location and mapping program on the computer. Out of curiosity, he typed in the address. Almost immediately the location appeared on the monitor. "No shit!" Cameron blurted. Federal Bureau of Investigations, Baltimore Maryland, field office, blinked on the screen. He half slid and half leaned over to the other computer. He quickly typed in the other car's

VIN.'RESTRICTED' instantly flashed on the screen. "Restricted! What the hell?"

He retyped the number. Again, 'RESTRICTED' flashed on the screen. Cameron shuffled through some of the papers. He found the coroner's report on the driver of the second car. They had a complete set of teeth and were able to extract DNA from some of the remains. However, the report was incomplete. The only information they had on the driver was what had laid on the coroner's table. The body was male, six feet tall and approximately forty-five to fifty years old. His hair was black and he had two teeth that had been replaced. And, he had suffered from a heart attack. Cameron picked up the two sheets of paper and counted the times the word UNKNOWN had been used in the report eight times. There was no name, no DNA match, no dental match, nothing. Just a glaring UNKNOWN.

He glanced at the wall clock, 7:32p. m. glowed in bright red numbers. Cameron stood and walked to the window. He flicked up the blinds and watched the cars on the highway speed by. In an almost inaudible voice Cameron said, "why would Mark's dad have a car registered to him but show the address of the FBI headquarters? Did his dad work for the FBI? And if he did, did Mark know?" He searched his memory trying to recall who Mark said his dad had worked for. He remembered their conversation while they had walk around the house in North Carolina. However, he couldn't quite put his finger on his employer.

Cameron looked back at the computer's monitor then returned his gaze to the not too distant California Interstate 210. Sounding perplexed, Cameron said. "And who the hell is Mr. Unknown?"

In his periphery Cameron noticed someone pulling into the station's parking lot. He glanced in their direction and noticed that it was the black and white California Highway Patrol cruiser that Lee and Dave had taken for the dinner run. He quickly looked back at the computer and then again out of the window. He watched as Lee and Dave stepped out of the car. Lee was holding bags from IN-N-OUT while Dave held a cardboard container of what looked like shakes. Both were laughing. Cameron was quite sure Lee had told one of his dry humored, inappropriate jokes. *Ah damnit*, he said to himself. Then, Cameron made the same decision he had made when he had first met Mark. He would not report what he knew to his superiors or his fellow officers. He reached over to the keyboard and repeated his action at Mono Lake, he deleted the information from the computer.

# 5

*January 27ᵗʰ.2003*
*Pentagon*
*The office of*
*Rear Admiral Shannon Lambert*

"Colonel Hanington, what do you think? Are we being too…cautious.?" Hanington's grey balding head was propped on the three fingers of his left hand. Both elbows were firmly planted on the table. With his right hand, he rubbed his sweaty temple.

He looked across the conference table at the two other men in the room. With narrowed eyebrows and locked jaws, they stared back. They slowly swirled their brandy in crystal clear glasses.

Hanington let out a long sigh as he looked down at the picture that had been lying in front of him. He studied the smiling faces of the five men and two women that looked back at him. Then said solemnly. "Admiral, they are seven of our finest."

"Yes, Colonel, but sacrifices must be made." Lambert harshly answered.

"The entire crew!" He shot back. Lambert pushed her chair away from her desk and walked over to the chair next to Hanington. She sat down and took the picture from his hands. Quickly she glanced at it, then turned it over and laid it on the table.

"Yes, the entire crew." She countered.

Hanington looked around the room once again. He knew why one of the men in the photo had to be silenced and he suddenly felt the question from Lambert was a test. He spoke his next words with measured caution. "Of course, you are correct admiral. This is really the only way." He looked at Shannon and continued. "It must be all of us if we are to change things. Having someone in NASA only extends our reach. We cannot trust that he will remain silent."

Shannon nodded her head and then pushed her thin five-foot, eight-inch, frame up from her chair. She walked over to the small table next to her desk and grabbed the bottle of brandy. She poured another glass and sat down. "It was his decision not to join us." She said. "I'm sorry for the rest, but this is the only way not to draw suspicion." Shannon picked up her brandy and drank half of her glass in one quick gulp. She continued, "Do you have a shooter?"

"Yes, Admiral." The answer came from an Air Force colonial sitting at the table. "We're flying an F-15 Eagle out of California's Edwards Air Force base. It'll be equipped with DARPAs experimental Tactical High Energy Laser. We'll laze them on reentry."

"Very nice!" Lambert quipped admirably.

*Jesus Christ!* Colonel Hanington almost said the words out loud. This was murder. He wanted out, but if he spoke his mind, he knew he would be next.

"And our pilot." Shannon asked. "Can he be trusted?"

The colonel finished taking a swig of his brandy and said with a smile. "Don't worry, Admiral. After this is taken care of, we can move on."


*Five days later.*
*February 1, 2003*
*Mission control, Florida*
*A television and radio news broadcast*


This is a special report: NASA has lost contact with the space shuttle Columbia. At 9a.m. eastern time, the spacecraft experienced trouble as it streaked across California.

It has disintegrated over Texas and Louisiana. It is believed all seven crew members have perished.

Our prayers go out to the crew and families of Columbia STS-107. God bless us all. And God bless the United States of America.

# 6

*January 20th 2003*
*Offices of Rowe Integrated Software*

D an Rowe laughed when Jack Springfield launched another rolled up paper ball from his cubicle. Three tightly crumpled 8 1/2 x 11 sheets of paper sat around Dan's desk. Of the twenty-six people who worked for Dan's company, Jack's arm was the most accurate. He, with a high degree of accuracy, could land a ball of paper on the head of his coworkers.

Jack had worked for Rowe's Integrated Software since its inception. The two men met in college and had become close friends. Two years out of college, Dan decided to make a go of it on his own. He had asked Jack to join him after he had landed his first contract. Three days after Jack's son Mark was born, he signed with Dan. Now, forty-three plus years later, both semiretired men used the business to fill their mornings and the paper bombs to help loosen up the next generation.

"Colleen, you're with me this glorious day." Jack quipped as he munched up another paper ball.

"Where are we off to, Mr. Springfield?" Colleen Kennedy was a new hire. The twenty-seven-year-old USC graduate had moved to the east coast to escape her family and experience the seasons. Jack had taken the young woman under his wing. She reminded him of and strongly resembled his own daughter, Mary. He constantly fought the urge to father her.

"Who's next?" He asked while batting the crumpled-up paper in the air off the palm of his hand.

Colleen gave Jack an apprehensive look. She wasn't quite sure which one of her colleagues should come under the attack of her mentor. She glanced around the office and smiled, then looked timidly at Jack and whispered."Angie?"

The giant smile and throaty chuckle from Jack told her it was the right choice. Jack swiveled his chair in the direction of Angie's cubical.

The loosely crumbled 8 1/2 X 11 paper ball arched two thirds of the way across the room. It disappeared behind the low beige walls and hit Angie on the side of the head.

"Damnit, Jack!" she yelled.

Jack let out a belly laugh and quickly twisted his chair back towards his desk. He rolled over and closed his computer. With the exception of a few framed photos of his kids and granddaughters neatly set on his desk, it was void of any personal items. "Well, we better get out of here," he whispered while slipping his computer into his well-worn tan leather satchel. He stood and walked over to Colleen's desk. "Shall we." The quick comment was more of a 'let's go' than a question.

"Where are we off to this morning?" Colleen asked, standing up and smoothing her dress.

"Fort Meade. And, Colleen, for the umpteenth time, it's Jack."

Colleen nodded her head and then quickly added. "Not the NSA, I hope. I'm not cleared for that part of the base."

"Nope. Today it's the Defense Courier Service. Apparently, a Mr. Allen can't get access to the share drive."

"Is that on the server or attached to the network?"

"Server." Jack answered, closing the door behind them. "The last time it ended up being a problem with the Transmission Control Protocol." The two walked across the parking garage towards the company car.

"How long did it take you to fix it?" Colleen inquired.

"About a half hour," Jack said, sounding annoyed with himself.

Colleen laughed. "Thirty minutes? That's not bad! As I think about it, it's pretty good."

Jack gave her a wink and opened the back door of their white sedan. He set his satchel on the back seat and closed the door. He turned and opened the front door. Colleen mimicked his actions.

The two settled in the front seats and Jack started the car while glancing over at Colleen and offering her a warm smile. They backed out of their spot and drove southeast to Fort Meade. Their IDs were checked and they were waved through the main gate. "Umm... I think you may want to slow down a bit, Mr. Sprin...Jack." Colleen said while pointing to the 35 miles an hour speed limit sign. A smile grew on his face.

"It's hard to drive thirty-five miles an hour," he laughed.

After a few minutes, Colleen let out an overzealous, "there it is!" when she had seen the building.

Her enthusiasm brought the smile back to Jack's face and with a raised eyebrow, he gave her a quick look.

"I know, it's silly," she said. "But this is only my third time on base and my first time to the Defense Courier building."

"Don't make me regret getting you that secret clearance, young lady," Jack jokingly admonished Colleen as he slipped the car into a visitor's slot next to the entrance.

Jack and Colleen sat in the outer foyer waiting for their visitor badges and the escort to arrive. Colleen had a grin as wide as the Grand Canyon. She was a striking young woman with shoulder-length auburn hair. She brought a smile to the faces of most men. Jack looked at her much differently. When he looked at Colleen, he saw his own daughter. It was her excitement that brought a smile to his face.

"Jack," a booming voice bellowed from across the room.

Jack looked up and instantly replied. "Marcus!" He stood with an outstretched arm. Jack continued after clasping their hands together. "How are you, my friend?"

"I'm well. Hey, thanks for coming out so soon." Marcus quickly replied.

"It's what we're here for." Jack quipped with a wide smile, then turned towards Colleen and said, "Marcus Smith, allow me to introduce my colleague, Ms. Kennedy."

Colleen timidly stuck out her hand. She was taken a bit off guard by Marcus. The husky framed, well-dressed, black man stood well over six feet. His baritone voice resonated off the walls of the small foyer, and his hands were the size of catcher's mitts. When the two shook hands, Colleen didn't think she would ever see her hand again.

"My pleasure." She finally said. Colleen glanced over at Jack and noticed he had been trying to suppress a smile.

"And before you ask." Jack started. "Marcus here played basketball for Philadelphia."

"The 76ers?" Colleen excitedly asked.

Marcus nodded his head and said. "Right up until I broke my knee. And that was that."

"Ouch, must have been bad." Colleen prodded.

"It was. And here I am." Marcus gave her a warm definitive smile.

After a short walk across the room, the three swiped their identifications through the electronic lock and buzzed into the inner door.

Michael Allen was easy to spot. When the small group stepped thru the inner entrance, he instantly stood up and walked to his office door. He raised his right hand and motioned for the group. "And that is our Mr. Allen." Marcus quietly said to Jack. "Please help him." Both men shared a quiet chuckle. Colleen missed the exchange but thought the men were sharing a private joke.

"Good morning, Mr. Allen, Jack Springfield at your service and this is my colleague, Ms. Colleen Kennedy." The two shook hands with Michael.

"Please fix my computer. I swear these things have set us back a hundred years." Michael Allen was in his early fifties. His thick black hair looked disheveled and appeared to have been pulled from both sides of his head.

"Well, let us take a look at it," Jack said.

"Good luck," Michael added. "I've been at it for well over two hours. I finally threw in the towel."

Jack pulled up an additional chair to Michael's desk and motioned for Colleen to take a seat. The two spoke quietly while Jack gently pressed the keys. After five minutes, Jack knew he needed a computer with Top Secret administrative access. The problem with Michael's machine stemmed from another source.

Jack leaned away from the computer and sharply said. "Marcus." Marcus was still conversing with Michael in the hall when Jack had gotten his attention.

"Sir" Marcus replied with a toothy grin.

"Can I use your computer?" Jack knew that Marcus would have the access he needed.

Marcus paused. In those few seconds, he considered what he had loaded on his computer and Jack's Top Secret clearance. He pursed his lips and slowly nodded his head unaware of just how gifted Jack Springfield was with reading code. He glanced at Michael then back at Jack.

"Okay." He turned to Colleen and said. "I'm sorry, you'll have to wait in the lobby. Michael will escort you back."

Colleen smiled and said, "oh no problem. I have plenty I can read."

"Shall we?" Marcus asked, Jack motioning to another door across the hall.

Jack smiled and nodded. After an elevator ride to the second floor, and a stop at the coffee pot, the two men sat at Marcus's desk. Jack watched Marcus log in and then roll his chair back giving him room to pull himself up to the computer. Within seconds, Jack had windows dumped, Dos running and lines of code scrolled across the monitor that Marcus had never seen.

"I noticed Mr. Allen had a proprietary block." Jack said while typing in commands. "Sometimes computers lose their minds." Jack continued with a grin.

Marcus pointed at his monitor and said. "I'd rather have the black screen of death than be faced with all that mumbo jumbo you have pulled up there." The two looked at each other and laughed.

"Hmmm… There's a message clogging up the works." Jack learned long ago not to try to explain what exactly was happening within computer code. He often used very loose and general terms. "You have a corrupted encrypted file that is…hmmm…give me a few."

Jack switched between dos, windows, and his special diagnostic code. Often, tapping the screen and uttering unintelligible verbiage under his breath.

"Coffee?" Marcus suggested it more so than asked.

It took Jack a few long seconds for the comment to register. Then, without looking at his host, he pushed his cup in the man's general direction and quietly answered, "Yesss."

Marcus, picked up their cups, and walked out of the room.

Jack pushed himself back in his chair. Staring at the computer, he stroked his chin. Leaning in, he started typing. Eighteen seconds later, what looked like a string of hieroglyphics spread across the screen. He pressed enter. Almost instantly a file popped up on the screen. "Gotcha!" Without thinking, Jack slid the mouse so the arrow was over the file and double-clicked it. On the screen appeared a two-slide show presentation. The slide that opened was titled REENTRY and below it was a flight profile with, what appeared to be, the outline of the space shuttle at the apex of its flight. From the root of the starboard wing, a thin line had been projected off the slide. Jack clicked on the next slide. On the screen appeared the second slide titled DARPA High Energy Laser /F-15. Under the title was an outline of an F-15, an Air Force tactical aircraft. It had a long cylindrical pod suspended from its port wing. The slide had just flashed on the screen when Marcus quickly entered the room. "Wait a minute, Jack!" Marcus spilled most of the coffee while abruptly setting the cups down on the desk. He quickly grabbed the mouse and minimized the screen.

Jack did not see much of the second slide, but he did see the file date. January 29th 2003.

"Oh, I'm sorry, Marcus. I got so tied up in the problem and it wasn't marked as being classified so I just opened it on instinct. I'm so sorry."

"Don't worry, Jack. I haven't seen that before. I need to figure out who it belongs to. You're fine." Inside Marcus's head, the words *shit shit shit shit* wouldn't stop scrolling.

"But the good news is." Jack quipped. "I may have fixed it." Marcus forced a laugh and said.

"Well let's go downstairs and find out. Sorry I spilled your coffee. I guess you caught me off guard. We have to be careful in this business. You know the motto, what you do here, see here, and learn here, stays here."

Jack said. "I do. Now, let's get your Mr. Allen back up and running."

Twenty minutes later, with Allen's computer fixed, Jack and Colleen stood in the lobby of the Defense Courier building. The two said their goodbyes to both Marcus and

Michael. As Jack turned towards the door, Marcus said. "Remember our motto," and slapped him on the back.

"Will do." Jack said with a smile and closed the door.

Halfway to the car, Colleen looked over at her partner. "What's their motto?"

"What you do here, see here, and learn here, stays here." Jack felt a scowl grow on his face. He felt uncomfortable. "But that's just not their motto." He added. "That's everyone's motto." Jack couldn't push the presentation from the front to the back of his mind. Something wasn't right and he could feel it. Sitting in his car, while waiting for his partner to fasten her seat belt, he stared at the building.

"Jack?" Colleen said, thinking he was daydreaming.

Trying to push it from his mind, he looked over at her, smiled and asked, "Hungry?"

*　　*　　*

Marcus returned to his office and immediately keyed his secured telephone and punched in a number from memory. He pressed the phone tight against his ear while waiting for the recipient to answer. When he did, Marcus simply said. "We have a problem."

# 7

*November 2012*
*North Carolina*
*Great Smoky Mountains*

Mark was patient with Cameron. He gave him time to reveal why he thought it was urgent enough to call so early in the morning. Mark could almost hear Cameron take a breath. What came next was not what he had expected.

"Mark…did your dad work for the FBI?" He asked. And in the recesses of his mind he heard Pandora's box slowly creaking open.

Mark leaned forward in his chair and shook his head. "The FBI? No, he was a programmer. Worked for Rowe Integrated Software. Why? what's this about?"

A thunderous boom from outside followed by an ear-splitting crack caused Mark to quickly look up from the floor and out of the window. When thick smoke drifted from around the corner he stood and took a few steps. "Cameron, are you still there?" Mark strained his eyes while trying to see through the rain-streaked windows and out into the smoke-filled dark. He turned and walked over to the couch that he had been sleeping on and carefully laid Ashley down. He covered her with the blanket.

"Mark?" The reply back from Cameron was static filled.

Suddenly, Mark felt as if he were standing next to Niagara Falls. The on slot of rain was deafening. Mark was sure the buckets of rain would extinguish any fire that may have caused the smoke. He stuck his finger in his open ear and tried again. "Cameron, are you there?"

"Yes, I'm here." Cameron said with a raised voice.

"That's better." Mark said tersely.

Calming himself, Cameron continued. "Mark, we found a car that was registered to your dad."

"Found where?"

There was a long pause on Cameron's side. Then finally, he added. "It was pushed into Mono Lake."

Mark searched his memory for the events surrounding the night his mom and dad had died. He was returning from Portugal. Shortly after landing in Amsterdam, he had turned on his phone. Waiting for him was a message to call the office. He vividly remembered the call. "Your mother and father were killed in a traffic accident." To this day, he could still hear the somber tone of the co-worker who had the misfortune to answer the phone when he had called the Los Angeles office. It was the longest day of his life. Instead of continuing onto Los Angeles, he changed the flight to one headed to Newark, New Jersey. From there, he rented a car and drove to Maryland and identified the bodies of his parents. It was gut-wrenching when he called his sister Mary to deliver the news. For a few seconds, Mark relived the pain he had felt. Pulling himself back into the moment, he asked, "Cameron, what are you talking about?"

"Mark, we pulled two cars out of Mono Lake. Are you familiar with the lake?"

"Vaguely, somewhere in Northern California. Go on."

"Roughly seven hours northeast of Los Angeles in the Eastern Sierra. Anyway, one of them was registered to your dad. The address was the FBI building in Baltimore Maryland."

"Jesus Christ, Cameron! Wha—"

"Mark, let me finish. The car behind it had someone in it. I ran the VIN and it came back restricted and the forensics came back with the same results. There was no name, no DNA match, no dental match, nothing. Not a damn thing. The only thing we know is the driver had had a heart attack."

"That's how he ended up in the water," Mark said flatly.

"And Mark. These cars could have been in the water since 2003."

Mark sat back down and slumped his head into his hand and rubbed his temples. He tried to make sense out of what Cameron had just told him. Mark pushed himself back into his chair while looking up into the loft. He glanced over at his nieces to assure they were still asleep.

There was a long pause while Mark tried to collect his thoughts. What Cameron was telling him was simply the impossible. He knew his dad. He was part of a very successful business that had been around for years. He displayed none of the telltale signs of working for a covert organization. He thought back on the few business trips that his dad had taken over the years. During the summer months when school was out and his dad had a business trip that wasn't too far away, he would load everyone in the car and make it a mini vacation.

*No!* Mark thought. *My father worked for Rowe Integrated software.*

"Cameron, who else knows this?"

"No one. But Mark, I can't keep this to myself for long."

"Give me a day on this. I'll make a call a little later this morning."

"And to whom might that be?" Cameron hesitantly asked.

"Dan Rowe, my dad's former partner."

# 8

*February 2, 2003*
*Sunday morning*
*The home of Jack and Christina Springfield*

Christina laid the paper on Jacks lap and set a cup of coffee on the small end table on his right side. A bout with the flu had kept him in bed and shivering under the covers the two previous days.

He thanked his wife and unfolded the large Sunday edition. Staring him in the face was the space shuttle Columbia. Written across the top in big bold letters were **7 ASTRONAUTS DIE.** Underneath the picture were the words. **Worse blow to NASA since Challenger.** Jack scanned the article and found the news hard to believe, both the tire pressure and temperature sensors on the left side of the spacecraft had been lost.

Jacks face had gone pale. He turned the pages while studying the article. The room began to spin. Over the last two weeks, he had pushed the nagging pictures he had seen at the Defense Courier building to the back of his head. However, now he was faced with an event that was strikingly familiar. "Good Lord!" Jack spoke the words with such deep conviction his wife stepped back into the room.

"What's the matter, honey?"

"Chrissy, come look at this!" Jacks top secret clearance had kept him from sharing what he had seen on Marcus's computer. But he had to show his wife the disaster.

Christina scanned the headlines and said. "I know, dear. It happened yesterday." Squeezing his shoulder, she continued. "You were feeling so bad that I didn't tell you. I'm sorry." She gave Jack a warm smile.

"No, no!" He said with desperation. "You don't understand!"

Christina studied her husband and asked. "Honey, are you okay? You look pale."

"I need to see Dan!"

"But Jack, it's Sunday!" She said in protest.

"I have to see him." Jack pushed himself out of his chair. When he walked past the kitchen, he tossed the paper on the table. "My keys. Find my keys." Absentmindedly, he patted his pajamas and added. "I need to change."

\* \* \*

Jack changed his clothes and walked back out to the living room. He grabbed his phone and punched in Dan's cell number and patiently waited. On the third ring, Dan answered. "Jack! How th —"

"Dan. I need to talk to you in person. I'll come to you." Jack said quickly, interrupting his friend.

"Can it wait until Monday. Jen and I are away —"

"Okay, I'll be in at seven. Please, Dan, meet me then."

"You got it. Oh, by the way, Jack. You were requested out in California. Some urgent task for our friends at Energy in Fresno."

Jack had hardly heard Dan's west coast news. Instead, he was fixated on what he had seen on Marcus's computer. He walked back into the kitchen, grabbed his newspaper, returned to his chair, and sat down with a heavy thud. Jack Springfield felt as if he would throw up.

*February 3rd, 2003*
*Monday morning*

Dan Rowe trotted out to his car that had been sitting in the driveway of his Tudor-style home. He opened the back door, tossed in his briefcase, and closed the door. After slipping into the front seat, he started his car and selected reverse. As soon as the car moved to the rear, he felt and heard a giant clunk from the passenger side. Dan got out and walked to the other side only to find a flat tire. "Shit!" As he checked his watch, his phone rang. Recognizing the number, he quickly answered it. "Dan Rowe."

"Good morning, Mr. Rowe. It's Lawrence from Soledad Energy. I hope this isn't too early to call?"

"I'm just on my way into work." Dan said while studying his flat tire. "Does this have anything to do with getting my man Jack out there?"

"It does and we can't wait. We are willing to pay whatever it takes to borrow him for just a day or two. I know he can quickly fix our problem."

"Let me see what I can do."

"Mr. Rowe, like I said, we will pay whatever it takes to get him out here as soon as possible."

"Sounds serious." Dan offered.

"It is. Part of our system is all but shut down." Lawrence added sounding desperate.

"I'll tell you what, I'll see if I can get Jack on a plane first thing this morning. However, this late, I may have to fly him out first class."

Lawrence chuckled and quipped "Whatever it takes, we'll pay."

"Okay then. I'll have my secretary contact you after the arrangements are made. And thanks again for giving us a call." Dan pressed the end button and then called the office. He instructed his secretary to purchase a ticket for Jack on a flight around ten a. m. to Fresno. Next, he called his partner.

"Dan!" Jack answered the phone sounding apologetic. "If this is about our meeting this morning, please don't rush in. I had a night to sleep on what was bothering me and when I tell you about it, it'll make you laugh."

"Well then this works. I got another call from the folks at Soledad energy, they need you in California. I'm sure you remember Lawrence Williams? They asked for you to head out today, and get this, you're going first class."

"That will be nice for a change." Jack laughed. "I'll drop by Sandy's office, get my itinerary, and we'll talk when you get in."

"And that's the other thing. I'm standing here looking at a very flat tire. I'll take care of this and see you when you get back. Keep me posted and let me know if you need anything while you are out there."

"Will do." Jack looked at his phone, smiled and hung up, he had talked himself out of thinking that some secret government agency was plotting to shoot down the space shuttle. The more he had thought about it, the more it had made him laugh.

# 9

*November 2012*
*North Carolina*
*Great Smoky Mountains*

"But Cameron, I want everything you have on this. Forensics, DNA, plates, the make and model of the cars and any pictures. I want the names of everyone around the crime scene. Any names you collected, I want everything, Cameron. Everything!"

Mark stood and stepped closer to the glass panes and waited intently for Cameron to acknowledge his request. When Cameron didn't, he continued. "Detective!"

"I'm here."

"I can't leave tonight, but I'll get out as soon as I can. When I get a flight to Los Angeles, I'll call you."

Cameron heard and felt the change in Marks voice. It wasn't the rock-solid baritone he had first heard a few years ago. It was different and had a twist of uncertainty laced within it. Cameron knew his friend was coming to California, and there was nothing he could do or say to stop him.

He simply said "I'll be there."

"Until tomorrow." Mark ended the call with a tap on the screen. He paused while looking at the phone, then he flipped it over in his hand a few times and looked up at the rain-streaked windows.

Mark walked back over to the leather chair and quietly sat back down. He closed his eyes and tried to push the conversation from his mind so he could sleep. He dealt with facts, hard evidence mixed with intuition, and he tried not to jump to any conclusions. He needed to see everything Cameron had.

Through his closed eyes, he could see flashes of light as the storm slowly moved east. The phone call played over and over in his mind while he tried to focus on the storm. A few more flashes of light and the sound of muffled rumbles had told him the storm was moving farther away. Now, he could hardly hear the rain. Finally, he fell asleep.

\*     \*     \*

"Uncle Mark, can we have pancakes?" Ashley asked while sitting on his lap and pulling his ears. "Mom and Dad are still sleeping and Christina said to ask you."

Mark quickly woke up from the pain of someone tugging at his ears. "Hey, knock that off. How am I going to hear your mom yelling at me if you pull my ears off?"

Ashley laughed and switched from tugging on Marks ears to punching him on his arm.

"I know what you need." Mark bellowed. He grabbed her, flipped her upside down, and slapped her bottom.

"Help!"

Christina bound across the room, dove over the air mattress, and landed on her uncle. Mark fell to the ground and the girls piled on.

"You kids knock it off down there."

"It's Mom." Ashley quickly said.

Mark stood, scooped up his nieces, and tossed them on the air mattress. "Now stay there or it'll be curtains."

"What does that mean?" Ashely asked while slapping the mattress.

"Stay there!" Mark checked his watch and walked into the kitchen, eight o'clock. He knew it was too early to call anyone. The rain had stopped but the clouds still filled the sky. Mark would give it another hour and call Dan Rowe.

*9:00a. m.*
*The cabins outer mud room,*

"Hello."

"Mr. Rowe, good morning. It's Mark Springfield, Jacks son. I hope it isn —

"Mark!" Dan quickly interjected. "Yes, yes. It's good to hear from you. How are you? It's been awhile."

Mark paused. In his mind, the call was supposed to be all business. Call and ask a few questions and move on. However, the lump in his throat told him it was far from 'just business.' Images of the dinner they had two years after his mom and dad were killed flashed in his mind's eye. He hadn't spoken to Dan since that night. It had taken Mark a few long seconds to answer, but he pushed the lump down. "I'm sorry. I should have called sooner. I can't believe it's been seven years. I —"

Dan cut Mark off and gently asked. "How are you doing young man?"

Mark heard the frailty in his voice. "Fine, thank you. Mr. Rowe, I would like to ask you a few questions concerning my dad and the time before he died."

"Your dad's death!? May I ask...why now?"

"It's my nieces. They are starting to ask about their grandma and grandpa. Mary has the grandma part covered but, we seem a bit vague on what our dad was up to before he died."

"Hmmm, I see. Well, I'll tell ya, your dad sure kept the office lively. The accident was a shock to all of us."

"I know, when I got the call, I almost dropped my phone." Mark paused then continued. "Mr. Rowe, what did his average day look like? What were some of the things he had been working on before the crash?"

Dan chuckled and said, "Well, I'm not as young as I once was, but give me a minute and I'll try'n remember."

"Mr. Rowe, if you'd like for me to call back I ca —"

"Oh, that won't be necessary. Let's see. The accident happened on a Tuesday, February 4th 2003 as I remember. So, the week before, your dad was at the... Business Transformative Institute, He made a trip down the street to... Environmental Concerns, and oh yeah, he made a trip to the Defense Courier building." Dan continued. "I don't remember who in those establishments he visited; it was a long time ago. In fact, I may be wrong with some of those."

"And to be clear, my dad worked on computers. Programming, writing code, that sort of thing, right?"

"Yup, he was the best," Dan offered.

A detail in Dan's recounting struck Mark, so he asked. "I see you remembered the actual day, Tuesday. That's a pretty good memory."

"Well that was a tough week for us. Your dads' protégé, well that's what he called her anyway, Ms. Colleen Kennedy had been killed, too."

"What?"

"Went out for a run, was robbed and murdered not one mile from her apartment. Poor thing, came all the way from California."

"Wait, the same week our mom and dad were killed so was Ms. Kennedy? This is the first I'm hearing this."

"I know, Mark," Dan quietly said. "We kept it from you kids. You didn't need any more... death."

Mark felt as if someone had pulled the rug out from under his feet. He leaned into the corner of the small room. He didn't think knowing about Colleen would have changed things back then but it certainly shined a new light on the events now.

Mark composed himself and asked. "Did she work with my dad often?"

"She did. In fact, she made the trip to the Defense Courier building with him. It was a big deal for her. She liked your dad a lot." Dan paused and added in a broken voice, "We all liked your dad."

"Will you find out who my dad met with at the Defense building? I'd like to get a perspective of my dad from the customer's view."

"Oh, sure. But you know, I'm one hundred percent retired now." Dan announced. "However, I'll go in and pull up our schedules for that time and see who he had met with. But Mark you just can't drive onto that base. You need a security clearance to get through the gate."

"My dad had a security clearance?" Mark asked trying to contain his surprise.

"He did. Some of the systems he worked on were classified."

"At what level?" Mark quickly asked

"Well, let's not get into that."

Mark had a slew of questions but stopped himself from asking anymore. He did not want to allude to the fact that he had had any knowledge of government security or how it worked. "Perhaps that's a conversation for another time." Mark said dismissing the security talk. "If you get me a name, address, and phone number, I'll find a way to talk to him."

"I'll see what I can do." Dan was relieved that Mark had quickly moved on from his dad's security clearance.

"Well thank you for talking with me this morning. I guess I should have asked him more about his job."

"My pleasure. And, oh wait, … Marcus Smith. Your dad met with Marcus Smith."

"Excellent! Thank you, Mr. Rowe."

"And Mark, please don't wait so long to call. Perhaps dinner at the house. We'll have you, your sister and those inquisitive girls over. I can tell them funny stories about their grandpa."

"That would be nice. Mary and I would love to hear them, too."

The two said their friendly goodbyes and then hung up. They had shared a common thread. And that thread had been frayed on a Tuesday night, in two thousand three.

# 10

*November 2012*
*Great Smoky Mountains*
*North Carolina*
*10:25a. m.*

"Hello."

Not only did Mark hear the 'hello,' he also heard all the commotion in the background and sensed his partner wasn't in the United States, but he asked. "Are you back?"

"No. We're on our way to catch a C-130 out of Baghdad. If our call drops, I'll call you when I can. We're going through a pretty remote area. I thought we'd be back a few days ago but we got hung up on a few small details I can't wait to tell you about."

Marks' hunch was confirmed. His friend and fellow agent had not returned from Iraq.

Mike Hollister and a new field agent had been on a two-week assignment investigating a weapons cache that was reported to have been from China.

Mike Hollister stood just over 6 feet. His short thick black hair, smooth complexion and solid build gave him the look of the classic CIA agent. He had joined the agency two years before Mark Springfield and used his seniority to harass his friend. Holding a Master's degree in computer programming he was highly sought after. Hollister swore his allegiance to the United States with six other Clandestine Service Trainees after a recruitment drive had left him wanting more.

"Who are you with?" Mark asked

"Cindell Little Foot." Mike said glancing over at his partner.

"The Cherokee?" Mark asked ardently. "How's she working out?"

"I think she might work okay. She talks a lot. Do you remember how Ramous went on about his mayflower roots? Well this one yammers on and on. Ramous would have been no match." Mike laughed and gave Cindell a wink. They were jammed shoulder to shoulder in a Humvee, wrapped in flak jackets with helmets strapped to their heads. Even though it was a noisy ride, he knew she could hear every word he said.

Other than seeing her at the graduation, Mark knew very little about the young woman. Her black shoulder-length hair had been pulled tight into a bun and Mark was sure that soaking wet, she only weighed one hundred and ten pounds. However, when she was in the academy, he heard stories of her being strong as an ox with a sharp wit. She had already made a name for herself.

Fearing a dropped connection, Mark switched back to business. "When you get back to the shop, run this name – Colleen Kennedy. She was murdered in DC, February 5th, 2003. Oscar Echo Oscar."

The acronym caused Mike to pause. He repeated it for clarity. "Oscar Echo Oscar."

"That is correct."

"Until then." Mike ended the call and slipped his phone into the inside pocket of his flak jacket. Staring at the boots of the marine sitting across from him, he thought, *what are you up to?* Oscar Echo Oscar was a term the two of them had used occasionally over the years. It not only meant Our Eyes Only, it meant do not let anyone know you're looking into anything and do not share the information with anyone.

When Mark arrived at North Carolina's, Charlotte Douglas International Airport at 2:30 p. m. he walked across the quiet terminal. With the storm passing through, it was impossible to leave as soon as he would have liked. Delta's 3:20 p. m. was the earliest flight available. While he drove to the airport, he racked his brain trying to come up with reasons why a car in a lake would have had been registered to his dad. No matter what scenario he ran, knowing what he knew about his dad, nothing fit. He wanted to believe that Cameron had had it wrong. But he trusted Cameron, and Cameron would not have called about something this important unless he was fairly certain of the facts. He had already texted Cameron his 9:35 p. m. arrival, so now all he could do was wait.

When you are federal law enforcement, carrying a gun on a commercial aircraft is not only possible, but encouraged, especially if you're CIA. After meeting the pilot, Mark walked past security with an escort. When he was cleared, he headed straight for Deltas' first class lounge. At the self-serve counter, he made himself a hot tea. After scanning the room, he walked over to a glass bowl sitting at the end of a table. A variety of finger foods had been laid neatly on the table. Using the aluminum scoop, he filled a blue plastic bowl with nuts.

Mark sat in a yellow padded plastic low back chair and placed his drink on a small wooden table that was in front of him. Holding the bowl, he picked through the assortment until he found his favorites. Then he tossed cashews into his mouth one by one.

Mark watched a woman dressed in a tight fitting black dress with white stripes down each side walk up to the table in front of him. She took a white ceramic mug and poured herself a cup of coffee. He tried not to stare, but even he knew there were times when a woman's chemistry transcended the bounds of decency. He looked away, but found his eyes wondering back in her direction. Distracting himself, he leaned in and took a sip of tea.

She sat down directly across from Mark and crossed her long tan legs, then leaned back and visibly relaxed while draping her left arm over the back of the chair. Slowly she took a sip from the mug. After two more drinks, she set her mug down on the same table that Mark had been using and looked directly at him. A sultry smile spread across her full supple lips.

Mark returned her soft gaze then his eyes drifted down her long legs and onto her black high- heeled shoes. He noticed a thin brown leather band around her leg resting on her ankle.

Finally, she broke the silence. "Do you think we'll actually make it out? It was a pretty bad storm last night."

Mark broke his stare and looked over her shoulder and out of the window. Nodding his head, he said. "It looks to be clearing. I think we'll be okay."

There was a long pause and when she spoke, the words floated softly from her ruby red lips. "Where do your travels take you this afternoon?" Leaning in, she interlaced her fingers around her knee. Her dress hiked up her perfectly shaped legs.

For a moment, Mark thought to say, Texas. But her shoulder-length blond hair and perfectly tanned skin screamed California. She could quite possibly be on his plane. "California," he said with a shy smile. For some reason, she had an effect on him. She was drop-dead gorgeous, and looking away from her wasn't an easy thing to do. But Mark also sensed an underlying toughness, an air of, 'Don't screw with me.'

"Oh, me, too" She said with a big smile. "Are you on the three twenty?"

Out of instinct, Mark grabbed his ticket and looked at it. "I sure am." Before he could look up, she moved around the table and sat next to him. *Honeysuckles,* he thought. *She smells of fresh, wet honeysuckles.* Mark felt her rub up against him when she leaned in and looked at his ticket.

"That's great!" She chuckled. "Me, too. My ticket is in my bag. Wait, I'll get it and we can see if we are sitting close together." She quickly stood and walked to a black bag that had been sitting on a table next to the counter that held the coffee pot.

Mark forced himself not to stare while she walked away. Instead he leaned in, picked up his cup of tea, and took a few sips. He sat back, crossed his right leg over his left, and looked out of the window while he awaited her return. When she didn't come back, he casually looked over his left shoulder. She was gone. Mark looked around the room and spotted an 8 1/2 X 11 sheet of paper folded in half like a tent sitting three tables over from where the black bag had been. Something was written across the front. Mark narrowed his eyes and stood. The writing was small however, he knew what had been written. He walked over, picked it up, and pursed his lips. He looked around the room and then back at the sheet of paper. 'Mark Springfield' had been handwritten across the front. Flipping it up, he read what had been scribed on the underside. 'Do not go to California, let the past be the past.'

There was something familiar about the ominous note. He waved it in front of his nose. Honeysuckles. Mark folded the paper and ran his thumb and forefinger across the crease while looking around for the woman. As a child he was taught to be polite to everybody and treat them with respect. His job had taught him to do the same with two additions, question people's motives and have a plan to kill everyone you meet. But he felt disarmed around the woman; the few minutes he had spent with her excited him and killing her had been the furthest thing from his mind.

# 11

*February 3ʳᵈ 2003*
*Off the Southeast Coast of South Africa*

E rasmo Jones stood on the conning tower of the Los-Angeles-class fast-attack submarine, USS Olympia. He held a pair of Bushnell 7 X 50 binoculars against his eyes while the submarine sliced thru the sea. Slowly, he moved his head from left to right. He lowered the binoculars and with his naked eyes scanned back the other way.

Erasmo, known only to his close friends as Raz, had been topside ever since the submarine had detected an explosion with their Common Broadband Advanced Sonar and Satellite Side-scan System. They surfaced off the southeast coast of South Africa and cruised at a slow 18 knots, its composite nose pointing in the direction of the Resolution Research Vessel. Through the binoculars, Raz could see its black smoke twist into the clear blue sky in the distance.

Maggie Cress stood next to the man she only knew as Mr. Jones. She, along with her counterpart on the port side, were the lookouts tasked with assuring their submarine would not runover any surface contacts or be caught off guard by approaching enemy ships or aircraft. A black watch cap was stretched over the twenty-eight-year old's short black hair. Over her head sat a pair of sound powered telephones. She too had a pair of Bushnell's and used them professionally to scan out to the horizon.

She was uneasy standing only inches from Raz. She felt their passenger was the kind of man that would throw her over and not think twice about it. But she stepped closer and nudged him to the side. She was new to the ship, one of the few females on a submarine and she wasn't going to let a man stand in her way, not even Mr. Jones. "Make a hole," she said bringing the binoculars up to her eyes.

Raz removed the glasses from his eyes while stepping to the left and looked down at the sailor scanning the horizon. He leaned back and looked her over, smiling at both her shape and her fearlessness.

"Contact." Maggie spoke firmly into the phones. "Bridge - Starboard lookout - small craft bearing zero three zero-six miles-closing."

"Shit!" Raz spat. "Where is he?"

Maggie pointed off the bow. She was annoyed by Jones's presence. They had picked him up three days earlier and the captain had moved the Executive Officer out of his quarters to give Jones his own space which was highly unusual.

Using the Bushnell's, Raz slowly scanned the horizon. Shaking his head, he asked, "are you sure?"

The look the young sailor had given annoyed him. Sure she would find nothing, he watched her lift the glasses and repeat her scan.

Maggie lowered the Bushnell's and slowly scanned with her naked eyes. She froze just off the forty-five-degree mark and then raised her classes. "Bridge – Starboard lookout – Contact four miles -Running broadside."

"Flash the contact," came the order from the bridge.

Larry Boshart fought the small boat as it constantly dropped down into the swells and shot back up the other side. The saltwater spray burned the bloody gash over his left eye. He gritted his teeth and adjusted the throttles, trying to maintain control. He felt like he was riding a cork in the middle of the ocean.

Far behind Boshart, the Resolution, the research vessel he had sabotaged, burned, its flames licking the water's surface. At the time, when he agreed to the work, the two-million-dollar pay-off had seemed a nice bonus for merely killing a man, something he viewed as a means to an end. But now, with the hassle of traveling across the rough sea, with what felt like the middle of nowhere, and the fact that his transport was thirty minutes late, that amount wasn't nearly enough.

Dropping into a deep swell, he noticed an intense white light off to the right. As he fought the sea, he glanced over his right shoulder and rode the wave to the top."God damnit. Where have you been?" he hissed thru gritted teeth. Negotiating the sea, he turned the boat towards the light.

"Bridge – Starboard lookout – Contact three miles - Running directly at us."

"So, he finally sees us?" Raz quipped.

Maggie understood the question for what it was and didn't answer. Feeling Jones push by her, she turned and watched him disappear down the ladder.

Raz found the captain and pulled him aside. They spoke for a few minutes and when the captain nodded his head, Raz smiled and headed topside.

As he ascended the ladder, Maggie heard the captain say, "Slow the boat to ten knots."

Maggie pushed her headset closer and said, "Say again."

"Lookout and signalman come below." The order was from the captain himself.

Maggie flashed a confused look across the conning tower at the port lookout and up at the sailor standing behind the high intensity signal light. Then she spoke firmly into the mouthpiece. "Aye aye, Captain." She shook her head in disapproval, then reached down and unplugged her phones. The two men descended the ladder in front of her, but before she went below, she glanced over at Jones and thought, "*Who the hell are you?*" Then she grabbed the sides of the ladder, slid down, and stopped at the laminated saying that had been taped to the side of the conning tower and quickly read the whole thing. *I am a United States Sailor. I will support and defend the Constitution of the United States of America and I will obey the orders of those appointed over me. I represent the fighting spirit of the Navy and those who have gone before me to defend freedom and democracy around the world. I proudly serve my country's Navy combat team with honor, courage and commitment. I am committed to excellence and the fair treatment of all.* Maggie finished her descent into the sub and stepped away from the ladder.

*       *       *

Raz felt he was being sized up but ignored the sailor. Instead he continued to watch the approaching boat.

Boshart slowed his craft, and as he came alongside the submarine, *Jesus this thing is big,* he thought

"Mr. Boshart, I presume." Raz yelled from forty feet above.

"Mr. Jones, I can't say I'm not impressed with your ride."

"I see by the smoke in the distance that you were successful." Raz said, tilting his head towards a small thread of black smoke twisting up towards the sky.

Boshart smiled and said. "Yes, I was, very."

"And the samples, may I have them?"

Larry Boshart was an experienced Troubleshooter, as he liked to be called in small circles, and he knew tossing up the small duffel was a fool's move. But bobbing around in a rubber boat next to a multi-billion-dollar submarine had left him little choice. He pointed to the ladder that ran up the side and said. "I'll sling the bag over my shoulder and climb up the ladder."

"No! We can't risk losing you both if you fall." Raz feigned concern, then held out his hand and said firmly, "Throw me the bag."

Boshart stood and turned towards his seat, lifted up the cushion, and withdrew the small blue backpack from within the chair's storage compartment. He looked at it and then at Jones. Dropping his hand low, he threw the bag to the man.

Reaching out slightly and using his other hand, Raz easily caught the bag. "Got it!" He set it on the deck, opened the bag and pushed the samples around looking for the other two. Not finding them he looked down at Boshart and yelled, "what happened to the other two, I'm supposed to bring four samples back, not two."

Boshart looked in the direction of the Resolution, smiled and said, "I suppose, by now, they are at the bottom of the ocean."

"How do I know you're not holding out on me?"

"Simple, I believe in what the group is doing." Boshart pointed in the direction of the bag and added, "I've given you all that I have."

"Ok," Raz said satisfied with the answer. "Come alongside."

"Asshole," Boshart whispered. Then he powered the boat and moved it in a circle to position himself next to the ladder.

Raz squatted down and reached into his own bag and withdrew his favorite pistol, a1911 stainless steel Colt Commander. He stood but kept the gun under the rim of the conning tower and out of view. With his empty hand, he motioned Boshart towards the ladder.

After he moved his boat into position, he quickly stepped on top of the inflatable tube and leaped onto the ladder. Relief washed over him when he firmly planted both feet onto the composite rungs. Slowly, he ascended, negotiating each step. When he was sure of himself, he looked up and right down the barrel of the 45.

"You son of a bitch." Raz spat, and pressed the trigger twice.

The crack of the 45 was swallowed by the sea, Raz heard what he thought was a high pitch squeal from Boshart when the rounds punched through his chest. He watched his arms fly out to the side when the impact threw him off the submarine.

Raz never heard Boshart hit the water. For an instant, the body disappeared in the swell, and as if the ocean didn't want him, it offered him up on top of a foam-covered wave. Raz studied the floating corpse. Then a satisfied smile spread across his face when the body slowly slipped below the waves. He stooped down, unzipped Boshart's backpack, and removed the samples, Knowing their potential, he checked the lids. Once he was sure they were secure, he reached into his bag and removed sheets of insulated paper and wrapped them around the vials. Then he placed the tubes inside plastic cases and slipped them into his own bag.

Erasmo Jones stood and looked out over the ocean. The submarine had moved quite a distance from the inflatable. He tossed the empty bag towards it, but with the slight breeze, it only made it about twenty feet before fluttering into the water. He took one last look before he descended the ladder into the submarine where Maggie was waiting for him.

"Are you finished topside, Mr. Jones?" she asked, looking up the ladder.

"I am."

"And the person in the small craft, will he be joining us?" she prodded.

"No." Raz said turning towards the captain. "The sub is all yours, skipper."

Maggie looked at her commanding officer and said. "Captain."

He pointed up at the hatch and said, "Close her up and let's get on with it. Mr. Jones, would you like me to lock that bag of yours in the safe?" He had been ordered to transport Mr. Jones to a set of GPS coordinates, surface, make contact and then clear the deck until his passenger was finished with whatever it was that was worth putting his fast attack in this part of the world. The captain knew that whatever the man had just received was of great importance.

Raz looked down at his bag then at the captain and asked, "Who has the combination?"

"The XO and I are the only ones."

"Thank you. But that's one too many." Raz turned and started to walk towards his quarters.

"Mr. Jones, where would you like us to drop you?"

Raz stopped, turned and offered. "Hawaii's nice this time of year."

"Helm. Set a course to Pearl. Coms, let them know we are coming. Will there be anything else Mr. Jones?" the Skipper asked.

"No, sir, you and your crew have been most accommodating." Before Raz left, he caught Maggie's gaze and held it for several long seconds. Then he turned and walked off the bridge.

# 12

*September 2012*
*CIA Headquarters*
*Langley, Virginia*

Mike Hollister walked past several of his colleagues' offices on the way to his own. He begrudgingly raised his coffee cup and mumbled a hello. He heard what he thought was laughter coming from the office adjacent to his. Not one to be left out of an amusing story, or a practical joke, he stuck his head in Bob Ash's office. Tapping on the open door, he got the attention of Bob and another agent who had been laughing at a photo.

Bob looked away from the picture and over at Mike. He turned the 8 ½ X 11 towards him and pointed to the lower right-hand corner.

Mike burst out laughing and said, "Bob, you're going to hell."

Mike stepped out of Bob's doorway, once inside his own office, he sat down at his desk, pulled his identification card from the plastic holder which hung around his neck and slid it into the slot on the side of the computer that sat in a docking station on his desk. It was flanked by two monitors. Then he pressed the on/off button. Leaning back in his chair, he closed his eyes and drummed his fingers on the plastic lid of his coffee cup.

He smiled again at the thought of the picture. When his computer beeped, he leaned forward and typed in his password and stared at the screen. Twenty seconds later, a red banner displayed along the top and bottom of all three monitors. Inside, written in white, were the words TOP SECRET. With a few strokes of the keys, Mike found and accessed the DC metro police crime log. He typed in 'Colleen Kennedy/2/5/2003' and pressed enter. Two files appeared on the monitor to the right. Just as he clicked on the file marked 'Photos' there was a knock on the door.

"Michael."

Mike glanced over the top of the center monitor and said, "Robert."

Laughing to himself, he reached over and switched the monitors off. The Oscar Echo Oscar code that he had shared with Mark came about because of Robert Ash. Years earlier, Mark had witnessed Bob, an older agent, break protocol, not once, but twice. It had led Mark to suspect Bob of espionage. He contacted Mike and instead of reporting their suspicions, the two young and ambitious agents had started their own investigation. They had devised the simple code to keep their inquiries to themselves. However, as it turned out, Bob was working at the discretion of the director of the CIA. When the two agents eventually approached the director with their suspicions, they were asked one question: why didn't you come to me right away? Their answer was simple. Bob had a stellar reputation and they didn't want to tarnish it if they were being overzealous. An hour later, the two left his office thinking they were going to receive a pat on the back but instead had gotten their asses chewed for conducting an unauthorized operation.

"Aren't you supposed to be in Bagdad?" Bob asked, stepping in and walking over to one of two brown leather chairs. He pointed to one and asked, "May I?"

"You're actually asking?" Mike chuckled.

Bob laughed, sat down, and said. "How was your trip and…why are you here?"

"No reason," Mike said taking a long drink of his coffee. "Ended up getting in at one and couldn't sleep, so here I am." He gave Bob a broad smile.

Bob sat back deep in the chair, pulled his left foot up across his right leg and over his thigh. "Do I have to wait for the report or are you going to tell me what you two found?"

Suddenly, Mike looked at Bob with a somber expression.

Bob felt the sudden change in Mikes demeanor and it made the room feel dark. He dropped his foot off his leg and lean forward in his chair. "Whatcha find?"

With pursed lips, Mike started. "Law rockets, TOW missiles, hand grenades, M16s." Mike watched the expression on Bob's face change and he knew why, but he continued, "The Beretta M9 and a shit ton of 1911s."

"Good Lord! A stash a U. S. made hardware!"

"And no one knows how they got there. The other problem for me is, everyone kept saying that this was a stash of Chinese weapons. But as soon as I went into the bunker, I could smell the apple pie."

"Who found it?"

"Our guys were on patrol and decided on a whim to expand their search grid. And there it was, out in the middle of F-ing nowhere, but at one time, that area was completely assessable by the Taliban." Mike grabbed his coffee, took a long drink, sucking the last few drops through the plastic lid, and then continued, "And that, Bob, is why I'm really here. I need to get all of this to the boss."

Bob stood, shaking his head. "Well, this will be interesting. I should let you get to it." Bob walked across the room and paused in the door frame. Looking over his left shoulder, he said, "I hear you traveled with Cindell LittleFoot."

"I did."

"And?"

He looked up at Bob with a tired smile and said. "She has a weird thing for mermaids, but I like her!" Mike finished with a slight chuckle.

As soon as Mike was alone in his office, he flipped on his monitor. Splashed across the screen were four photos of a murder victim. The first photo was a frontal picture from the chest up. It was of a woman lying on the ground seemingly dressed in a running suit, her green eyes wide open. There had been no indication of trauma. The second photo was from the side and Mike could tell from the hair that something had happen to the back of her head. The rear photo told the tale. It showed her blood-soaked hair matted around a small hole in the base of her skull. The fourth picture was taken from what Mike thought was ten feet and showed the crime scene. Under the pictures, was the name, Colleen Kennedy.

Mike clicked on the second file icon and a police report opened. It was dated February 5th 2003. It described the crime scene, the young woman, her family, employment, where she had lived and the 22-caliber bullet that had killed her. Mike studied the crime scene photos again and paged through the report. When he had finished, he leaned back and mumbled, "And who are you, Ms. Kennedy and why is Mark interested in you?"

# 13

*March 1777*
*Les NeufSoeurs, Paris*
*(The Nine Sisters Masonic Lodge)*
*Grand Master – Benjamin Franklin*

"I have spoken with the King and although he has not said directly that he would help fund our revolution, he encouraged us to fight on against our oppressors." Ben Franklin quickly picked up his ale while letting his last statement sink in. Shadows shimmered against the walls and ceiling when the flames from the fire danced out over the stone hearth. He was flanked to his left by Adam Weishaupt, a German philosopher and professor, and to his right by Mayer Amschel Rothschild. Across the large wooden table was the Marquis de Lafayette, to his right was Alexander Hamilton. At the head of the table sat Johann Daniel Lawaetz. All six men had pints of ale in front of them. Franklin was unaware Hamilton had been in Paris, but knowing the man was a confidant of General Washington, he held his tongue in case this was a covert visit.

"I will set sail for the colonies in one month's time and I will promise six thousand men for the American fight." The comment and promise came from the nineteen-year-old Lafayette, a French aristocrat convinced that the American cause in its revolutionary war was noble. He wanted to travel to the New World and seek glory. Secretly, he had had ideas for his own country.

At the request of Lafayette, Adam Weishaupt invited Franklin to the secret meeting. The young nobleman needed a recommendation from Franklin if he ever expected Washington to give him a position within the Continental Army.

With a questionable look, Franklin peered over the top of his mug and wondered, *who is this young man to command six thousand troops?* He glanced over at Weishaupt, then back at Lafayette. The purpose of Franklin's trip to Paris was to ask for support for the American cause. Earlier, he had been approached by an agent with the promise of blankets, powder, and ships. Now, he sat across from a nobleman who was offering troops. It was obvious that the monarch was covertly helping. But he asked. "Do you come on behalf of your king?"

Lafayette observed the men huddled around the table. Clearly, he was the youngest and felt in the presence of greatness. Dr. Franklin, who had snatched lightning from the heavens, was a figure whom he had known of his entire life. Rothschild was a recent acquaintance who was an important banker that wielded great power. Hamilton, he had just met and only knew him as a very influential

American Statesman. Weishaupt, he had met the past year. At the head of the table sat Lawaetz, who had been introduced as a merchant and textile industrialist and seemed to know everyone but Franklin. "Dr. Franklin, I am here to offer you six thousand men in exchange for a position with General Washington." Lafayette would not elaborate if he was there on behalf of the King.

"We will take the men, but I can only scribe you a recommendation. Whether General Washington will accept you is entirely up to him."

The young Lafayette excitedly raised his mug and exclaimed. "Dr. Franklin, I accept. I will rally the troops. It will take some time to get them to America, and as I said, I will go next month as it is the first available packet scheduled to sail to the colonies."

Franklin took a long drink of his draught, pulled it away from his wet lips, and said, "You will have your letter in two days' time." Then he continued to drink until the mug was empty.

All five men raised their mugs and followed Franklin's example. Each slammed their mug on the wooden table when they had finished.

When their mugs were drained, Adam Weishaupt addressed Lafayette from across the table. With a motion from his outstretched arm to the rest of the group, he said, "Kind sir, we would like to have a private word with Dr. Franklin."

Lafayette stood, pushed back his chair, and said, "Gentlemen, it has been a great honor. Dr. Franklin, to be in your presence was an even greater honor. I bid you all a good evening." Lafayette walked to where the garments had been neatly hung on hooks and grabbed his black cloak trimmed in blue. He turned, walked to the door, and pushed it open. Looking back over his shoulder, he said, "Au revoir." Then he walked through the doorway.

Several minutes passed before Weishaupt stood and moved around the table. He took Lafayette's empty chair, and when he spoke, his voice was hushed. "Dr. Franklin, you are a great man, an inventor, writer, philosopher, but most importantly, you sir, are a free thinker." Weishaupt paused and waited for the barmaid to set fresh mugs of ale on the table. He thanked her and when she walked away, he continued, "I would like to offer you membership in what I call Order of Perfectibilists."

For the first time in the evening, Rothschild spoke. He faced Franklin and whispered, "The order is being renamed to fit its cause." Gesturing to Weishaupt with his mug, he continued, "When he returns to Ingolstadt, he will rename it 'The Order of the Illuminati.'"

"Yes, the enlightened," Weishaupt confirmed. "We are going to infiltrate all of the Masonic lodges."

Franklin turned to Rothschild and asked, "What is your part in all of this?" Franklin understood money and was wary of bankers, but he saw the importance of it when he left Boston as a teenager. The colonial economy languished for want of means of exchange. When he first landed in Philadelphia most shops where closed-up in the city but when the assembly had seen fit to print money, the city and country flourished. Now he had just asked a banker what he wanted and almost laughed out loud at the answer.

"Money, my dear friend. You need money for your cause and I would like to take advantage of your good fortune should your country win its independence. It is a gamble I am willing to take."

Franklin glanced at Weishaupt for several long seconds and thought, *this is why I was really asked to visit the Three Sisters.*

"When you win your independence," Rothschild continued, "we would like the honor of establishing the Bank of the United States."

"A bank backed by *our* government?" Franklin asked suspiciously.

"No, Doctor. Backedby Mr. Lawaetz, a few friends here in France, and, of course, me."

Franklin looked into his ale while he shifted his mug between his hands. Slowly, he shook his head.

Rothschild had seen the hesitation and shrewdly added, "Of course, we will form a charter. It will give your fledgling government time to establish itself. It will have the money required."

Weishaupt reached across the table and laid his hand on Franklins forearm. He gave it a squeeze and said "The Illuminati, Ben, I think we can use the power of the banks to reach all of the free thinkers. And perhaps draw new ones to America. Our order will put us on a path of enlightenment."

Franklin looked his friend in the eyes. The thought had appealed to him. It was why he had spent his last eighteen years in London. He felt he had outgrown Philadelphia. Kindred scientific spirits were few in America, kindred intellectual gifts still fewer. He sat back and took a drink of his ale. He held his mug to his lips while looking at both Weishaupt and Rothschild. Moving the mug away from his face, he asked. "And you will agree to a charter for a period of time?"

"It is the right thing to do." Rothschild answered.

"We will write it into law." Franklin said, testing Rothschild.

"What will you need, thirty, forty years? I'm sure, Dr. Franklin, these things can be worked out."

Ben Franklin tilted his mug high in the air and drained it. Warm liquid dribbled down the side of his chin. Wiping his mouth with the back of his hand, he stood and looked at the men around the table and said, "This has been a successful trip. We have been promised ships, blankets, powder, men." Stopping his gaze on Rothschild, he added, "and money." Franklin pulled out a small purse and removed a few coins from its pocket and laid them on the table. "Gentlemen, I must take my leave. I have a chess game that awaits. We will talk soon, Mr. Rothschild. We will talk soon." Mimicking Lafayette, he grabbed his cloak and walked thru the doorway out into the cold night.

Several minutes went by before Hamilton spoke. The worry in his voice was evident. "A charter? A law? Dr. Franklin is not one to be trifled with."

A smile spread across Rothschild's lips. He looked at Hamilton and said. "Let me issue and control a nation's money, and I care not who writes the laws."

# 14

*November 2012*
*Los Angeles, California*

Delta's mid-afternoon flight left fifteen minutes late but touched down in Los Angeles, California on time. Mark turned on his phone and texted Cameron, '*Landed.*' Thirty seconds later, his phone vibrated. '*Got it. Text when curbside.*'

When the plane parked, Mark watched the passengers get up, retrieve their belongings from the overhead bins, and stand in the aisle and wait. He too waited and slowly looked around at the passengers like he had done when he boarded in North Carolina. The blonde was not someone who would have been easily overlooked. He assessed she simply wasn't on the flight. His solace was that he was armed. He assumed she was as well and God only knew where she kept it.

After retrieving a backpack stuffed with enough clothes for three days from the overhead bin, Mark walked out into the Southern California night air ten minutes after he stepped off the plane. He moved thru the terminal at a quick pace, watching and wary of everyone.

Halfway thru the terminal, he sent Cameron another text. He only waited four minutes curbside before a 2012 maroon Ford Fusion pulled alongside with its passenger window rolled down and Cameron staring at Mark as if he were lost.

Mark slid onto the front seat and threw his pack over his left shoulder onto the back seat. He faced Cameron and said with an outstretched arm. "Good evening, Detective."

The friends shook hands and Cameron blurted with a grin. "Detective! Not that again?"

"Nice car. Please tell me it's not a hybrid."

"It's not." Cameron chuckled.

Mark smiled but it didn't last long. He liked seeing Cameron but this wasn't a social call.

"What do you have for me?"

Cameron handed Mark a vanilla folder and then pulled away from the curb and drove toward Century Boulevard. "It's the strangest thing. Like I said on the phone when I tried to look up information on the second car, it came back restricted. When we ran DNA and asked for a dental match on the body, it came back as unknown. I've never seen that before."

"I have." Mark blurted. "You've heard of WITSEC, the Witness Protection Program haven't you?"

Cameron nodded his head and said. "Yes, I have."

Mark looked at Cameron and pondered telling him of the SLIPP, the CIA's Top Secret version of the WITSEC. However, the Secure Location International

Protection Program was rarely used so Mark decided to keep the information to himself. In the folder was a trove of pictures and lab reports. Cameron and his partner took so many pictures that the normal person wouldn't see the need to actually go to the lake where the cars were discovered.

As Mark looked thru the folder, he said. "How about we take a trip to this Mono Lake?"

Cameron raised his eyebrow while looking down at the folder. He quickly did the math and said, "Traffics light but that still puts us there a bit over five hours. Probably closer to six. That's four in the morning, and besides, I didn't take enough pictures?"

Mark sat quietly and paged thru the contents of the folder. He finally said. "If this really is where my dad died, I'd like to see it."

"Recline that seat and close your eyes, I'll drive the first half."

Mark moved the seat back, hit the recline lever and then stretched out his legs. His eyes felt heavy but he had to ask one more question. "Detective, how's that girl of yours, what's her name?"

"You know damn good and well what her name is!"

"Oh yeah, I remember now." Mark said with an evil grin. "It's Veronica. Well!?"

With a heavy sigh, Cameron countered, "This is going to be a long drive."

The two men bantered about Cameron's love life, but shortly after he transitioned from the 14 North to the 395 North, bright white and blue lights lit-up the interior of his car at the same time the sirens started. He glanced down at his speedometer, eighty-five was locked into the cruise control. He slowed and pulled over to the side of the road. He knew he had a few minutes while the officer ran his plates so he retrieved his wallet and opened it so his badge was visible. Then he turned on his dome light, lowered his driver's window and placed his hands on the steering wheel. He looked at Mark and quipped. "No need to get shot this time of night."

The officer cautiously approached Cameron's window with his hand resting on his gun. He stopped a few inches aft of the door handle and said. "Good evening, May I —"

"Officer, before you get started, my name is Cameron Butler. You and I work for the same folks," he said with a smile. Cameron flipped his wallet over and showed the officer his badge and ID.

The officer quickly changed his demeanor when he recognized Cameron from all of the interdepartmental write-ups. "Officer Butler, sir, it's an honor," he said offering Cameron his hand.

"It's 'detective' to you," Mark blurted louder than he should have.

Cameron looked over at Mark, shook his head, and laughed. Then Cameron turned back to the officer.

"Thanks, but all that nonsense in the hills seems like such a long time ago."

The officer stuck his hand thru the window and shook Cameron's hand. "Well, it's an honor, sir."

Quickly changing the subject, Cameron asked, "Hey, we're headed up to Mono Lake to take a look around. Any animals I should be looking out for?"

"Yeah, there's been a bear sighting a bit farther up. But you're driving at this time of night?"

"I have an out-of-town visitor who's on a tight schedule." Cameron said tilting his head towards Mark. "We wanted to be there at first light."

"Are you working the body and cars they pulled out?"

"I was, but sorry. There's nothing I can share."

"That's okay. I'm sure I'll read about it." He quipped. "You two be careful and a… slow down a bit. There really have been sightings."

"Will do and thanks again."

As Cameron drove away from the side of the road, Mark kidded. "A little fame, I see."

"Happens once in a while." Cameron said sheepishly.

"And did that fame come with any sort of financial gain?"

"It may have come with a bonus in my check. And before you ask, I bought Springfield Armory's M1A1 SOCOM, chambered in three o eight. I was going to surprise you with it the next time you were out."

Mark nodded his head in approval and asked. "Is it a sixteen or II?" Looking at Cameron, he continued, "Picatinny rails verses the Cluster rail system."

"How is it that you seem to know more about firearms…" Cameron jokingly protested. "But to answer your question, it's a II, a little heavier with the extra rails, but you never know when you need to hang more stuff off your gun."

Mark chuckled. "True." He closed his eyes, pushed his body back into the seat, and tried to relax. The encounter with the woman pushed itself to the forefront of his mind. To him it had actually spoken volumes. Quite a few hours had passed after Cameron's phone call before he even knew of that particular flight. And there she was, in the first-class lounge, sweet, innocent, and if the word 'stunning' had a picture, it would have had been of her. She looked as if she were meeting with dignitaries. *Was Cameron's phone tapped? Was his? If so, who knew to tap them and why? And the note, 'Let the past be the past.' What a crock of shit.*

Mark wasn't happy he was taken off guard by the stranger. Beautiful women can go anywhere and do almost anything. He had given talks about it at the academy and he had watched his sister Mary get away with murder when they had been out together. Men went out of their way to help her do the most mundane things. The two of them often joked about it. *Let the past be the past*, he thought again. *Am I supposed to forget about this? Do they know they are threating a federal agent?* The answer was easy. Yes, they do, they know exactly who he is. He felt it. He was dealing with a very well-connected organization possibly at a government level. The question he had had was, what government?

Cameron noticed Mark was finally quiet. Knowing the man had been up most of the night, he reached over and pressed the 'heated seat' icon on the display to help him fall asleep. And not talking about a past love all night suited him just fine.

Mark fought the need to sleep. There was still too much to figure out. However, the road noise slowly disappeared as he was being immersed into a warm blackness.

# 15

*November 2012*
*Mono Lake, California.*
*0630*

"**M**ark." Cameron waited a few seconds before he nudged Mark's shoulder for the second time. "Mark."

"Yes, I'm up, I'm up." Mark forced open his eyes, shifted in his seat, and looked around.

"There's been movement in the office for about thirty minutes. I don't think they open for another hour or so, but I bet we can get in and take a look around."

"You should have awakened me earlier," Mark said through a muddled throat.

Cameron pushed open the door and stepped out into the chilly morning air. He walked around to the trunk, popped it open, and pulled out two light jackets. Mark was closing the door when Cameron walked around the rear quarter. "Any normal person would've been happy with the pictures we took." Cameron quipped with a smile. "But, Mark Springfield, you are far from that. Here, take this. I thought you might want to come up here." Mark gave Cameron a warm smile as they pulled on their jackets and turned towards the entrance to Mono Lake. When they got close to the kiosk, they watched thru the front window, a woman in her sixties with short reddish-blonde hair, opened the side door.

"Sorry, guys. We don't open until eight."

Cameron noticed the name *Rhonda* had been embossed on the woman's name plate. Underneath was written *Manager*. "Good morning, Rhonda," Cameron said, taking her hand and shaking it. "My name is Cameron Butler, and this is my partner, Mark Springfield." He reached for his ID holder while she shook Mark's hand, flipped it open, and showed her his badge. "We're investigating the submerged cars."

"Oh, I remember. You folks had a boatload of people up here last month. It's been the talk of the town." Rhonda leaned in close to Cameron and whispered. "Tell me, was it murder?"

"Honestly, Rhonda, we don't know what it was." Cameron said with a smile. "But if it's okay, we sure would like to take another look around."

Rhonda nodded her head, leaned back into the booth, and grabbed a ring of keys. "Well, let me unlock the chain so I can open up the gate and you two boys can have at it."

Both men waved when they drove pass the booth. Ten minutes later, they were standing next to where the cars had been pulled from the lake. While comparing the site to the photos, the two looked the area over while Cameron explained how the cars were found and what tests had been performed on them and the driver of the rear car. "It was here that I had first run the vehicle identification numbers and came up with the information on your dad." Shaking his head, Cameron continued, "Since I had to guess at some of the numbers, I knew it had to be wrong. So, I waited until the labs came back then I ran it again."

"And here we are." Mark added. Looking out across the lake and back at the surrounding terrain. Then he added, "one thing this area has going for it, it's isolated." Squatting down, he asked. "But why here?" Mark stood when he felt his phone vibrate in his pocket. Pulling it out, he checked the screen. The name Mike Hollister was displayed across it. "Hello."

"Good morning, Mark."

"Are you back?"

"I am and sitting at my desk."

"What do you have for me?"

"Let's see. Colleen Kennedy was killed September 5th 2003 by a single gunshot to the back of her skull. A .22 caliber bullet was retrieved. It's listed as a robbery, no sexual assault. It says she was out for her normal run but apparently at the wrong time. No suspects, no witnesses. And Mark, it says here she worked for the same company as your dad." There was a long pause. "Wait a minute." Mike opened another window and typed in 'Jack Springfield' followed by what he could remember of his address. Two files appeared on the monitor. One marked as photos and one marked as a police report. He clicked on the report and started to read it out loud, but then quickly started reading to himself when it became apparent what was going on. Jack Springfield died one day before Colleen Kennedy's murder.

Mark was certain Mike had made the connection and added. "You know how I feel about coincidences. And a .22. How textbook can you get?"

"What else do you need, Mark?"

"Have someone pull the security tapes from in and around Delta's airport lounge at the Charlotte, North Carolina airport. Start at 1 p. m. and run it until 4 p. m."

"What am I looking for?"

"A blonde dressed in a black dress with white stripes down both sides. Trust me, you'll know when you see her."

"Done. Anything else?"

"My dad and Ms. Kennedy made a trip to the Defense Courier building January twentieth, about a week before they were killed. It was a Monday. They met with a Marcus Smith. I need info on him and anyone else they might have met with. And another thing, my dad had a security clearance Fi —"

"Your dad had a security clearance?" Mike blurted. "Isn't that something you think you'd know?"

The question caught Mark off guard. It had been the same question he had asked himself ever since he spoke with Mr. Rowe. "I guess. However, I had no reason to investigate him. He was my dad. But find out what level clearance he had."

"I'll get right on it. By the way, how are the Smokies this morning?'

The question caused Mark to pause. Even though these were company phones with their own encryption built in, the whole thing had started to feel…different. He wanted to tell his friend he was in California but thought better of it. "Cold. Cold and rainy."

Mark ended the call and slipped the phone in his pocket and looked out over the lake wondering, *what else don't I know about you, Jack Springfield.* Looking at Cameron, he said, "I want to show you something." Mark walked over to the car, opened the door and retrieved the folded paper from his back pack and handed it to Cameron. "This was sitting on a table in the lounge yesterday afternoon." He watched Cameron unfold and read it. Then he continued, "As I was waiting for my flight, I was visited by one of the prettiest women I have ever seen. When she mysteriously vanished, this appeared on a table."

A confused look grew on Cameron's face. "I don't understand. I just called you."

Mark slowly nodded his head. "And that, detective, is a problem."

# 16

*February 5ᵗʰ 2003*
*A club in Virginia*
*Meeting of the Membership*

The thin blue cloud that hung over the room would have offended some. However, the smokers creating it could not have been happier. Cigar smoking was encouraged and Cubans were as plentiful as candy at Halloween. Frank Sinatra, Bing Crosby and Nat King Cole took their turns softly crooning over well-placed speakers set around the room. Tapestries from the fourteenth century were hanging neatly from the walls. A Roman fresco of a young man which had once adorned the walls of a first-century villa now stood inlaid in an oak frame in the west corner of the room. It had been flanked by works of art painted by, Oscar-Claude Monet and Rembrandt van Rijn. Eloquently displayed were artifacts from the Ming and Tang Dynasties. Treasures worth millions from around the world adorned the room. And displayed on a marble desk from the Vatican and various shrines were relics representing the world's religions, they had been positioned to face the centerpiece, an eighteen-inch silver S with two thin solid gold bars set vertically thru the center. The display represented the organizations core: money and control.

The panel of a tall cabinet that stood near the three-inch-thick solid mahogany door had been slid open exposing a bank of sophisticated listening and electronic monitoring equipment used to constantly sweep the room. The five-story building was owned by the Essex Corporation which had leased the first three floors to a law firm. The fourth floor was empty, acting as a security buffer for the Membership which occupied the entire fifth floor. The fifth floor was divided into two sections: the main offices on the north side of the building and a recreational area on the south. a small gym, sauna, lap pool and locker room took up the south side of the building. The secure office space, bar and entrance occupied the north side.

Eight of the thirteen members were in attendance and lounging in the bar. All of them in their sixties and seventies except for Rear Admiral Shannon Lambert. The fifty-one-year-old sat across a love seat wrapped in a thick white bathrobe. Her shoulder-length auburn hair was wrapped in a towel and her feet were pulled up under her rear. She swirled the last sip of her second brandy while waiting for Martin Chase to finish retelling the story of his granddaughter's birthday.

The Membership was the tip of the greatest pyramid organization ever conceived. It was born out of want and set its roots in the United States during the revolutionary war. Over the centuries, it had been perfected in Europe. They controlled the global markets, using people from nine compartmentalized organizations from the pyramid, who are led to believe they are part of a secret society.

Lambert was shepherded by her grandfather and weaned from the tit of power and greed. Ten years after she became a naval officer, she had been brought into the Membership. Three weeks after her initiation, her grandfather had died. Sixteen years later and a one-star admiral, Shannon Lambert controlled the reach into the military corridors. Now she was being positioned for Assistant Secretary of Defense for Global Strategic Affairs.

Timothy Rothschild stared at Lambert, patiently waiting for Chase to finish. The seventy-one-year-old banker sat back in a dark green tweed chair holding a nearly empty glass of ice wine by its stem. He wanted an answer to why there was a breach in security and what was being done about it. But he was patient with his colleague and the members politely laughed at the end of the retelling.

After a short pause, Rothschild asked. "Shall we discuss the markets?" Nods from around the room told him he could continue. "We are set to see growth in the relative strength index for New York Stock Exchange Composite somewhere north of eighty percent." Rothschild sipped his wine and continued. "Of course, there will be the 'suggested' periods of decline."

"That, of course, will never happen." Chuckled Chase from across the room.

"No, not likely." laughed Rothschild while standing. "Two thousand three will be a very good year. Two thousand four however..." He let his comment sink in and walked over to the bar and poured himself another glass of ice wine and turned toward Lambert. "And that brings us to the breach in security, Admiral. We cannot risk one of the lower tiers exposing any of this. No matter how small the breach, it needs to be dealt with."

Lambert pulled the towel off of her head and vigorously rubbed it over her hair. A few seconds later, she laid it in her lap and ran her fingers along and massaged the top of her scalp.

Her casual actions took Rothschild by surprise, but then he said. "You've taken care of this already, haven't you?"

Lambert smiled and said. "Timothy, I have the same concern as you." Reaching over, she grabbed his hand and said with finality. "It has been taken care of." Then she gave it an affectionate pat while adding. "It is unfortunate that Colonel Kirby did not work out. Having someone from the astronaut corps in a tier and the head of NASA would have been perfect. However, I have already taken steps to identify a replacement, and before you ask, he will be the new NASA administrator before next year's weather event so there is no need to cancel anything you have put in motion." Lambert glossed over the three people she had ordered killed to conceal the shooting down of the space shuttle, however, inwardly, she was concerned. It did not bother her that she had ordered the disposal of three human beings. Her concern was that two of them had been the parents of a CIA agent. She knew field agents were professional investigators mixed with attack dog. She hoped that their demise would always appear to be an accident and never point to a more malevolent ending. Pushing the thought to the back of her mind, she went on to say. "Speaking of next year's weather event..."

Rothschild walked back over to the bar and muttered, "Hmmm...Yes." He turned back to the group and said, "As you all know, my lower tier knows this as Carlotta 5. We will strive for a category F5 tornado but we will settle for an F4. What matters is that the town will be destroyed."

"Timothy, you have done an excellent job with this and I think I can speak for the rest of the group when I say, we never thought anyone would be able to actually control the weather. The test next year in Nebraska will be the culmination of years of planning and research. Well done."

Lambert looked around the room and then back at Rothschild and continued. "We lift our glasses to you."

Here, here's were heard from around the room and then everyone raised their glass and toasted their friend by taking long drinks. Shannon too, raised her brandy glass and finished her drink.

"Yes, our ability to control the weather. The F5 is set for Nebraska. We will target the town of Hallam and we will do it May 22, 2004. Our predictions show the entire town should be affected."

"And, of course, the more devastation, the better." Chase said with a grin. Again, everyone raised their glasses.

Shannon handed her glass back towards Timothy and jiggled her ice around and quipped. "This isn't going to fill itself."

He smiled, took the glass and walked back towards the bar.

"Now our last order of business before I go for a swim." Morgan laughed while snapping the elastic of his red bathing suit.

"Very well," nodded Rothschild. "The microbes." He handed Lambert her drink and said, "Admiral?"

Lambert took a sip from her brandy glass and started. "The samples should be on their way back. Then we transfer them to another tier and off they go to the lab."

"Very good. Moving these from one tier to another assures our shell game goes undetected."

"Yes, Timothy, and once it's demonstrated that we can weaponize the samples, our friends across the pond will be set for the Vatican attack."

"On a biblical scale." Laughed Chase, "on a biblical scale." Everyone in the room laughed and continued with their drinks.

# 17

*February 7th 2003*
*Pearl Harbor, Hawaii*

Erasmo Jones felt the moment the submarine kissed the buoys of Pier 14. The tug boat slowly nudged and held the fast attack in position while the mooring lines were tied. Raz had been lying across the bed lightly sleeping, the unintended interaction with the female sailor now pushed into his subconscious. She had gotten under his skin and it caused him to grin.

Two pillows and his backpack were stuffed under his head and a world map with his hand-written notes had been spread out across his chest, the Colt Commander was lying on the bed next to him.

Twenty minutes after the submarine docked, a sharp whistle over the public address system broke the silence in his compartment. "Liberty. All ashore who's going ashore."

Raz flipped his wrist and checked his watch. *I'll give it fifteen*, he thought. Gathering up his map, he slipped it into his backpack and the Colt, he slid into the waistband holster he had clipped to the inside of his pants. He pulled on his shoes, stood and looked around the small space. He reached over to the desk and instinctively straightened a few items that belonged to the XO. Again, he checked his watch and mumbled, "close enough." Grabbing his back pack, he slid one strap over his right arm and rested it on his shoulder. After a quick glance down to ensure his shirt was covering his gun, he stepped thru the doorway, turned left and strode down the passageway.

Raz put one foot on a rung and looked up thru the open hatch at the clear blue Hawaiian sky. After living aboard the submerged submarine for eight days, the air gave him a feeling of renewed life. When he was about to ascend the ladder, he sensed someone watching him and turned around. Looking back down the passageway, he instantly recognized the culprit. "I have to say, Ms. Cress, nice job spotting my friend."

Maggie was headed topside and when she saw Raz at the ladder she stopped, she had no intention of associating with him. However, his compliment took her off guard and she returned a half smile.

He nodded, then turned and climbed the ladder out into the warm Hawaiian air.

Erasmo cautiously stepped thru the hatch and looked around the submarine while turning on his phone. Before walking across the gangway, he carefully studied the area looking for anything out of the ordinary. As he stepped on the dock his phone vibrated displaying one single text. *Aircraft delayed/maintenance pick up tomorrow Hickam/1400 hours.* Raz pursed his lips but quickly turned them into a shallow smile when he saw Maggie stepping onto the gangway. He hunched up his back pack and walked towards her. "Well it seems my departure has been delayed." He said stopping in front of her in such a way that it prevented her from stepping onto the pier. "I'm here until tomorrow. Join me for dinner?"

The last person Maggie thought she would ever spend time with was Mr. Jones. Although attractive in an odd way, he had a solid build, and was easily twice her age. However, something resonated thru him that she couldn't put her finger on. There was a quiet intensity, an inner power. She looked up and retorted. "Your binocular work needs, shall we say…help."

Raz looked around, cocked his head and whispered, "It was that bad?"

"Well…it sucked." Maggie leaned in, nudged Raz out of the way, stepped down from the gangway, and walked across the pier.

Watching her walk away, he smiled and thought, *she not only makes that uniform look good, she is indeed, fearless.* Still smiling he looked down and checked his phone. He knew he had to get the microbes to a secure location but, he wasn't unhappy he had been stranded in Hawaii.

"Three hours."

Raz looked across the pier in Maggie's direction.

"I'll be ready in three hours." She repeated.

Raz held up his phone and walked closer. "Give me your number and I'll call in three hours."

She pointed to the guard shack across the pier, "Mr. Jones, meet me there in three hours."

The two stared at each other for several long seconds before Raz blurted, "fourteen."

"Fourteen? What is —"

"Our age difference. Fourteen years. I saw the question in your eyes."

Maggie shifted on one leg and added. "I had you older than forty-two."

"Then you *are* twenty-eight."

"You guessed?"

"And correctly."

Suddenly, Maggie noticed the softness in Raz's eyes as his hard look seemed to soften. Then she heard herself say out loud "it doesn't seem to matter."

Raz tried to control his smile but it spread wide across his face. It was a smile that had melted a hundred women's hearts, but this time, hers would be the last heart he would ever want to melt. Erasmo Elisha Jones was smitten.

\*     \*     \*

*"Why the hell have I been waiting in this rental car for forty minutes? Do I really need this now? I don't even know this girl. Maggie Cress, who are you? I know you're not a one-night stand. I will say you are defiant mixed with a little*

*toughness. And you do know your own mind. Yup, that about sums it up. But what am I doing?"*

Erasmo's thoughts kept him company while he waited for the young sailor to arrive, flicking the keys to the car, pondering whether he should leave. "Too late now, this must be you." He murmured as he watched a short gray bus stop before the pier's entrance. Thirty seconds later, the bus slowly rolled out of his peripheral, he let out a low whistle that sounded like it had come from someone else. *Jesus,* he thought.

Almost unrecognizable without her uniform, Maggie stood with both hands in the back pockets of her white shorts, which accented her smooth tanned legs. The loose-fitting mint green shirt did little to hide the size of her breasts. He preferred women with long hair, but Maggie's pixy cut had him rethinking his tastes. A small black duffel bag embroidered with the word NAVY in yellow sat on the ground next to her. He watched one of the two Marines standing guard duty rush to assist her in any way possible. Raz opened the door of the rental, stepped outside and slowly walked towards his date. After making eye contact, he gave her a small wave.

"Thank you, I see my friend now." Maggie had been polite to the sentry but spent most of her adult life wondering why guys fell over themselves to talk to her. "You haven't been waiting long have you, Mr. Jones?"

"No, maybe five, ten minutes," He lied.

"I hope this is allright. I guessed a Hawaiian dinner meant shorts."

"Well it looked like your friend seemed to think so." He jested, nodding his head towards the marine.

Maggie looked back at the guard shack and shook her head.

"So, what's in the bag?" Raz inquired with a tilt of his head.

"In case a Hawaiian dinner didn't mean shorts."

Raz chuckled and said. "Maggie, we're going to take a drive to the other side of the island. There's a small bar over there that makes some of the strongest rum drinks on the planet. They may even serve us up some food. What you are wearing is just fine."

"Great"

Raz snatched her bag off the ground and said, "Shall we?" However, before he finished speaking, Maggie stepped in front of him and quickly walked to the drivers' side of the car.

"Mind if I drive?"

Raz returned a big smile and motioned to the driver's door. From the passenger seat, he watched her pull the seatbelt over and latch it. The big toothy grin she had given him warmed his heart. He found it hard to look away and felt he could touch the energy between them. He leaned in stopping close enough to share their hot breath. Feeling Maggie's hand on the back of his neck stirred something inside of him he had never felt. Leaning in further, he cupped her cheek and did something that shocked him more than it did her. Slowly, he ran his tongue over the inside of her upper lip.

# 18

*April 2, 1865*
*The White House*
*Washington, D. C.*
*United States of America*
*13 days before the assassination of Abraham Lincoln*

"I wish this godforsaken war had just been about slavery, John. With it winding down, we could start rebuilding this great country of ours." Abraham Lincoln stood straight as an arrow with his hands clasped behind his back while looking thru the window out onto the streets from his office in the White House. The fifty-six-year-old president's six-foot, four-inch frame was frail. His face was thin, drawn and set with deep lines. The four-year war had claimed over six hundred thousand American lives and it wore heavily on Lincoln.

"Mr. President," Lincoln's secretary said while closing his memo pad. "It is an important undertaking that you have chosen for the country."

Lincoln turned from the window and walked to his desk. Sitting down, he rested his head in his left hand. The man from, Hodgenville Kentucky, was tired and the fight that was looming could be as disastrous as the war. Lifting his head from his hand he continued, "Our founding fathers' intentions were honorable, but if they had only known, if they had only known." Grabbing the parchment from his desk, he gave it another quick review. "And this letter from, Weishaupt to, General Washington that had been found amongst his things confirms my suspicions." Lincoln stood, walking slowly around his office he read aloud the letter. "An association has been formed for express purposes of rooting out all religious establishments and overturning all existing governments. The leaders would rule the World with uncontrollable power, while all the rest would be employed as tools of the ambition of their unknown superiors." The president flipped over the letter and offered. "And on the back, General Washington's reply penned as a rough draft." Lincoln intently read on. "It was not my intention to doubt that Doctrines of Illuminati and principles of Jacobinism had not spread in United States. On the contrary, no one is more truly satisfied of this fact than I am. The idea that I meant to convey was that I did not believe that the Lodges of Free Masons in this country had, as Societies, endeavored to propagate diabolical tenets of first, or pernicious principles of the latter if they are susceptible of separation." Lincoln returned to his desk and eased his tired frame into his chair, still gripping the letter. He shook it at his secretary, then tossed it on his desk and continued his rant. "And the banks John, the god awful banks."

Lincoln's secretary, John Nicolay knew the bankers well. He had heard his boss complain time and time again at their attempt to divide the country and had experienced it firsthand when he and the secretary of the Treasury had traveled with Lincoln to New York in an attempt to secure a loan to finance the war. They agreed to loan him the money but at interest rates from twenty-four to thirty-six percent. Lincoln refused; he knew perfectly well that it would lead the United States to ruin.

"And my greenbacks John. That was the answer. They were the greatest blessing the American people have ever had. Why couldn't congress see that the people would have been flush with a currency as safe as their own government? Money would not have been the master but the servant of humanity. Democracy would have risen superior to the power of money. Why did they revoke it?"

Nicolay knew Lincoln hated the bankers and needed time to vent. The war had been hard on him. He had lost his son to the fever and his wife had enlisted mediums to talk to his spirit.

"I'll tell you why!" Lincoln continued straightening in his chair. His face turned red with anger as it often did when he discussed the bankers. "Most of them have been bought, their campaigns and elections financed by these money grabbers." Clearly agitated, he continued. "I will show them, if it is a battle they want, it is a battle they will have and it will resonate all the way to Europe. They too do not want us to succeed as one nation. They are afraid of us John, afraid of us."

Nicolay leaned forward and inquired. "What is our plan Mr. President? They already yield great power."

A stone-faced Lincoln offered. "I plan on vetoing that god awful Banking Act after the war. But I must save the Union first. Then, I will attain our economic and financial independence. No more will the banks be part of our fabric." Lincoln stood and turned towards the window. Gazing out across the town, he quietly added. "It will end their financial domination over the world."

# 19

*April 5, 1865*
*Mary Surratt's Boardinghouse*
*Washington, D. C.*
*United States of America*
*10 days before the assassination of Abraham Lincoln*

"He will be at Ford's theatre on the fourteenth. We will seize him from his carriage while in route." John Wilkes Booth swirled his whiskey and looked around their small setting. He sat on a chesterfield with George Atzerodt and sitting in the chair next to them was Lewis Paine. Samuel Arnold and Michael O'Laughlinsat on an adjacent window frame. The small group seemed to be in disarray, their earlier plan to kidnap Lincoln and restore the confederacy had failed. Their plan to try again was taking shape.

Across the room in a corner chair sat an older, squat gentleman drinking tea prepared by Mary Surratt. Next to him stood a coat rack which he had hung a light jacket, propped against his chair was a gold handled, silver tipped cane. Observing the group for almost an hour and hearing broken whispers had told him plenty;

the discussion was about Lincoln, and Booth was clearly the leader. His spies had been in place for months and the men they had been observing was right for the task. Slowly, he stood and took a step to steady himself. After he grabbed his cane, he picked up his tea and ambled towards the group. When he was close, he said with a meek voice. "Good evening gentlemen."

Everyone looked up suspiciously at the new arrival. Finally, after several long seconds, Booth blurted, "Good evening."

With a sharp tone, Atzerodt added, "May we help you?"

Lifting his cane, he pointed it at the men and said, "It is what I can do for you gentlemen, and the confederacy."

Everyone in the group shifted uncomfortably in their seat. They glanced at each other but looked at Booth for guidance.

"May I, gentlemen?" asked the stranger, pointing his cane at a small section of sofa between Booth and Atzerodt. However, before they answered, he made himself at home by wedging his fat butt between the two. His belly squished into his lap when he bent forward, his torso tilted towards the two against the window frame. The action forced Booth and Atzerodt to lean in when he started talking. Setting his tea on the table he propped both hands on top of his cane and went straight to the point. "You can kidnap the President and turn him over to the confederacy." Pausing, he studied the small group and then continued. "They, of course, will negotiate his release which will drag on for months."

"Who are you?" Atzerodt quickly asked.

The stranger pursed his lips and then held up a finger. Then he continued while looking at Booth. "Mr. Booth you are a well-known actor; someone will surely see you." He paused and pointed at the rest of the group and continued. "Then you and the rest of your co-conspirators will eventually be picked-up." Looking back at Booth, he added audaciously, "And hanged."

The men started to protest the stranger, but his tiny voice became hard and he forcibly spat,

"Or…or to have the most effect and preserve our great confederacy, you can kill the president, the vice president, and the secretary of state. That will decimate the North's leadership." The stranger sat upright, picked up his cup and slurped the hot tea as he let his words sink in.

The men stared at the floor and considered the stranger's words.

Then he added. "The head of the snake will be severed. Can you even imagine the welcome you will receive from our brothers in the south?" He was careful not to push too hard. Lincoln had to die, the war was all but over and he had become a powerful man and could not be permitted to mettle with the banks. Assassinating the other two only gave merit to his plan. "I have money to aid in your escape to the south and as far as your question – who am I – I represent a group loyal to our confederacy."

An odd silence overtook the group while the men again considered the stranger's words. Minutes later, emboldened by his fame and small group of friends, Booth broke that silence. "Yes, that is right. Lincoln must die. I can easily get into the theatre. I will do it then, in front of everyone."

In a hushed voice, Atzerodt spoke next. "Johnson, I will kill Johnson." For the next few very long minutes, no one said a word. The silence was nerve racking. Having Booth commit to killing the president would reverberate thru history in ways he would never be able to grasp.

However, the stranger knew, and knew all too well. Hes poke quietly. "It needs to be all or none. A statement must be made. Who will kill the secretary of state?"

Lewis Paine, a former Confederate soldier, finally spoke up. "I will kill Seward."

The stranger nodded his head and then pulled from his pocket three purple velvet pouches and handed one to each would-be assassin.

"This will get you out of town and is enough to live on for quite some time." The three men opened the pouches and looked inside. Almost simultaneously, they said, "But, Sir, this is…"

"Just remember, the attacks must be simultaneous. If not, the others will be alerted." He dismissed their surprise at the stacks of gold coins in the velvet pouches. Pushing himself up on his cane, he said, "Gentlemen, I look forward to the good news on the fourteenth. Until then, I bid you a good evening."

The group watched the stranger slowly walk across the room, retrieve his jacket and leave thru the front door. Then they turned and planned their attack.

# 20

*November 2012*
*Bakersfield, California*
*California Highway Patrol*
*Office of Veronica Gibbs*
*Crime Scene Investigator*

Veronica had spun around in her chair so fast that her long coal black hair stood out from her head. The smile on her face lit up the room as she looked around her new office. Her workers occasionally looked through the glass panes and gave their new boss a thumbs-up. She had just finished decorating her desk and walls with mementos of an eighteen-year career. Set in the center of the desk were two framed pictures of Cameron Butler. They were of them vacationing at Two Harbors, Santa Catalina Island. One photograph was of them sitting on the beach together, one drinking buffalo milks on a patio of an outside bar. A photo of Cameron's legs sticking out from under their tent had been hung on the wall. They had started a relationship two years earlier when she had worked the crime scene the first time Cameron had met Mark Springfield. It had ended six months ago. The pictures were proof that, Veronica had never given up on their relationship.

Sitting on her desk was the same report that Cameron had seen a few days earlier. As the supervisor of the department, it was her responsibility to assign the case to one of her staff. However, since Cameron had seemed so intrigued with it, she would look into it personally.

Veronica went over the reports for more than an hour and with no more to go on had run into the same brick wall that Cameron had. Spinning again in her chair, she stopped and stared at the coffee machine in the corner of her office, trying to resist a third cup. But before she knew it, she placed a coffee pack into the machine and within minutes, it was making its all too familiar gurgling sound. She grabbed the cup from the Keurig, sat back and took a long, slow drink. Then she had an idea. Standing, she walked over to her office door and, looking around the frame at her colleague, she said, "Stephanie, I'm going to email you the info on the body we pulled out of Mono Lake. I would like you to check the missing persons database." Pausing, she took another drink of her coffee and then continued. "Start in the county and broaden the search. And Steph, I need this ASAP."

"You know Boss," Stephanie started, looking up from her computer and over her purple framed glasses, "I'd be happy to bump you right up to number one if I had one of those." Smiling, she pointed to Veronica's cup of coffee. With a chuckle she continued. "I'd even make it myself."

"Oh no, girl!" Veronica laughed. "Give me a minute to send this over to ya and I'll get you all setup with one of my faves." She quickly walked back to her desk, shuffled through the pile and pulled the folder on the body, then typed an email containing the little information that they had. She hit *send* and seven seconds later, Stephanie gave her a thumbs-up.

As she waited for the coffee to brew, she again looked around her office, stopping at the picture of Cameron hanging on the wall. She laughed at the memory of him crawling under their tent to remove a rock he had missed while they were setting it up. The memory suddenly made her sad and for a second, she thought she might call him, but his long hours and her move to Bakersfield strained their relationship to the point of Cameron calling it off. She decided to wait and see what they could find on their John Doe.

A quiet beep shook her from her thoughts and with a slight smile she grabbed the steaming coffee cup and walked it over to Stephanie. "I have your —"

"Not now." Stephanie said pointing to the corner of her desk, then she continued to talk to her computer.

Veronica chuckled and set the cup down, smiled at her friend, turned and headed back towards her office, sure Stephanie wouldn't remember she was even there. As Veronica walked back towards her office, she was stopped by one of her staff to discuss upcoming training required by the department. As she stepped thru her office doorway she heard, "I have three names. And...I'm working on a fourth."

"Excellent!" Twisting around she was greeted by Stephanie with another raised finger. Veronica shook her head and smiled, turned and continued into her office and sat in her chair.

"Peter Byers, Robert Ross, William Wick and James Black. I'll send you the names, descriptions, addresses and last known locations." Stephanie watched as Veronica rolled back in her chair and stopped in the doorway. "Was that A-S-A-P enough for ya?" she laughed.

"Shit! What was that, twenty minutes?

"More like seventeen but, I didn't pay *that* much attention," laughed Stephanie.

"Are you bucking for employee of the year?" Veronica quipped. A few seconds later, she heard her computer beep. She rolled her chair back over to her desk and opened the file that awaited her.

The four names were built into a spreadsheet containing information starting from one year before they had been reported missing. She studied the names, trying to get a *feel* for whom she should start with, however, when nothing came to her, she picked up the report and read the description of the body they had found. They didn't have much, but the information they had had seemed to stick out.

*Beep*. Stephanie's computer made the familiar sound of an awaiting email. It was a task from her boss. - Start in February nineteen-ninety-eight and find out who had seen their doctor. Even a specialist like a cardiologist. Also, another question for the families, and this should be pretty straightforward. Who had two teeth replaced, and if they don't know, get their dentist contact information, they'll know. Thanks, and tic toc – Stephanie smiled at the *tic toc,* closed her email and started her search.

*       *       *

"I have it!" Veronica declared.

Stephanie scooted her chair back, stood and walked into her boss's office. "What do you have?"

"Mr. James Black. Reported missing, February 8th 2003 by his girlfriend."

"Wasn't 'I' looking into these characters?" Stephanie asked, feigning sadness.

"You know me," Veronica quipped. "A bit impatience. I just started from the other end of the list and there it was." Veronica passed the enlarged photo copy of the driver license over to her friend. Under the picture were handwritten notes.

"I'm guessing you called the girlfriend, which I assume led to this dentist," she said, pointing to a name under the picture. "Who I assume you called."

"Yes, on all accounts." Veronica laughed. "And if my math is correct and if indeed our John Doe is really James Black, he's fifty-two years old. We'll have the dental x-rays in about an hour. Everything else matches."

"Nice," Stephanie said, sitting down on the side of the desk. "I see here he's from Monterey."

"Yeah, but he's been living with his girlfriend in Carmel. If this is our guy, I'm going to head over and talk to her."

"You're going to the coast to talk to someone?" Stephanie asked, glancing around the office at the pictures. "This is about Cameron, isn't it?"

Veronica looked at the pictures on her desk, then up at Stephanie. Slowly, she nodded her head.

# 21

*November 2012*
*California*
*South 395*

"What's our plan?"

"Can we drive for a while? I need to think." Mark looked over at Cameron and said. "Hey, I'm glad you're with me on this. Mark got a nod from Cameron, sat back in his seat and looked out at the trees. The drive thru the Inyo National Forest would normally have been breathtaking. And although Mark was looking out at the tress, his mind's eye had only seen the woman at the airport. *How the hell do you get someone with looks, poise and guts in position so quick. And to what end? Why try to deter me, why? Do they know what I might find?* Suddenly, Marks head jerked up and his eyes flashed open. He caught himself dozing however, he tried to stay awake. Finally, he said. "Cameron, I need to sleep."

"Bishop is about forty-five minutes away. We are going to drive right thru it. I'm sure we can get a hotel for the night."

"I only need a few hours."

Mark looked at his buzzing phone and said, "It's Mike," pressing the phone icon he answered. "Yes"

"Let's start with the easy part. Your dad had a Top Secret clearance. He'd gone thru two reinvestigations, so that means he had had it for at least ten years. Before that, he had a secret clearance. I looked through the background info, pretty normal stuff, actually kind of boring. The tapes were easy."

"Great!" Mark quickly answered. "Then you know who the woman at the airport is."

"The tapes were easy because… there were none."

"God damnit! What the hell is going on?"

His friend's remark caught Mike off guard. Mark was not one who normally used profanity. He continued, "I have somewhat better news on Marcus Smith, although it's not very helpful."

"Just don't tell me there's a head stone with his name on it."

"No, he still works for Defense Courier, but as of yesterday, he went out on emergency leave, and before you ask, no one knows what the emergency was."

"I'm guessing he won't be found." Mark added. Mark both heard and felt Cameron's phone buzz and gave him a quick glance.

Cameron looked at his phone and said in a hushed voice, "It's my boss." Answering, he said, "Yes, sir. Outside of Bishop."

Mark watched Cameron suddenly sit straight up in his seat and his face turn beet red.

"Yes. Yes, where?"

Mark sensed the seriousness in his friend's demeanor and said, "Mike, let me call you back." Then quickly he ended his call.

Cameron also ended his call and looked over at Mark. The corners of his eyes moistened and his voice broke when he said, "There's been an accident."

*     *     *

Veronica set her coffee in the center console's cup holders, slid onto the front seat of her small CSI van and checked her watch. "Hmmm, six-o-five, not too bad for this time of morning," She quietly said, complimenting herself. After her team had verified the dental x-rays, she called the girlfriend of James Black and set-up a ten-o-clock interview. She was looking forward to the three plus hour drive to Carmel. The mostly scenic trip would help clear her mind and the drive thru Big Sur with its jagged coastline would be breathtaking. She pulled out of Sheriffs' department parking lot and headed towards the central coast.

After her fourth cup of coffee, she pulled into a rest stop. The next part of her trip would be through Big Sur and she did not want Mother Nature calling during one of the most scenic drives in the United States.

While walking back to her van, she noticed a large black Cadillac Escalade parked in an area set aside for big rigs, and two dark figures, hardly visible, sat low in the front seat. Though not a big fan of crime dramas, she recognized it for what it was, *suspicious*.

Stepping behind her van, she slightly raised her phone over the top and took a picture of the Cadillac. Checking the photo, she realized that only the last three numbers of the license plate were visible. Tossing her phone on the front seat, she slid in and adjusted her rear view mirror again to check the Escalade. The driver's window had been rolled down and there was an extended arm hanging out over the door frame and holding a burning cigarette. Seeing the individuals appear relaxed made her feel better. If they were truly interested in her or had been following her, they would be ready to pull out. She checked them one last time as she accelerated north onto Highway 1.

Veronica was thrilled to be driving thru Big Sur. She felt the draw of the Santa Lucia Mountains with their abrupt rise from the Pacific and the dramatic views of the jagged coastline. She understood why the area had the same number of visitors as Yosemite National Park. The way the land had thrust itself up through the surf excited her. Veronica glanced in the rear view mirror to see if she was slowing anyone down and she caught a glimpse of the Escalade. It appeared to be trying to stay out of the line of sight since it was hugging the outside of the road. She slowed going through the small town of Big Sur and sped up. When she realized the black Escalade was making no attempt to hide itself and was now trying to gain and overtake her, the Crime Scene Investigator knew, she was in trouble. For an instant she thought about pulling off the road, but the narrow roadway made it all but impossible to escape the SUV. Every second that passed, the Escalade drew closer. When she reached for the phone, her van quickly crossed over into the opposing lane. She jerked the wheel and swerved back onto her side of the road. At the faster speeds, it took both hands to negotiate the winding road and to keep from running off the cliff. Veronica accelerated even more and felt the sweat roll down her forehead and into her eyes. She batted her eyelashes, trying to clear her vision but her eyes burned.

Sliding her van around a corner, she almost hit the Bixby Creek Bridge sign. When she regained control, she saw the bridge, its narrow width caused her to inadvertently let up on the accelerator. The escalade easily overtook and rammed the rear of her van. Veronica jerked forward and screamed. Again, the black escalade sped-up alongside of her and slammed into the side of her small van. She screamed again and mashed down on the gas pedal, her van sped-up but its small engine was no match for the giant eight cylinder that lived under the hood of the Escalade.

The driver of the Cadillac turned his wheel to the right and swerved all the way over to the side of the narrow bridge, throwing the loose gravel onto the railing. He paused until he was perfectly aligned with his victim then accelerated until he was in front of the van. With gritted teeth, he jerked the steering wheel hard to the left and collided with the van. The small SUV seemed to cower to the Escalade and it was rammed into the bridge railings with such force that the concrete posts shattered.

Veronica screamed, realizing in that instant that she was being pushed from the bridge. Everything seemed to slow then abruptly speed up. Pieces of the concrete railing had embedded themselves into what was left of the front of her rapidly disintegrating van. To her right was the black Cadillac Escalade which seemed stuck to her van, and to the left, nothing but a two-hundred-and-eighty-foot drop. To Veronica it had felt like an infinite abyss, she couldn't stop screaming. Finally, the grinding metal and smashing concrete noise stopped, her van flew from the bridge and slowly rolled to the left. She reached up and over her head trying to grab anything that would stop her fall. Her hair floated upwards over her head and flattened itself against the roof. An eternity turned to seconds as the ground raced up to meet her. No one heard the terrifying screams of the doomed woman.

The van slammed into the ground with such force the back-axle tore away from the frame. The airbags deployed, then instantly deflated when the windshield exploded. Veronica's screams ended.

The driver of the escalade made no attempt to check his most recent victim; he knew no one would survive such a fall.

\*　　　\*　　　\*

Marks phone vibrated as soon as he asked Cameron about the accident. He looked at it and not recognizing the number, he ended the call. "What happened?"

"Veronica, she's been in an accident."

Marks phone vibrated once more showing the same number. Again, he ended the call.

"Apparently, she was pushed from the Bixby Bridge."

"What! A bridge, what the hell! What bridge?"

"It's North of Big Sur." Cameron answered again feeling in a daze.

"Cameron, according to the sign we just passed, Bishop is just a few miles ahead. Drop me there and get your ass over to the coast."

"But" was Cameron's' stunned reply.

"But nothing. Get me to Bishop and I'll take it from there."

# 22

*November 2012*
*CIA Headquarters, Langley, Virginia*
*Office of Michael Hollister*

Mike looked up from his desk after hearing a sharp knock on the frame of his open door and smiled at one of the secretaries from the first floor who had appeared in his doorway. He stood, walked across his office and greeted her. She had a stranger in tow and was obviously playing escort. In her care was a well-dressed, familiar looking man. "Yes, may I help you?" With the exception of agency personnel, Mike did not receive guests and he could tell by this visitor's demeanor the visit was not a social call.

"Agent Hollister, I'm Senator Jones. Erasmo Jones."

The two shook hands and Mike led the senator to a chair in his office, turned, thanked the secretary and then returned to his desk. "Senator, what can I help you with?" Mike quickly opened up Google and typed in 'Senator Erasmo Jones'

"Agent, I need to get ahold of Mr. Springfield. It's imperative I speak to him."

The Google search showed Mike that Senator Erasmo Jones was a Republican from North Carolina and serves on the Committee of Oversight & Government Reform. "I'm sorry, Senator, but I can't give out Agent Springfield's number."

Raz shook his head, waved his hand, and said, "I already have it, but he won't answer my calls. The director gave me his number but also told me he's out on leave and that I should talk to you since you two are friends. Said you may know how to contact him in the Smokies."

"Senator —"

Raz quickly interrupted. "Agent Hollister, Mike if I may, shelve the senator. Erasmo will do."

Mike nodded his head and continued. "Agent Springfield, Mark, has a lot going on right now. It's true if he doesn't recognize your number, he won't answer it."

"I need you to call and convince him to contact me." Raz leaned in and continued. "Mike, I'll get right to the point. I believe your friend is in grave danger."

"And that danger is…" Mike asked with a sideways look.

Raz raised his hand and said. "I know I have come here looking for Agent Springfield's information, but please, I'd rather not go into that."

Mike tapped his desk with his finger while looking at the picture of Erasmo Jones. Underneath the photo was written United States Senator. The man staring back from the computer monitor was dressed in a dark blue pin striped suit with a light purple shirt, and like the man sitting in front of him, appeared to be formidable. He pulled open his lower right desk drawer and retrieved two bottles of water, opened them, and set one in front of Raz. Finally, Mike broke the silence. "I don't believe he's in the Smokies anymore. He was, but he must have left. I took a call from him recently, but he ended it abruptly."

"What makes you think he left, and why wouldn't he just tell you?"

"He has a friend in California, Cameron Butler, works for the Highway Patrol. While I was on the phone with him, I think I heard Cameron in the background. It's not unlike Mark to get up and leave on a moment's notice, not that he's impulsive, just motivated. And why didn't he tell me? I've been thinking about that." Mike picked up his phone and showed it to Raz and added. "I don't think he trusts the phones."

"Good, good. Then he knows to be careful. Do you have Cameron's number?"

"No, but I can get it. Give me your number and I'll call when I have it."

Raz pulled out one of his business cards, flipped it over, and scribbled on the back. "This is my personal number. Call me as soon as you know something." He handed the card to Mike and added. "Twelve hours. If we don't find Mark Springfield within twelve hours, I'm afraid we'll never find him."

"Mark doesn't die so easily." Mike quipped.

"Yes, I read his file. He's a good agent, but there are forces at play here that I don't even understand." Raz stood, took a long drink of his water, lifted it towards Mike and nodded his head.

"One more thing." Mike added while standing. "I heard Cameron say 'outside of Bishop.' If Mark is in California, and indeed, with Cameron, I can only assume, Bishop, California."

"Hmmm. That's a place to start. Call me as soon as you have his number." Raz turned and walked thru the doorway.

Mike walked over to his desk, pulled out his address book, and opened it to Cameron's number. He tapped the entry with his index figure while considering his next move. Then with the decision made, he texted the digits to the number Senator Jones had written on the back of his card.

Mike sat back down and stared at the senator's picture, hoping he had done the right thing.

# 23

*November 2012*
*Bishop, California*

C ameron rounded a sweeping right turn into Bishop and pulled into the first hotel off the 395.

"Vagabond Inn. This'll work," Mark said. Then he grabbed his backpack from the rear seat, opened the door and stepped out.

"Mark —"

"Cameron, get to the coast, just keep me posted." Mark closed the door, turned and walked towards the hotel hoping his leaving would encourage his friend to get a move on. He checked his watch. He had not had any real sleep for nineteen hours.

Cameron tapped his horn and drove away.

Mark had continued to carry the false identification that had been given to him years ago. The name Daniel Ricci was becoming as familiar as his own. He used it and the credit card when he checked into the hotel.

The second floor, street-side room had given him a nice view of everyone coming into the hotel. He peered thru the curtains, looking up and down the street and around the parking lot. No one was around. He felt as if he had had the town to himself. The thermometer which hung outside his window indicated fifty-nine degrees. He looked at the bed and then over at the open bathroom door. The silent call of the shower won.

Marks' normal three-minute shower turned into ten. He stepped out of the shower, pulled two towels off the rack, one he wrapped around himself and walk over to the window while he continued to rub another towel over his head. Again, he pulled the curtains far enough away from the window to see out and around the street. Only this time, his eyes stopped on Scat's Roadhouse.

"Nice," he softly said. The name conjured up an old-style hearty meal, which suited him just fine; he was starving. He returned to the bathroom, picked up his Glock 23 and wiped the moisture from the steam off with a washcloth. Out of habit, he pulled the slide back and checked the round in the chamber. Next, he removed the magazine and gave it a wipe for good measure.

The first thing Mark smelled when he stepped into the roadhouse diner were the pies that were laid out on the counter before him. The sign above read 'Happy Hour - a slice of pie and coffee $5'

"Sit anywhere that's open, dear."

"Thanks!" Mark gave the woman behind the register a quick nod. With the exception of a few occupied seats, most of the restaurant was empty, so he sat in a booth that faced the parking lot and in the general direction of his hotel. When he was finished eating, he pushed his plate towards the center of the table but still held onto his fork and tapped it lightly on the edge of the plate as he stared at the remains in the dish. He sat up against the back of the booth and looked around outside. Mark picked up his vibrating phone and when he saw it was Mike, he quickly answered. "Tell me you have something on the woman."

"Sorry, not yet. However, I had an interesting visitor. Have you ever heard of a, Erasmo Jones? He's a senator from North Carolina."

"The name might be familiar but I just can't place him."

"You would recognize him." Mike added. "Says he has been trying to call you. He asked if I'd call and have you return his call."

"I did get a couple of calls. Any idea what he wants?"

"He said you might be in danger. Actually, grave danger." Mike paused and then added. "He passed the water bottle test so I also told him where I thought you might be."

"You and your water bottle test. Are you sure it's not just your gut?"

"Nope… it's the water bottle."

"And as far as knowing where I am, I can't get anything past you." Mark was careful with what he said on the phone.

"Is there anything you need me to do?" Mike asked

"Yeah, find the woman, and tell me what the hell is going on." With that, both men ended the call.

Mark jogged across the street and walked onto the property of the hotel. He trotted up the stairs to his room, looking forward to some sleep. However, when he opened the door, his eyes fell on the woman they had been looking for. She was standing next to the bed wearing only long black stockings, her high heels, and a shoulder holster that was draped under two perfectly shaped breasts. A faint smell of honeysuckles hung in the air. Above a whisper, her sultry voice floated across the room. "Now didn't I tell you not to come to California?"

The image froze Mark in place. Before he could act, he was hit over the back of his head with a blackjack. With his knees buckling, he reached back towards the sudden blackening pain. But he was unconscious before he hit the floor.

"I can end this now." One of the men said, slipping the blackjack into his back pocket. Then he pulled his jacket back and gripped the stock of his pistol.

"Not quite yet." Tia said, pulling the shoulder holster up over her head. She laid it on the bed, then pulled on her panties, slacks and a shirt. The two men in the room made no off-color remark about their naked boss; if they had, they would be dead before night fell.

The third man, who had signaled Marks arrival, entered the room. Looking down at Mark then across the room at the woman, he said. "We have eyes on his partner and his girlfriend may still be alive." When Tia gave him a questioning look, he continued. "Twenty minutes ago, a helicopter was standing by while they cut her out of the van."

Tia picked up her holster and slipped it over her arms and latched it across her chest. She pulled the Walther P380 from the leather holster and the silencer from the inside pocket of her jacket. After she screwed the silencer into the barrel, she pointed it at Mark. All three men smiled. Then suddenly and smoothly, she swept her arm over to the driver of the black Escalade and shot him in the throat.

Grabbing his neck, he fell back into the TV, knocking it up against the wall and rolling to the right, he hit and knocked a lamp to the floor. Blood sprayed out from between his fingers, over the carpet and onto Marks Pant legs. Dropping to his knees, he gasped for air thru the gaping hole in his neck. He looked around the room as his eyes bulged and he screamed for help. He tried to speak but blood was the only thing that emanated from his mouth.

Tia raised her arm and pressed the trigger again, shooting him in the left side of his head. The .380 caliber round punched into his temple and threw his head to the right and he dropped where he knelt. Tia looked at the other two men and said. "We will have no more mistakes." She pointed the gun in their direction and waited for a reply.

Both men nodded their heads in agreement. One quickly blurted, "Yes, Tia."

Hearing his adversaries helped him quickly assess what had just happened. Mark had only been knocked out briefly but feigned unconsciousness until he could fully regain his faculties. The back of his head pounded and he felt as though he would vomit. However, having the wherewithal to launch an attack eluded him while he felt the room spinning around him. Someone fell on his legs but he didn't move.

"Get him up, take his gun and give it to me." She smiled and added, "They make nice souvenirs." Tia considered killing the agent but she needed to know who else knew why he was here. The hotel room would never work as a place to question him. However, the woods outside of town would be perfect.

The two men slid their arms under Marks thick frame and tried to lift him. It took all they had to lift his dead weight and pull him up on his knees. One of the men patted his torso and found a gun on his side. He reached down and pulled the Glock 23 out of its holster.

Mark lifted his eyelids and through blurred vision he saw where the woman was standing. When the man who had relieved him of his gun started to turn back from tossing it on the bed, he acted. He smashed both men in their groins. From his kneeling position, he pulled one foot up and lunged at the woman, forcing her to take a step back and giving him time to get to his feet and charge her.

She gritted her teeth, raised her Walther and fired.

The round hit Mark under his right shoulder but it didn't stop his two-hundred-twenty-pound wild charge. He wrapped his arms around Tia and pushed her through the window, across the small balcony and over the railing.

Tia raised her gun and slammed it into Marks back, the stock of the Walther digging into the exit hole of the .380.

Mark let out a muffled groan as pain emanated throughout his body, but he knew the upcoming fall would be much worse.

The two tumbled over the railing and down two stories through the low shrubbery and onto the decorative white rock that had been laid around the grounds. Tia ended up on top of Mark and both let out loud grunts when their lungs were jolted from the fall. Shards of broken glass was embedded in Marks back. He grabbed Tia by the throat and yanked her to the left. Then he balled up his right hand into a tight fist and slammed her in the ribs. In the fight for his life, he didn't hear two of them crack.

Tia was hurt but not out, she brought the gun down hard on Marks already bruised head, causing him to loosen his grip. She hit him again and twisted away, rolling onto the walkway and staggering to her feet.

Mark pushed himself up to his knees and the ground around him exploded. Both men were shooting from the balcony. Looking over at the woman, he saw her holding her side and smiling. The Walther was point directly at his head. Quickly, he scooped up a handful of the white rock and flung it at her while twisting his body to the right.

She fired.

# 24

*November 2012*
*Bixby Creek Bridge*
*North of Big Sur, California*

C ameron stood over the embankment and looked down at the van Veronica had been extracted from. Two tow trucks had had their cables and ropes extended down to the van and tied around the front end and window post to keep the vehicle from sliding further down the embankment.

A highway patrol man handed Cameron a slip of paper which he had torn from his notepad and said. "This is where they flew her."

Cameron glanced down at the paper. As he tried to keep his voice from breaking, he asked, "What happened?"

"She was run off the road." Both men looked over the side. The Highway patrol man continued. "Her van hit the ground hard, and quite frankly, she's lucky to be alive."

The words stung Cameron. "How do I get down there?"

"To the van?!"

Cameron looked at his colleague and his look was clear; he was going down to the van.

The highway patrolman shook his head, laid his hand on Cameron's shoulder and pointed him in the direction of the rigging and harness equipment used by the rescue crew. "Those two lines were laid for the firefighters and rescue folks. Here, I'll help you." He retrieved a harness and handed it to Cameron and then guided him to the ropes.

It took Cameron some negotiating, scrapes on his ankles and legs, but he made it to the crash site. He looked back up at the bridge and wondered how she survived. It was obvious from how far she had landed from the bridge that the van had been going at a high rate of speed when it broke thru the barrier.

Cameron looked over the outside of the van. It had evidence of external damage caused by another vehicle, long scrapes of black paint were obvious along one side. Although there was extensive damage to the van from the fall, he was sure the vehicle that had rammed her caused a large part of it on the passenger side. Inside, he found papers strewn around and something else that had caused him to pause, blood. Veronicas blood was everywhere. Her driver's seat, door, the rear driver's side, head-liner and floor had been covered in blood. If they hadn't told him she was alive, he would have been sure the person in this accident had died. He reached thru the side of the van that had been cut open and gathered up the loose sheets of paper. Recognizing the report, he flipped thru the pages. It was the same report that he had gone through two days ago. "What the hell!" He slowly paged through them and stopped when he saw something new, a name. He read it out loud, "James Black." Next to it was a question mark and the name John Doe/Lake. He also found a name marked 'girlfriend' and a phone number, address in Carmel, and a photo copy of his driver's license, and more blood. Cameron pushed down the sickening feeling he had and for a moment looked away from the van and took a few deep breaths. He flicked the stack of papers and wondered, *what were you up to?*

"Butler!" The call came from atop the hill. "If you're finished, they'd like to pull up the van."

Cameron waved his arm, stuffed the papers in his shirt and walked over to the ropes. With some difficulty he made it back to the top.

"How long is the drive to the hospital?"

"It's really not far, this time of day. Just over an hour. She's in Community on the Monterey Peninsula. We flew her there because… She's in bad shape."

"Please, take down my number. If you find anything on who or what ran her off the road, call me." Cameron gave the officer his number, took one last look at the van, then turned and walked back to his car. Forty-five minutes later, he was sitting on the floor outside of the double doors leading into the operating room. A quick stop at the nurse's station and he had learned she had been rushed into emergency surgery for internal bleeding, a concussion, collapsed lung and broken bones. Cameron had been to many accidents, but none that had caused this many tears to stream down his face. The hallway and area outside of the waiting room was filling with colleagues and friends. Six hours later, a doctor pushed through the door. Cameron quickly stood and stopped him. "How is she?"

"She's not out of the woods, but she's stable for now."

"When can I see her?"

"We are getting ready to move her to intensive care." The surgeon looked over Cameron's shoulder at the clock on the wall and added, "Give us about an hour."

Cameron nodded his head and said, "Thanks doc." Then turned and walked towards the group that had gathered in the hallway. After the retelling, he walked into the waiting room and directly over to the coffee dispenser.

\*　　\*　　\*

One hour later, Cameron stood next to Veronicas hospital bed. When he looked down on her, his lower lip started to quiver. The myriad of tubes and wires that ran from her bruised and broken body was almost too much to take. Even her eyelids were discolored. Pulling his phone from his back pocket, he called Mark. When Mark didn't answer, he left a message. 'Veronicas alive. I'm standing next to her at the hospital in Monterey. I think I'll stay. Mark, she's in bad shape." Cameron paused for several long seconds, taking deep breaths and trying to compose himself, then he continued while inquisitively looking around the room at all the monitoring equipment, IV pumps and stands that held bags of blood and serum. "Thanks to Veronica, we have another name, James Black. He may be our Mono Lake John Doe, driver's license number C4758319. I found all of this in Veronicas van. I can only assume she was on her way to pay a visit to the girl he had been living with... Okay, we'll talk soon." Cameron ended the call without saying what he was really thinking. *This is all my fault.*

"Excuse me."

Cameron looked up and lightly smiled at a nurse standing in the doorway. Instantly, he thought of his grandmother.

She quietly said. "No cell phones in this area, sweetie."

Cameron nodded his head and switched his phone to airplane mode. He grabbed a chair from the corner of the room, pulled it next to the bed, and sat down. "If you wanted to see me, all you had to do was call." He whispered. Then gently, he picked up her hand, lightly stroked it and did something he had not done for quite some time, he prayed.

# 25

The handful of white decorative rock that Mark had scooped up and thrown at the woman did the trick, but it still cost him dearly. The bullet that she was able to fire before being pelted with the rocks ripped into his left side. But it slowed her second shot down enough for him to charge and ram her into a post that held up the second-floor balcony. Another shot rang out from the floor above when the men tried to shoot over the balcony rail. Hearing them running across the balcony towards the stairs, he knew, he had only seconds. He grabbed the woman by the shoulders, pulled her up and head butted her, stripped her Walther from her hand, lifted her off her feet and then pushed her thru a window into a room. Mark raised his arm and covered her head with the front sight of the pistol.

Suddenly, the post next to his head exploded. His face was peppered with chunks of splintered wood. He stooped low, twisted his body and returned fire. The .380 spit two rounds at the first man down the stairs, who retreat long enough for Mark to run west across Main street. He fired again from halfway across the street then ran through several businesses, while looking, over his shoulder. The front of Marks shirt was soaked in blood. He faltered and went down on one knee but willed himself to press on. Both his right shoulder and left side felt like someone had stabbed him with red hot pokers. Looking out across the field he could see trees and thought, *If I can just make it across this clearing.*

Mark stopped running when he stepped from the pavement onto the field of grass that lay before him. He looked back again and was relieved no one was perusing him. However, in the distance he heard sirens. Mark knelt down behind some tall shrubbery and faced the town. Through the pain, he took several very slow, deep, shaky breaths. He set the gun on the ground and pulled a handkerchief from the inside pocket of his jacket. Mark tore a strip off and stuffed a piece into the hole in his left side. The pain was so intense it had caused him to sit down, sweat poured from his brow. Finally, he stood and struggled another seventy yards out into the field towards the trees. He felt his phone buzz and then stop, buzz and stop, buzz and stop. "What the hell!" As he reached for his phone, he heard a helicopter in the distance. It grew louder, then finally, he could see it coming over the horizon from the west, and it was headed straight for him. He ejected the magazine from the gun and counted the remaining rounds. He wished he had had his Glock, but four rounds of well-placed .380s would ruin anyone's day.

With the powerful seven-hundred horsepower Allison gas turbine engine beating the air into submission, the Bell Jet Ranger slowly descended on Mark and as it descended he could see someone kneeling in the open doorway. The thirty-three-foot diameter main rotor pounded his ears. As it approached, he could see the words 'ENDANGERED SPECIES' had been painted across the bottom, and an emblem had been painted on the side of the white and pink helicopter. It wasn't until the chopper had turned itself broadside that he actually got a good look at it. The emblem matched the shirt that the crewman was wearing when he jumped from the side door. A pink flamingo, wearing sunglasses and a bright yellow Hawaiian shirt, stared back at Mark. He stood up and raised his newly acquired gun and pointed it at the stranger hurrying towards him. "Who are you?" he yelled.

The crewman slowed to a walk, raised his hands and shouted. "Mr. Springfield, Senator Erasmo Jones sends his regards."

Mark instantly recognized the name. Using the back of his left hand, he wiped the sweat from his brow. He started to feel nauseous and unsteady. "What do you want?" he shouted in return.

The crewman motioned with an extended arm back at the helicopter and said. "Want to take a ride?"

Mark did not know Jones, but he knew Mike and if he trusted the senator, then he would trust Mikes gut, or his ridiculous water bottle test. Mark lowered the gun and slowly walked towards the helicopter. He didn't stop the crewman from helping him climb inside, but he didn't put his gun away either.

The crewman slipped on his headset, and then slid a set over Marks' head and said. "I'm Jack. Sitting upfront is Mr. Flamingo."

The pilot, hearing his partners' comment thru the headset, turned around and gave him a blank stare and then looking at Mark added, "It's Diane." Both crewmen started laughing then suddenly the pilot yelled. "Hold on, here we go!" The Bell JetRanger jumped off the ground and screamed up to two thousand feet, dipped its nose and headed west.

The crewman reached over and pulled Marks jacket to the side, looking at his blood-soaked shirt, and shook his head.

Mark pointed to the wound in his shoulder and said. "This is thru and thru." He then pointed to his bloody side, winced and exclaimed, "however, this is not."

"Well let's get you patched up." The crewman unlatched a first aid kit from under the seat, slid it out and placed it on the seat next to him.

"Nice cork." he quipped, studying the fabric Mark had jammed in the hole. "I bet that hurts."

Mark returned a hard stare.

"I think I'll go after your shoulder first since you did such a nice job stopping the bleeding in your side, but first a little something for the pain." The crewman quickly stuck a hypodermic into Marks arm. A few minutes later, he went to work on his shoulder. When he was finished, he turned his attention to his second wound and said. "I may have to get aggressive with your side, I'm going to give you something that may put you out but, I'm going to need your gun."

Mark flipped up his gun and looked at it. "Who are you guys, and don't tell me Jack and Diane," he finished with a half-smile.

"Your pilot is Teddy, I'm Ziggy. We worked together in Vietnam. He was my pilot, and I was the medic. Now we work for the senator's wife."

"And she lets you two borrow her helicopter?" Mark smiled and handed Ziggy the gun.

"Let me get you fixed up." Ziggy prepared another hypodermic, smiled and sarcastically quipped, "This may pinch a little."

Mark raised his hand to momentarily stop from being injected. "If I die, don't tell anyone I was rescued by a pink flamingo."

Ziggy gave Mark a low chuckle, straightened out his arm and injected him. "It's been a real pleasure, Mr. Springfield. Nite, nite."

# 26

*November 2012*
*San Jose, California*
*International airport*

Teddy's high-speed approach to the San Jose International airport had won him another warning from the tower and after one complete high-speed skidding circle around their outlying home office, he gently set the helo down in the center of its designated spot. Eighty feet away sat a business jet, the Gulfstream G650 which sported the same painted emblem.

The two men helped Mark from the helicopter and slowly walked him over to the jet. Two striking, blonde female pilots dressed in blue slacks, white shirts and form-fitted blue jackets, stood at the stairs that led up to an open door. "Ladies, may I introduce Mr. Mark Springfield. Mr. Springfield may I introduce the real Jack and Diane. Actually, Jacklyn, Ziggy said motioning to the woman on the right.

She gave him a crooked smile, then turned her attention to her passenger. "Mr. Springfield, let us help you. These stairs can be tricky."

Mark mumbled his reply. The lingering effects of the drugs had not only kept him groggy and off balance, they had also kept him from speaking clearly.

The ladies helped him up the stairs and laid him on a tan leather couch. They stuffed a few pillows under his head and covered him with a blanket. Before Diane joined her partner back at the tarmac, she slid a large bottle of water into a rack next to him. Walking down the stairs and looking at Teddy, she said, "If you keep that up, the senator is going to get another phone call. And I don't particularly think he was too happy after the last one."

Teddy pointed up at the sky and said. "My approach... nah, they love me here!"

"I know you scared me!" Ziggy said, slapping Teddy's arm as he laughed. He handed a small bag to Jacklyn and added. "This is his shirt, jacket and a few other odds and ends. I don't know if he wants the clothes. They have holes in'm. Oh, by the way, there's a firearm in there as well. The magazine has rounds in it, but I emptied the chamber."

"I'll see that he gets this," Jacklyn replied, holding up the bag.

"It's a beautiful day to fly and we wish you girls a good flight." Teddy added. The men turned and walked away from the jet. Ziggy looked back and said, "Hey, when he wakes up, tell him Teddy was the one who dressed him in the flamingo shirt."

The two Navy veteran F18 pilots looked at each other and shook their heads. Then they stepped inside and closed up the Gulfstream.

After clearance from ground control, the Gulfstream taxied to the hold line for the active runway and Diane gently applied the brakes and waited for clearance to takeoff. The jet had had its preflight inspection and the engines had been checked for anomalies. From the left seat, Jacklyn looked over her right shoulder at Mark sleeping on the couch.

Diane glanced over at her, smiled and lifted an eyebrow.

"Well, he is kind of cute." Jacklyn chuckled.

Several long minutes later, the radio squawked. "Gulfstream zero-fifty-eight bravo, taxi into position and hold."

Diane quickly shot back into the boom microphone of her headset. "Gulfstream zero-fifty-eight bravo understand taxi and hold, request left-hand departure."

Jacklyn poked her finger at the instruments and said, "She's all yours."

Diane smiled and followed the command from the tower by slowly advancing the throttles and coaxing the fifty-six-million-dollar jet over the hold line and onto the active runway. Slight pressure on the left rudder pedal toe brake caused the G6 fuselage to swing left and set its nose wheel perfectly on the runways center line. After they were lined up, she gently applied the brakes and waited for the tower's next command. While waiting they looked outside of the jet, searching the runway, the opposing taxiways, and the sky above for any traffic that may cross in their path.

"Gulfstream zero-fifty-eight bravo cleared for takeoff, left-hand departure approved."

"Zero-fifty-eight bravo, understand left hand departure approved." From the right seat, Diane slowly pushed the two throttles forward, accelerating smoothly down the runway. The G6 was well below her max take-off weight of ninety-nine-thousand-six-hundred-pounds and she smoothly transitioned from go-cart to flying machine long before the required six-thousand-foot take-off roll. With the Rolls-Royce engines each developing sixteen thousand pounds of thrust, the Gulfstream easily maneuvered and climbed to their cruising altitude at the skillful hands of Diane.

Once they wished their last radio contact a good day, the ladies set their cruise and checked the GPS to ensure their Gulfstream was pointed east to Charlotte Douglas International Airport, North Carolina.

\*　　\*　　\*

Thirty minutes into the flight, Jacklyn asked, "Are you going to fly for a while or going auto?"

"I'll fly for a while," Diane chuckled. "You know me!"

Laughing, Jacklyn quipped, "Yeah, that means I'm going to need to pry that yoke out of your hands when it's my turn. Okay then, don't go anywhere, I'll check our passenger." She punched the harnesses' center latch and tossed the restraints over her shoulder. Twisting in her seat, she pushed herself up and stepped into the aisle only to see her passenger sitting up and rubbing his head. "Well, hello there!" She said, then grabbed the bag next to her seat and walked it over and set it next to the seat she had just taken.

"Where am I?" Mark asked while rubbing his head. "Strike that, where am I going?"

Jacklyn reached across Mark and grabbed the bottle of water that had been sitting in the rack next to the couch. Then sat back in a low leather recliner across from him and twisted the cap off of the bottle. "Here, drink this. Ziggy gets a little heavy handed with his knock out juice."

Mark took the bottle and gulped down its entire contents. "Thanks!"

"We are headed to North Carolina."

"Am I being kidnapped?" Mark asked with a half grin.

"Not hardly!" Jacklyn laughed her reply.

Mark briefly scanned the interior of the jet then pulled his new shirt away from his body and studied its design. "I remember, the helicopter, and that god-awful pink flamingo. Does this have anything to do with Senator Jones?"

"It does. We work for his wife."

"Yeah, I keep hearing that."

"We were asked to find, recover, and take you back to their home. Well, Diane and I are the take you to his home part, Teddy and Ziggy are the search and recovery part. That's right up their alley."

"You do this often?" Mark inquired picking up on the word *are*.

"Mr. Springfield, I'm sure the senator will clear some of this up."

"But how did you know how to find me or know who I am?" Mark pressed.

"Well, we know who you are because while Diane's been doing the flying, I've been going thru the bag Ziggy had given me when they dropped you off, and while we have ferried some folks around, you are the first person from the CIA. To add to that, you're shot-up, that's a nice touch, real cloche and dagger if I may say." Jacklyn returned a caring smile and pointed to Marks wounds. "Speaking of being shot, how are you feeling?"

"I've been shot before," Mark grinned. "It's the dying part of being shot you want to avoid." Mark raised his right arm and made small circles with it. "I think your Ziggy did a pretty good job patching me up." What Mark wasn't saying was that it hurt like hell.

Jacklyn laughed and said, "Oh no, not *my* Ziggy. Diane and I love him and Teddy to pieces but, those two are from another era." Reaching down, she picked-up the bag sitting next to her chair. "And speaking of them, Teddy wanted me to give this to you when you woke up."

Mark opened the bag, reached inside and pulled-out his cell phone. Tossing it on the small table, he said, "This is of no use to me right now." Again, he peeked inside and this time munched his eyebrows, looked up at the blonde beauty sitting across from him and retrieved a small plastic bag. He held the bag up to Jacklyn and said. "I can add this to my collection."

"There's a collection? Is that a three eighty?"

Mark flipped the bag around and took a look at the smashed bullet. "Very good, I'm impressed."

With a smirk, Jacklyn reached into her vest pocket and removed four cartridges. "I was just being a smart ass, I knew what that was." She picked up Marks left hand, turned it up and laid the rounds in his palm. "As you'll find in the bag, the guys gave your gun back but I took the liberty of removing the rounds." She was ready for Marks questioning look. "I didn't want anyone shooting holes in my airplane. I thought it might be a good idea to talk to you first."

"Smart." Mark quipped returning her smile. "And to set the record straight, that's not my gun. I carry a forty caliber Glock, and before you ask, I'd rather not talk about it."

"That's fair, but tell me one thing. Twenty-two, twenty-three, or a twenty-seven?"

"You know the model numbers!" Mark chuckled.

"I'm a Glock girl, Mr. Springfield. Been shooting since I was five."

Mark watched Jacklyn lean forward in her seat waiting for an answer. This interaction was completely different then the last time he had sat across from an attractive woman. He hoped he wouldn't end up pushing her through a plate glass window or two. "It's a twenty-three." He blurted out.

Jacklyn nodded her head, "I prefer nines. I get a much more controlled second shot."

"Or third or fourth, you given them what they need," Mark added and then tapped his empty water bottle. "And speaking of needing, can I get another one of these?"

"Oh, I'm sorry, I'll be right back." Jacklyn stood, smoothed her pants, turned and walked towards the back of the airplane.

"Let's blame Diane for not getting enough in the first place." Mark kidded.

"I knew it was her fault." She giggled.

Mark watched Jacklyn stoop down, open a small refrigerator and retrieve two bottles of water. He wondered what her story was, then suddenly, he thought of the woman he had fought with and how he wished he would have had the time to shoot her.

Jacklyn returned and handed Mark a water bottle then slid the other in the rack. "Well, Mr. Springfield, there's nothing I like better than talking guns, and I'd like to tell you how my nine is better than your forty, but I should go forward and check on Diane. But not only that, you should try to get some rest. We have a few more hours before we land in Charlotte."

Mark smiled and looked down at the couch and pillows. "I have been lacking sleep and since there's not much I can do here. I might as well take advantage of this couch." Then he added. "Thank you for taking care of a shot-up government guy. And Jacklyn, it's Mark."

Jacklyn patted the side of Marks leg and retorted. "It's been our pleasure Mark."

He watched her walk into the cockpit and slide into the left seat. He smiled inwardly at the pleasant encounter, then threw his legs up onto the couch and stuffed a pillow under his head. He rubbed his side, knowing the woman in his hotel room had once again out-smarted him, but now, he had a name, Tia. His thoughts drifted back to Jacklyn while he fell into a light sleep.

"I was… unsuccessful."

Lambert listened intently to the voice on the phone. It was labored; the woman struggled with each word, slowly inhaling shallow breaths. Receiving the call in her office, she could not ask what had happened, however, she could only assume Springfield was still alive.

Tia struggled with every word. Each breath brought a wave of agony. The pain of two broken ribs, a punctured lung and being attacked by what felt like a brahma bull would have been unbearable if it had not been for the drugs that were administered by a company doctor. She knew she was lucky to be alive, but continuing the pursuit of the agent was out of the question. She failed when normally she would had exceeded Lamberts expectations. It had been her first failure and she hated to admit it to her boss, but all she wanted to do now was to fill her lungs. In an unsteady voice, she regretfully said, "I cannot continue…the assignment."

"God damnit! Lambert snapped. She had not expected a single person so late to the game to be so much of a problem, especially for, Tia, who was one of her most effective weapons. Very much like she had been groomed for the Membership, Lambert had groomed the thirty-one-year-old for sex and to kill. Her chemically enhanced pheromones along with her natural beauty and intelligence increased her sexual power. It had even had an effect on Lambert. And once Tia had set herself on a man, she would enter his dreams and married or not, they would be defenseless against her. Without waiting for a response, Lambert asked, "What do you need?"

"Time," Her answer was labored. "I will finish what you have asked me to do."

"No! There is no *time*. I will deal with this myself," Lambert stated tersely and then hung up the phone. Picking up a rubber band, she spun her chair around and gazed out the window. Snapping the elastic between her fingers, she thought of the events that had led up to today. Since the reported activity that Cameron had first started with Veronica, connecting James Black to the John Doe of Mono Lake, she knew something had to be done. And when she learned that an employee of the Central Intelligence Agency with access to classified information was involved, it had become somewhat urgent. And now, more seriously, he was on the run. She was sure Springfield was in California and she knew exactly how to get him back to his cabin: kill his family and he would surely return. Then she could finally put an end to this inconvenience and move forward with the electromagnetic pulse strike to the midwest. Sixty-six million people on the grid instantly removed by a Chinese-built nuclear missile detonated in the atmosphere. She smiled. A war with China and the money it would bring was staggering. The lives lost due to the ensuing panic could not have been further from her mind.

# 27

*November 2012*
*Charlotte Douglas,*
*International Airport,*
*North Carolina.*

The Gulfstream's approach into Charlotte was as routine as the white billowy clouds that hung over the city. The rough air had given the jet several hard jolts and had been enough to jar Mark awake. Another hard shake sent him to the chair which Jacklyn had occupied earlier, and when he heard the landing gear unlock, he searched for a seatbelt. After finding one, he snapped it closed across his lap. A few additional light jolts and they were free of the clouds and the green countryside seemed to stretch out to the oceans.

Over the intercom, Jacklyn kidded. "This is your captain speaking. As we make our final decent into Charlotte, please fasten your seatbelt and put your tray tables and seat backs in their upright and locked positions."

Mark leaned into the aisle, looked forward and gave the crew a thin smile, but looking through the galley, it felt like he was a mile away from the flight deck. Leaning back in the chair, he took toll of his injuries. *Not bad.* He thought. *In just a few short hours, I've not only been shot twice but also clubbed on the head twice.* He ran his hand over the back of his head where he had been knocked unconscious and then hit with the woman's gun. Feeling the bump, he considered looking through the refrigerator's freezer for ice. But the thought was fleeting as the glance out of the window showed they were turning onto their final approach. The last few minutes of the flight were smooth and if it wasn't for the outside stimulus it would have felt like he had been at home in his favorite recliner.

Mark watched through the oval window as the runway seem to speed by and after a light tap of the main landing gear they were down. An American Airlines terminal came into view, then disappeared from the window as the Gulfstream passed it by and continued its roll out. Minutes later, they turned off the active runway and taxied towards an outlaying building.

Mark never felt the jet come to a full stop, but suddenly the two Rolls-Royce engines were spinning down, then were silent. Tilting his head, he watched Jacklyn and Diane effortlessly move their arms and hands around the instruments and the cluster of switches, shutting down the jet and her engines. At the same time, he reached across and grabbed the bag that held his phone. He pulled it from the bag and paused. With pursed lips, he tossed it back into the bag. Instead of using his phone, he pulled the last water bottle from the rack and finished it in three gulps.

"Mr. Springfield, you have a car waiting." Diane said while sliding out of her chair.

Mark turned towards the front of the plane, nodded his head, unlatched his seatbelt, stood and stepped towards the door. He paused while Diane unlatched and pushed it open. After she finished, she stepped to the side, smiled and motioned with her arm towards the stairs.

"Thank you. If I ever meet the elusive senator's wife, I'll be sure and pass on my compliments." Taking a few steps past Diane and into the cockpit, he added. "And thank you for the lift."

Jacklyn turned towards her passenger and gave him a thumbs-up. Speaking softly into her headset, she turned back towards the instrument panel.

Mark smiled, turned and walked out of the door.

When Mark stepped out onto the plane's stairs the black town car wasn't easy to miss. Tan Dockers, and the very distinctive sun glass wearing pink flamingo Hawaiian shirt, adorned the man holding open the rear door.

"Good afternoon, Mr. Springfield."

"Let me guess, you work for the senator's wife?"

The driver smiled and said, "Niles at your service." And then, he motioned Mark towards the back seat of the car.

Two hours later, the town car was slowly being driven through an affluent neighborhood. From what Mark had seen between the houses a body of water was a stone throw away. A slow sweeping turn to the right and he could see the end of the road was well-defined by a wrought iron fence and stone wall. Iron gates closed after the car had entered the driveway, and when Mark had stepped from his ride, he immediately notice two large, sunglass wearing, metal flamingos built into the gates. Mark pursed his lips and shook his head.

Raz strode through the front door with an outstretched arm. "Mr. Springfield, Erasmo Jones. Welcome, welcome to our home!"

Mark turned towards his host, took his hand and gave it a hard shake. "Senator Jones, I'd like to say it's a pleasure but... I'll wait."

Raz tilted his head. "I'm sure you have questions. Hopefully, I can clear some of them up." Motioning towards the front door he added, "Shall we."

The two men walked through the foyer and into the senator's office. "I'll forgo the usual tour of the house and grounds and get right down to business." Raz pointed Mark to a seat and then sat in the opposing chair.

Having interrogated hundreds of suspects, Mark had found being a good listener was sometimes better than a loud interrogator. He sat back and stared at Raz with the chiseled look of a four-hundred-year-old statue.

"Mr. Springfield, I'll get right to the point. You're being hunted." Raz let his words sink in but they seemed to have had no effect. "In August, someone from a California Highway Patrol car ran a set of numbers and that raised some eyebrows." Raz studied Mark, looking for a reaction. Not getting one, he stood, walked over to a cabinet, and retrieved a bottle of eighteen-year-old Macallan single malt scotch whiskey and two glasses. He poured them half full and returned to his chair setting both glasses on a table that stood between them. "A few weeks after that, a lab in Bakersfield, California started their own search for information on something that my boss was assured would never be found." Raz took a drink of the whiskey, hoping the pause would get Mark to say something, but when it didn't, he went on. "And then this happened." Raz reached down and retrieved one of three files that had been leaning against his chair and handed it to Mark. "A Crime Scene investigator made the connection and that quite frankly, started a shit storm."

Mark opened the file and slowly scanned the complete manuscript of Veronicas phone calls regarding the investigation into the John Doe along with all of her personal and professional information. It even contained phone calls from six months ago. It had all been recorded on the pages before him. As he flipped through the file, he realized that there were several screenshots of her computer screen with information linking James Black to the Mono Lake John Doe. Also included in the file was what looked like a photograph of her from her computer's camera. It didn't escape him that all of this information was only days old.

Leaning in Mark, finally spoke. "Senator, who is that you work for?" He let the question stew, then continued. "I know a little something about getting information and how long it takes." He raised the file up and said. "This was achieved in record time; this isn't just someone's address or the car they drive. This is detailed information retrieved from different platforms, complete with someone transcribing audio."

Raz suddenly felt uneasy. He had handed the file to the agent to share what he had; he did not expect him to dissect how the report was collected, let alone do it in minutes.

Mark laid the file on the table and added. "And my pick-up from your team, you not only knew where I was, you knew I was someone who needed help. And senator, you knew that at the same time the crime scene investigator needed help."

Raz felt the pleasantries they shared earlier vaporize. He was exposed and it felt like the agent was about to pounce on him. Springfield knew what information he had had access to. Reaching over for his glass, he took the last drink of his whiskey. Being rattled was new territory for him and he needed a few minutes to regain his composure.

"My compliments, Mr. Springfield, for being so astute. I only shared the information with you to bring you up to speed. I'm afraid you know more about me than what I'm comfortable with."

Mark ignored the comment and tersely asked. "Why did you come after me and not the woman? She had been involved in an accident and I can only think this has something to do with it." Mark added, pointing to the file.

Raz stared at Mark for several long seconds, grabbed his glass and stood.

"Take mine." Mark said gruffly.

Raz looked at both glasses, then took the few short steps to the cabinet, refilled his glass and returned to the chair. The two studied each other before Raz spoke. "I thought you required rescuing. Although sitting across from you, I'm not so sure that was the case. I only knew your location after I spoke with your colleague, Mr. Hollister, and learned of the Cameron Butler connection. It was because of him that I was able to find you. My team triangulated your phones and then focused on yours." Raz shook his head as he looked off into the corner of his office and reflected on his next words. "The information on the investigator was given to me last night. But truth be told, had I known about the woman sooner, I honestly don't know what I would have done. I only had enough assets in place to get one of you."

Mark felt the remorse in the senator's voice and read his demeanor, and it spoke volumes. "What do your sources tell you about her condition?" Marks tone was less harsh than it had been.

"She's alive, and safe for now. I understand there's quite the law enforcement presence at the hospital."

Inwardly, Mark was relieved and pictured Cameron standing vigil, however, outwardly, he remained cold. He leaned in, tapped the folder and asked, "Now tell me, how did you get his information?"

# 28

*November 2012*
*EasternShores Road*
*North Carolina, the home of*
*Mr. and Mrs. Senator Erasmo Jones*

The two folders that Raz had next to him were revealing, more so than what he had already given to the agent. But he was at his wits end trying for years to grasp what he was sure was a bigger picture. The agent could be the perfect partner, however, the story he would tell him was unbelievable and if for some reason it didn't go well, his pistol, the Colt Commander sitting in the pocket of his chair would help even things. He had no misconceptions that he could best even a wounded Mark Springfield. But he needed to be honest with the bull dog sitting across from him.

It was difficult for Raz to go down the path of no return. He loved his grandfather and still felt a loyalty. So, he would start from the beginning. "Before I go on, may I offer you anything? How are your wounds? I know you're not a hard liquor man but that whiskey may help take the edge off." Raz pointed to the untouched drink in front of Mark.

Mark was in pain and even though it was true, he did not prefer hard liquor. He knew the dark amber drink before him would help. Leaning in, he took the glass and gulped down the contents. "I'll have another." He said, handing the empty glass to Raz.

Raz produced a thin smile, took the glass and quickly refilled it and returned to his chair while handing it back to the agent.

Mark took another drink and pointed to Raz. "You were saying."

"Mr. Springfield, I'm from a rather wealthy family. My grandfather was a banker, a very wealthy man. His grandfather was a banker and also a wealthy man. And so on and so on. Each other's grandfathers were wealthy. They in turn had seen to it that their children are taken care of. But now it's my turn. I'm the grandson of a very wealthy banker. But it's not just that, the wealth, there's something else. It's an over-the-top 'need', enough money to last ten lifetimes." Raz slowed himself down. He felt he was rambling, but how do you tell someone you had just met in an afternoon that you're really the good guy. He paused and then continued. "I was gently coaxed by my grandfather to study finance, which I did and of course at the most prestigious schools. I had spent a lot of time with him early on in my childhood and as a young adult. During the summer breaks, I would visit him at his bank. I had watched him, the way he bought and sold money. He was a patient mentor, and I started to understand how money really worked, what it meant to people, and what they would do to get it."

"And how does money really work Senator?"

Raz shook his head and took another long drink. "It's quite simple. Money is the jail and the bankers are the wardens." Raz let his words sink in, then continued. "Think of a time when you may have received a considerable amount of money. Let's say, an inheritance and let's say that amount was, including property and stocks, one-million-seven-hundred-eighty thousand dollars."

Mark looked at the senator and his eyes narrowed. The man sitting across from him knew exactly how much he received when his parents had died.

Raz felt Springfield's dark look but it didn't stop him. "How did you feel with all that money? Suddenly you think, I am a rich man. Money was no longer a burden. It was no longer something that had to be chased, and for a short time, it started to lose its value and more dangerously, you felt free. But we fool ourselves. Those dollars are really the bars of our jail cell and the men on them, our jailers. Our great president, Abraham Lincoln, desired for us to be the masters of money, not the other way around. I believe his intentions to break-up the banks are what had gotten him killed. Are you aware that Mary Surratt, the owner of the boarding house that the infamous James Wilkes Booth rented a room in, talked of a stranger sitting with the now famous group? So out of place was he that a few guests had complained of his rudeness. Shortly after her telling of the strange man, she was arrested and, of course, hanged." Raz again paused to let his words sink in, then added, "So, I guess we will really never know who the stranger was, even though Booth and his co-conspirators were named, tried, and hanged."

Mark sat back in his chair and took another drink of his whisky. He did indeed remember getting his parents' inheritance and even after the split with his sister, it had been a considerable amount. Suddenly, a question occurred. "Why did you say 'more dangerously?' Why is it dangerous to feel free?"

"Yes, you must not be free, this is by no means a free country. If you are truly free, *they* lose control." Raz studied Marks face and saw the uncertainty in his eyes. "I know, I know, I sound like every other conspiracy nutcase out there."

"Senator." Mark interjected.

Raz held up his hand and said, "please, allow me some leeway." Without waiting for a reply he continued, "to cement their control, they came up with an ingenious system in the late eighteen hundreds. The Woolford brothers from Woolford, Maryland, began the Retail Credit Company in Atlanta. They started their credit investigations by going door-to-door among the different merchants, asking about their customers, and noting the findings in ledgers. Cator, a former bank employee, and Guy, a lawyer, employed simple notations to reflect merchants' comments about their shoppers' payment habits: "Prompt," "Slow," or "Requires Cash." They published these findings as 'The Merchant's Guide,' sold it for twenty-five bucks, then went on to offer individual credit reports. They became very wealthy men."

"Senator what does this have to do with —"

"Mr. Springfield, that was the beginning of Equifax, and it developed into those all-important three numbers that drive your credit score. What started as just columns in a ledger turned into a driving force." Raz took another drink and continued. "Spend money, make your payment and your score goes up. Pay off your debt and your score goes down and money becomes harder to get. Makes a lot of sense, doesn't it? But it's all about control and keeping you in debt."

"Twenty-five dollars in the eighteen hundreds, that was quite the sum," Mark alleged.

"Yes, but it shows us just how important those numbers were becoming. But, forgive me, Mr. Springfield, I get a bit ahead of myself at times. Allow me to back-up. I had already received my degree by the time I was twenty-one and working on my masters. But guess where I was working during the summer months?"

"Of course, the bank," Mark concluded.

"Yes, and then in stepped my dad. He didn't like me spending all that time with my grandfather. I think he saw a change he didn't like and I don't think he liked his father-in-law very much either. And personally, I think he was right. I was becoming just like him. After a while, I couldn't look at people or property the same way. My dad had a solid moral compass, and that's how he had raised me. He was not going to tolerate who I was becoming. He was very aware of the cycle and wanted to break it. A Navy man who had spoken of honor and duty, his quiet calm had won the day, and four months later, I had joined the army."

"How did your dad take the news his son had joined the army?"

"He didn't care as long as I was away from my grandfather, who, by the way, he played."

"Your grandfather doesn't seem to be one that gets played." Mark offered in a lighter tone.

"It seemed when it came to me, he would do almost anything and that anything was getting me a leg up. And that was thanks to my dad mentioning I would need to serve as the run of the mill solder for a while. That didn't sit too well, and it wasn't long after that, I was handed a letter stating I had been congressionally nominated for a direct commission and after I finished my combat training, off to Fort Benning I went."

"A congressional intervention. Your grandfather has friends in high places."

Raz nodded his head, debating telling Mark just how high, but he decided to wait. "Of course, I still had to attend all the required schools and put my time in but that letter opened a few doors for me. I had a financial background but it allowed me to do something completely different, so I choose intelligence which led me to work with the cyber folks." Raz paused and took another sip of his whiskey. "I have to tell you, I had only joined the service because of my dad, but it was the best thing I could have done. It refocused me and quite frankly unstuck my moral compass and, Mr. Springfield, it's what brings the two of us together. I would have put on the rank of Major, but I left the army after my dad died." Several long seconds passed while Raz looked nostalgically into his glass. After glancing down at his watch, he stood and motioned towards a closed door across his study. "But before we go any further, Agent Springfield, I'd like to offer you some dinner."

Mark nodded his head, stood and faced Raz. "Senator, Mark will do."

"Very good, I was hoping for a more amicable relationship than the one we started with."

"I get a bit defensive when I've been shot," Mark quipped.

"This way." Again, Raz pointed to the door. "I have a small staff, and I had given them and my house manager, Mary Mel, the day off." Giving Mark a smile he added, "I hope you find my wife's cooking to your liking."

Mark stopped and asked, "Your wife is here?" He watched Raz nod his head and added, "I look forward to meeting her." When Mark walked through the door that Raz had opened, he stepped into an old-fashioned dining room. Six padded oak chairs sat around a solid oak table. The ensemble sat on a large off-white area rug trimmed in red. Along a wall to his left was a cherry wood hutch filled with the same china that was sitting neatly around the table. Hanging above the table was a dimly lit chandelier. Of the room decorations it was the item that caught Marks attention the most. It had been made from a thin hammered wrought-iron band encircling a frosted glass sculptured globe. Attached to the band were eight equally spaced square twisted rods each holding up a frosted, amber tipped, floral glass shade. The fixture was attached to the ceiling with five lengths of hammered chain. In the low light it appeared the walls had been painted in a mustard and trimmed with white wainscoting. Standing next to one of the chairs were two very pretty women.

"Mark, may I introduce my wife, Maggie."

"Ah, the senator's wife," Mark kidded while giving Jacklyn a quick glance.

Maggie stuck out her hand and exclaimed, "Mr. Springfield, it's a real pleasure."

"Please, it's Mark." He said shaking her hand. "You have quite the team," he added looking at Jacklyn. "And a beautiful home."

Raz chimed in. "And I'm sure you remember Jacklyn. Maggie thought it might be nice for you to see a familiar face."

"I'll not soon forget my rescuer." Mark said taking Jacklyn's hand in both of his and giving it a light shake.

"Hello again. You seem to be doing better."

"The senator and I have been having a nice chat. And the Gulfstream allowed me to nap a bit. I feel rested. Thank you."

"Please, everyone, sit." Raz said pulling out the chairs for both Maggie and Jacklyn. Once everyone had been seated, he walked into the kitchen.

Mark looked around the room and offered, "Your dining room has a nice feel to it." Looking up he added, "I like this chandelier."

"Thank you!" replied Maggie. "My brother does a little metal work on the side." Pointing to the chandelier she added. "That and a few other items were house warming gifts."

Mark laughed and said. "So, I'll assume that the metal flamingos on the gates where his handy work as well."

"As is the entire gate." Maggie laughed. "He insisted on an elaborate wrought-iron system for Raz but we held him to just building the entrance gates."

"He certainly does nice work," Mark concluded.

After a few long seconds, Maggie stated, "You'll have to excuse Raz, the nights that we send the staff home, I cook, he serves and does the dishes," Maggie offered with a wide smile motioning towards the kitchen. "And by the way, I like your shirt. A little small, but we can fix that."

Mark glanced at Jacklyn and then down at his shirt. "Why pink flamingos?"

Maggie laughed and said, "it all started with my dad. When we were kids, he would stick plastic pink flamingos with their long metal legs in the front yard. I really think it was done to tease us kids." Maggie smiled at the memory then continued. "When Raz and I started our organization, we needed a mascot. The flamingo seemed a natural fit."

"Let me guess, your husband dressed him up." Both Jacklyn and Maggie laughed at Marks comment.

"No, actually it was this one." Maggie said motioning towards Jacklyn. "We were at a conference in Portugal, and one night during dinner she had asked if I would consider some changes to the mascot. I said sure, draw something up and let us take a look at it." Maggie looked at Jacklyn and smiled. "One drink later, she reached into her purse and produced a picture she had already been working on. As soon as she showed it to me, I knew it was what our flamingo needed."

Mark, remembering his *god-awful pink flamingo* shirt comment, gave Jacklyn an apologetic smile.

Raz pushed a silver cart piled high with serving bowls thru the door. Everyone looked over at the commotion.

"Dinner is served," he announced. Raz took the platter with the rib roast from the cart and carefully set it in front of Mark. "You have the honors." From under the cart, he retrieved a carving knife, a large serving fork and passed them to Marks waiting hands.

The following ninety minutes were filled with light conversations covering a variety of topics from Jacklyn's ten-year navy career to what was really Maggie's endangered bird project that had grown into a globally recognized organization. When dinner was finished and the table was being cleared, Mark pulled Jacklyn to the side and apologized for his rudeness. She in turn handed him her business card and said, "I'll be in the area for the next three days. If you find yourself with some free time, call me. I'd like to see you again."

"I haven't had much luck with blondes lately," Mark chuckled.

Jacklyn leaned in, kissed him on his cheek and whispered, "call me."

Mark flipped her card over and noticed that her phone number had been written on the back. He looked at her and retuned a warm smile, then turned to the sound of something behind him. Raz was standing at an open door that led into his office.

The senator felt the mood in the room had changed to a somewhat lighter feeling. However, he knew what was coming and poured them both another whiskey.

# 29

Mark returned to his chair and watched the senator refill their glasses. He had considered bowing out of the third but decided to join him. He took the swill, sat back and crossed his legs.

Once the office door had been closed, Mark fell back into business which was evident with his first question. "Senator, why are you telling me all of this? Why did you really bring me here?"

Raz answered, "it's a fair question." He reached down, grabbed another folder and paused. After glancing at it, he handed it across the table. "Mr. Springfield, let's call a spade a spade."

Mark returned an inquisitive look while taking the folder. When he opened the document, a picture that had been clipped to the inside cover was not whom he had expected to be looking back at him. Staring back was the picture that had been used on his CIA identification along with a copy of the actual document. Mark looked at the senator, then returned his attention to the folder. Not only did it contain his personal data, but the information went back ten years and even covered top secret assignments.

"I only show you that to let you know I know that you're not only a spy, but one of the top spies."

Mark clenched his jaw and asked, "How did you get this?"

Shaking his head Raz answered. "How I got that is not important at the moment. What it told me is what's important." He watched Mark page through his file searching for anything that stood out and stopping every so often to review a page.

"Other than you're not supposed to be able to get this, the file itself looks right. What am I missing?" Mark asked.

Erasmo studied Mark for several long seconds, knowing what he was about to show him could possibly send him over the edge, but if there was anything that would convince the agent that hidden forces were at work, this was it. In an even tone he said, "I draw your attention to the deceased family members' page." He watched Mark thumb through the folder and stop on the page in question. After giving him a few seconds to review it, he reached down and withdrew a yellow sheet of paper from the third folder and held it up to Mark. "This is that same page copied in yellow," Raz offered, then, he handed it across the table to his guest.

Mark leaned in and took the page while staring at Raz. Then he sat back and studied the page.

'Deceased family members' was written across the top, and with the exception of it being yellow, everything else looked the same. He gave Raz an inquisitive look.

"Of the people recorded, what do you notice about your mom and dad's name?"

Mark studied the list while scrutinizing his parents' names. Shaking his head, he said, "nothing."

"Hold the sheet up to the light."

Mark followed the senator's instructions and held the sheet up to the light, removed it from the light and then returned it to the light once again. "I see a small T1 next to their names when they are lit-up. I assume that has meaning." He suspiciously added.

"Yes, it does. But first I need to answer your question. Mark, I'm on the committee of oversight and government reform. Clearly, I have access to information that is classified and as you can see, I can get information rather quickly. I'm also sure it hasn't escaped you *that* information," Raz said, pointing to the file that Mark held, "was retrieved outside of the normal channels. But I didn't pick your name from a list of applicants. You had been recently dropped in my lap." Raz stood and walked over to a small desk and picked up two picture frames. When he returned, he handed one to Mark. "This is my Grandfather."

Mark studied the picture. "Why does your grandfather look familiar? Should I know him?"

"His name is Timothy Rothschild."

"Holy shit. You're a Rothschild?"

"I am, but I am also a Jones." Raz said pointing to the other picture frame. "My dad had met my mom, Elizabeth by chance. They dated for eight months before he knew who she really was."

"How did she get around the last name?"

"She used her middle name and became Liz Emelen. And according to my aunt Michelle, my dad's sister, *Mr. Rothschild* wasn't too happy his daughter was involved with a navy man, someone so low on the status scale. But that is a story for another time."

"Your mom is a pretty woman." Mark said handing back the frames.

"Yes, yes, she was. After my dad died, she wasn't herself and two years later, she followed him." Raz returned the pictures to their rightful places on his desk, turned and asked. "What do you know about secret societies?"

The question caught Mark off guard and he almost snapped his answer. "Senator, don't try to tell me this whole thing is about secret societies."

Raz held Marks hard stare while walking back to his chair and his irritation was clear when he spoke. "It's the answer to your question. It's the answer to your highway patrolman's question. It's been the god damn answer to every question throughout history."

"They don't exist, Senator! Secret societies are what fictional books are written of."

Raz held Marks gaze for what seemed like an eternity. "You were literally dropped in my lap. I read your file, and then I made some calls. Why did I really bring you here?

I decided to bring you here and feel you out, get an idea of the man I have been learning about. And now, I'm ready to ask you for help."

Mark leaned in, propped his right elbow on his knee and asked. "And what is it you want? What is it you think I can *or will* do for you?"

"To go after the very thing that fictional books are written about." Raz watched Mark lean back and shake his head, he only had seconds before he lost him. "Mark, I am a member of a secret society," pausing to let it sink in, he continued. "The Freemasons to be exact."

"Senator!" Mark said.

"Hear me out Mark and when I'm finished you can decide to walk out of that door and this meeting will have never taken place."

Mark stood and walked around the office. "There's one thing missing that may have helped give credence to your claim." Mark pointed to the shelves and walls and added. "Nothing, you have nothing in this office that says, I'm a Freemason."

"The answer is simple, there are Freemasons and there are Freemasons. No one in the Society is identified as a member, not even on the periphery as your books and movies would allude to. There are no plaques, posters, statues, trophies or rings. There's nothing that says Freemason." He stood and walked over to Mark. "Please sit, and I'll explain." Both men returned to their seats and took another drink of their whisky. "Halfway through my army stint, I went on a trip with my grandfather as I often did. We spent a long weekend in one of his many homes. The first two days were spent with him and a business acquaintance. On the third day, I was indoctrinated into the Freemasons, the ring wearing kind. I was excited, I was part of a group that helped people. Over the years, because of my grandfather, I have met the upper echelon, and unbeknownst to me, I was being groomed. Five years to the day after my dad died, I was brought into the Society and then I was tested. I had given the members information on very specific questions concerning what I did in the army and the cyber command. I did it willfully. I was part of the fabled *secret society*. It all made sense, the extreme wealth. I was taken with it all. Then someone made a mistake. I caught wind of a test and my dad's moral compass came spinning back." Raz stood and stepped over to a picture hanging on the wall. His dad, wearing Navy dress blues, stared back. He quietly avowed, "I found out, and did nothing about, Hallam."

"Doesn't even ring a bell." Mark stated sounding far from convinced.

"Hallam, Nebraska." Raz returned to his seat and picked up the last folder that was leaning against the leg of the chair and offered it to Mark. Reading his face, he professed, "don't leave yet."

Mark took the folder and leaned back in his chair. Inside was an eight by ten chart, in the upper left-hand corner written within a box were the words, HALLAM, NE. TORNADO. MAY 22, 2004. From the lower left corner running up towards the upper right-hand corner was a black swath of a storm track running through several Nebraska counties. Hallam had been accented with a time stamp, 8:35p. m.

"Thirteen towns around the storm's path. Look how the storm widens as it closes in on Hallam." Raz's voice grew angry explaining the chart as if he had had it front of him. "You can clearly see it's moved around the other towns causing only slight damage. However, it becomes an F4 when it strikes Hallam." Then remorsefully he continued. "One dead, thirty-eight injured, an entire town decimated." He finished his drink and quietly added, "and I did nothing."

"You're trying to get me to believe that someone had caused this storm, killing and injuring innocent people?"

"Mark, I'm quite sure you are aware that the government has been controlling the weather for years."

"Sure, some seeding to remove dense fog around airports and targeted battle space arenas but nothing like this. We would never do anything like this."

"Don't think for one minute your government is beyond this. Two thousand four was the culmination of years of trial and error. Someone demonstrated that the weather can be controlled." Raz twisted his glass between his fingers, giving his words time to settle, and after a few reflective minutes, he continued. "I have a map that I have been working on for years. It's a map of the world. I have been jotting down events on the map that I know have occurred through the Masons. I started correlating other events happening all over the world but, my reach was limited."

"And that's why I'm sitting across from a senator." Mark stated.

Nodding his head Raz continued. "Sitting on the oversight committee allows me to see information not available to the normal taxpayer and it paid off, and my map started getting crowded." Raz stood, walked over to his liquor cabinet and poured himself another glass of eighteen-year-old Macallan. He turned back towards Mark and said, "I have seen events that have happened on a global scale and I can't help but wonder if there are some hidden forces at play. Someone, or perhaps some entity, driving the whole damn thing."

Mark returned a questionable look but said. "World events?"

In the confessing mode, Raz continued. "In two thousand three, we were getting ready for an act of god. Of course, we were the ones playing god and…the Vatican was the target."

# 30

"The Vatican as in Rome?" Mark questioned.

"Actually, Christianity. It was to be one of the most horrific attacks on an organized religion. And it was being perpetrated by science. A scientific expedition was funded to collect microbes from below the sea floor. These microscopic creatures flourish on inorganic molecules, one of them being hydrogen, a building block of the human body. What do you suppose would happen if we remove hydrogen from your body?"

Mark looked at the floor, pondering the question. "How could you possibly remove hydrogen from a body?"

Raz was waiting for the question and quickly answered. "Replicate, weaponize and introduce the microbes into the air. When they are inhaled, they become active in their natural, warm, wet environment." A shiver surged through his spine when he spoke his next words. "And then, Mr. Springfield…they eat."

Mark pictured a shriveled, grotesque human body after its hydrogen had been devoured. "This is absurd. No government agency would ever condone this type of behavior." Mark said the words but deep down he wasn't so sure. "Senator, I seem to remember there was an expedition years ago. Your microbe comment rings a bell." Mark paused, searching his memory for a moment. Then he continued. "Yes, an explosion on a research vessel that killed the entire crew. The Resolution?" Mark probed.

Raz returned a surprised look and while nodding his head said. "Yes, yes, very good! And you are correct, no government agency would condone such an attack, but it's something other than that. I knew there was more going on than what I was being told. My eyes were opened after Hallam, and then this, the microbes. I was sent to collect those very samples and I watched the Resolution burn in the distance knowing the entire crew had been murdered." Raz pursed his lips and spat, "and then I killed the son of a bitch who brought me those samples."

"Why didn't you try to stop it?" Mark barked, his mood turning sour.

"Why, indeed." Raz sat back and pondered the question. He knew the answer, but he had to convey the 'why.' "Mark, I'm just one man and, I am quite sure, there are forces at play that go far beyond my understanding. I need to operate slowly and far below the radar."

"What happened to the samples?"

Raz quickly answered, "It had taken me a couple of days to come to terms with what I had actually been given and what they were going to be used for. Shortly after I hit Hawaii, I incinerated them. Then I told the Admiral they had been lost at sea during the transfer when her man was accidentally smashed between the submarine and his inflatable." Raz paused and reflected on his next words. "People do things willfully without really knowing the big picture. They think they know, but they don't. It's an allegiance, but it's a blind allegiance."

The words hit Mark hard. He was well aware of the evil that men do. He studied the senator for several long minutes. He felt his passion and knew he was putting himself out on a limb talking to an agent of the federal government. Mark started to put it together and offered, "that's why you're on the oversight committee."

Raz nodded his head and added. "In order to peek through the keyhole, you must first get to the door."

Instantly understanding, Mark uttered. "That's why you ran for senator. I'm impressed."

Raz chuckled, stood and said. "Blame my dad," then walked over to a decanter and poured two tall glasses of water. Handing one to Mark he said, "and now, I must give you the last piece of *your* puzzle, one you had no idea was missing, and the reason for all of this."

"Senator, I feel like I've been battling an unseen evil with a very long reach."

Raz, knowing the agent was not going to take the information well, tapped his glass with his finger as he contemplated if telling him was really a good idea, but it had to be done. Suddenly, his mouth went dry. Taking a drink, he leaned in and started. "Mark, I happen to know that when someone is marked for termination it's identified, not on some secret data base, but right out in the open." Raz watched Marks face slowly contort into understanding. "When the mandate went out for your information, I had that file pulled." Raz said pointing to the folder that Mark had set on the table. "I then took your deceased paperwork and printed it on yellow paper." Raz paused while watching Mark glance back at the file, recognizing that the razor-sharp agent knew what was coming.

Mark suddenly stood and grabbed the file. Looking around the office he spotted a printer sitting on a small table next to the desk. Ninety seconds later, a black and white copy of the deceased page was lying in the tray. He looked back at Raz while grabbing the copy, turned and held it up to the light. Nothing, the T1 was not visible. "Where's the yellow paper?" He asked in a demanding manner.

The two locked eyes for several seconds before Raz pointed to a closed cabinet behind the printer. "Left side, bottom shelf."

Mark retrieved the paper, slid open the copier's tray and placed the yellow sheet on top of the stack. His finger paused above the green copy button. The old saying made famous by the fortieth President of the United States, Ronald Reagan, *trust but verify* never rang truer. He pressed the button, not believing what he was about to see.

Seconds after the flash of light under the cover, the yellow copy rolled onto the tray, and the copier went silent. Mark looked at Raz with that same chiseled look. He looked down at the simple yellow sheet of paper, took it and held it up to the light.

T1 was clearly visible next to his mom and dad's name. No one else on the list had any indications.

*　　*　　*

Mark Springfield, in his lifetime, had felt happiness, sadness, and frustration, but nothing would prepare him for what was coming, an emotional overloaded that will shake his very core.

Mark lowered the paper and glared at Raz. In a low restrained voice asked, "what exactly does this mean?" The understanding started flooding his mind. The missing Defense Courier employee and the car that was registered to his dad that had been clearly pushed into the lake. "I get the implication of the code. I know a car was found that was somehow tied to my dad. I know his colleague, Ms. Kennedy had been killed one day after him." Mark aggressively walked over to his chair and pulled it close to Raz and sat down, the two were almost knee to knee. "Do you expect me to believe my dad's death was no accident, that my mom had been killed because of something that he had been involved with?" Still holding the yellow paper, Mark shook it in front of Raz. "And this, this is not right out in the open as you said!" Mark stood and moved behind the chair trying to understand what was going on. "You knew how to get this and you knew to check my file."

"I knew to check your file god damnit because I am a member of the society, I know how things work. I don't know how the code ends up there but the truth of the matter is, it does. That is why I have been trying for the past ten years to figure this out and somehow put a stop to it!"

"To what, put a stop to what?"

"I… don't… know!" Raz almost shouted. He stood and walked over to his desk and opened the drawer, looked down at the picture and then up at the fuming agent. "I have the notion there's more than one society."

Mark wasn't getting answers and he didn't like it. "More than one secret society, something outside of your Freemasons?"

Raz snatched the picture from the drawer and slammed it on the top of the desk. "This, this is what I think got your dad killed. Not something he had been involved with, but something he wasn't supposed to see." Raz stepped back from his desk and pointed Mark to the picture.

Mark tossed the yellow sheet down on the table, walked over to the desk and picked up the photograph, seven smiling astronauts in their space suits filled the scene. At the center of the picture was an outline of a space shuttle with the names of the astronauts written around the outer edge. STS-107 was predominantly displayed under the tail section. Mark glanced at Raz with a questioning look.

"The Columbia." Raz offered answering his expression. He watched Mark look back down at the picture and after a few seconds he added. "Colonial Kirby was tapped to head NASA."

Mark quickly located the name along the shuttle's starboard wing's leading edge. "Go on."

"He met with one of our society members three weeks before he and his six other crewmen mysteriously met their fate."

"You don't think this was an accident," Mark stated looking down at the picture.

"One hour before the shuttle broke up over California, an F-15 Strike Eagle launched out of Edwards Air Force Base in California. Do I think this was an accident? Perhaps if the Eagle wasn't carrying a laser."

"A laser?!" Mark spat.

"DARPAs Tactical High Energy Laser was undergoing operational testing." Raz read Marks face and continued. "I know what you're thinking. You don't just hang a laser on a jet and take it flying."

Mark laid the picture down on the desk and sat in Raz's desk chair. He had not felt his gunshot wounds for a while, but now with his heart racing, they both throbbed.

"But you do if the society is involved. But it wasn't the masons; I would have known. Ever since the weather event in Hallam, I knew there was more going on... I found out about it and watched it happen," after a long pause, he regretfully added again, "and did nothing."

Both men stared at the floor, each coming to terms with their own demons. Raz broke the silence. "We use the Defense Courier folks to pass information back and forth. According to their records, your dad and Ms. Kennedy signed into the building January twentieth, a little more than a week before the shuttle incident." Raz contemplated giving the agent the hardest pill he'd ever swallow. "I think your dad had seen something he wasn't supposed to. They couldn't risk him telling anyone and panicked, so they called him out to California, perhaps they were going to set him up and something went wrong and that's why he ended up in the FBI car registered to him. They can do anything." Raz's voice broke with his next statement. "They killed him, then your mom, stuck them in their car, and made it look like an accident."

Mark heard the senator but it didn't immediately register. "What!?"

"The key to all of this—"

"Wait!" Mark shot. "Wait! Are you telling me that both of my parents were murdered?"

Rage started its slow burn in the pit of his stomach. He stood and walked around the small table. His anger growing at the realization that someone may have murdered his parents. He walked to the desk and tapped the photograph of the shuttle crew, then glanced over at the yellow sheet of paper. *This doesn't make sense*, he thought. *My parents could not have been involved in anything like this, I would have known, or would I.* Mark dwelled on the fact that he was out of the country when the accident had happened, straining to remember the details. *This can't be happening; our parents had died in a tragic accident.*

Raz watched as Mark paced around the room coming to terms with his parents' death. He had expected the agent would question him and hoped he had made a believable case. The time for names was approaching.

Mark had a hard time focusing, his thoughts were chaotic and before he knew it, he was facing the senator and between clenched teeth heard himself ask, "The key to all of this is what?"

"Is whomever your dad helped at the Defense Courier building."

Mark quickly searched his memory for the name Dan Rowe had given him. "Marcus Smith." He offered.

"How do you know that?"

"I have my sources."

"I'll have him picked up. We can ask—"

"He's gone as of yesterday." Then Mark sternly asked. "Who did the Colonial meet with?"

"The same person who had asked me for your information. And the same person who was rattled when they found the car in the lake. Which I knew nothing about," Raz added.

"Who!?" Mark demanded.

"Shannon Lambert." Raz quickly blurted.

"Damnit, another familiar name." For a moment he searched his memory, but drawing a blank and wanting answers barked. "Who is she?"

Raz not only felt the anger in the agent, but it almost burst out of his dark eyes. "She is a retired admiral. Now she's the Assistant Secretary of Defense for Global Strategic Affairs.

"That's how I know the name!" Mark snapped.

"Do you know what she does?" Raz dubiously asked.

"I'm sure she oversees programs in the SecDef's office."

"She has his ear when it comes to our nuclear forces, missile defense, cyber security and..." Raz paused to highlight her last responsibility. "Space." He watched Mark make the connection and then narrow his dark eyes until he had the look of a soulless jackal.

"Where can I find her?"

# 31

*November 2012*
*Bishop, California*

Sirens in the distance told the killer that returning to the hotel was out of the question. However, watching the helicopter fly away made it worthwhile pursuing the agent. It would be easy to run-down who owned the pink flamingo painted craft. Walking down Rome Drive he could see, in the distance, flashing red and blue lights on the roof bars of the cruisers. Wailing sirens told him that the town would be crawling with the law. He eventually made it to West Line then over to Main. He turned left, back towards the hotel, and it looked like Christmas, every police and highway patrol car in the area looked to be parked in and around the lodge. He stuffed his hands in his pockets and strolled closer to Main, looking like everyone else wondering what was going on. Feeling his phone buzz, he removed it from his pocket and answered, "Hello. No don't come back, I have something I can follow-up on. I saw a hel—" Before he could finish, he observed a highway patrolman turn the corner one block to his right and slowly drive towards the lodge.

The officer appeared to be studying the crowds that had gathered. "Got to go." He blurted quickly ending his call. Then he walked over to three women and asked them if they knew what was happening.

After the cruiser had passed, he turned right and walked south on Main, again consulting his phone. After typing in a few search suggestions, the familiar sunglass wearing pink flamingo was prominently displayed in the upper right-hand corner of an information page. In the left corner was the picture of the founder of the endangered bird organization, and written under the smiling photo was the name Margaret "Maggie" Jones. A quick perusal of the document showed San Jose was one of three California locations for the organization. Considering the direction of the helicopter's flight it was headed in the general direction of San Jose. He opened up his maps and studied the Bishop area, quickly, finding a nearby airport and the services they offered. Slowly he walked back towards the three women with the intent of asking the fastest way to the airport. However, as he approached them, a black Ford Escape with a small yellow taxi sign on its hood was driving in his direction. Quickly he stepped out into the street and urgently waved his arm until the driver pulled the car over to the curb. "I desperately need to get to the airport. My mother has had a heart attack and I need to get to San Jose."

"Shit! let's get you to the airport." After the rear door slammed closed, the taxi driver quickly accelerated away from the curb and turned left onto East Line. Ten minutes later, the killer was reading a sign hanging from a small building. Adorned with wooden cut out letters was the name, Black Mountain Air Service, and underneath in smaller letters had been written, Charter and Sightseeing Flights. Suppressing a smile, he walked into the flight center. Forty-five minutes later, and after using the same story he had told the taxi driver, the small four seat, Cessna 172 lifted off the runway and was turning left towards the coast.

*November 2012*
*San Jose, California*
*International airport*

The assassin had never flown in an aircraft so small, with only the two seats behind him, he knew that he preferred the jumbo jet version. The approach into the international airport was daunting and the fact that he didn't see it at first was worrisome. Thru his headset he had listened to the pilots speak an unintelligible language, understanding very little of what was being said. Shortly after his pilot spoke into his boom mic he heard, 'Cessna seven five seven mike pop altimeter two nine'r nine'r five, winds out of the west at ten, clear to land runway three zero right' His pilot quickly returned, "seven mike pop, understand clear to land, three zero right."

He heard - cleared to land - and was happy to soon be on the ground.

The touchdown was smooth and when the nose wheel hit the runway it was official, he had survived. The roll-out was uneventful and while they taxied to one of the Fixed Base Operators, he scoured the airport looking for the company's familiar logo, the sun glass wearing bird. When they had gotten close to a small Fixed Based Operators office building, a man wearing a white jump suit appeared with two blocks of wood connected together by a long rope draped over his should. After receiving hand signals from the attendant, his pilot shutdown the airplane. The blocks of wood were quickly placed in front and behind one of the tires.

"Well that's it, I sure hope your mom is ok." His pilot said while removing his headset.

With his unquestionable loyalty to his boss and lacking a moral compass of his own, the henchman would have just as soon killed the pilot, however, he was in a hurry and out in the open. He reached into his pocket and retrieved a roll of bills. Counting them and feigning grief, he said, "I can't thank you enough," he opened the door, stepped out of the plane while the attendant pointed him to the flight centers entrance. Once inside, he went immediately to the counter and asked. "I'm looking for the group that flies the helicopter with the pink —"

"Let me guess, flamingo!" The pretty red head quipped finishing his sentence.

"Yes, where can I find them?" he abruptly asked.

Pointing out of the door she said. "Through the door and turn right, walk almost all the way to the end of the block. You'll see the bird on the right."

The killer turned and left without saying a word. After walking down the long sidewalk, he spied the pink flamingo logo above an entrance to an office building. To the right of the structure he could see the top of the helicopter and the tail rotor behind a smaller building. The fuselage was obscured. He walked around the building and saw the sunglass wearing bird slathered in pink soap. He momentarily watched an older man wash the tail of the helicopter. A tall fence around the facility forced him to enter the main entrance. He walked up to the counter, pointed to the craft and said. "I'm looking for the guys who flew that helicopter in."

Another pretty red head answered. "My lil sis just called and said someone was looking for us. That must be you?" she replied with a smile.

"Yes, I need to talk to them," he curtly answered.

Cloe Hansen, a striking red head stood behind the counter. Her smooth skin and deep blue eyes had caused many to pause when first meeting her. The forty-seven-year-old had worked for the endangered foundation since its inception. She was one of the few that had been handpicked by Erasmo himself. He viewed her as the first line of defense. While serving together in the army, Cloe had become a good friend and confidant. Her advantage was she could read people like some read a good spy novel, intently and from cover to cover. She felt the man who stood in front of her was bad and his presence had given her a chill.

"We had a helo out!?" she quickly questioned while picking up the schedule. "Hmmm... I know the boys have an upcoming maintenance flight, but that's not until tomorrow." Cloe paged thru the schedule perpetrating a ruse. "Please have a seat, I'll be right back. Oh, and what is your name?"

"Stanley." He quickly answered.

*My ass.* She thought. Cloe turned with the schedule still in her hands, walked to the door, ran her card thru the door reader and then typed in her code, which was followed by a loud audible click. After walking through, she turned, assuring that the door had closed and locked. Cloe smiled back through the glass door at the new arrival then proceeded to walk towards the smaller building where the helicopter was being washed.

Ziggy and Teddy both had joined the fight against the North Vietnamese in nineteen seventy at the tender age of twenty-one. Teddy was assigned the co-pilot position in the left seat of the Bell UH-1 but was quickly moved to the right seat when he had demonstrated that crop dusting on his families' mid-western farm had given him admirable flying skills which he had honed to a razor edge over the following years. He collected a chest full of medals during his career, the purple heart was awarded after he had been shot through the leg when a hot round punched through the bottom of his helicopter while flying a mission into North Vietnam. Ziggy had been sent to medic school when it was discovered he was studying to become a veterinarian. He had joined Teddy's crew eight months after he had enlisted. The two had developed a friendship but, when Teddy went back for his medic who had been shot by a sniper and had fallen twenty feet from his outbound helicopter their friendship forged and would last a lifetime. Working for the senator's wife and flying what they called 'odd jobs' for the senator was something well suited for them.

The two men maintained the helicopters and treated the aircraft they flew as if they were their own. The last-minute call from the senator was not unusual; what was unusual was their cargo. A shot-up CIA agent on the run was not an everyday mission.

Teddy had been listening to Elton John's Rocket Man while washing the helo when he noticed Cloe walking towards him carrying the schedule. Normally she would not have walked out to the wash rack. He pulled out his earphones and took a few steps towards her. "What's up?" he asked.

Holding the schedule up as if they were reviewing it, she said. "We have a visitor. Says he's looking for the guys that flew the helicopter in."

Teddy knew that what had kept him and Ziggy alive over their twenty-five-year army career was to trust, not only themselves, but their team and he trusted Cloe.

Teddy turned, tossed the sponge into the bucket, wiped his hands on his shorts and took the schedule, continuing the ruse. "And you're here because you got a bad feeling about this guy."

"If I could read auras, his would be coal black."

Teddy gave her a thin smile and added. "Ziggy's out getting hamburgers and shakes," reading the hurt look on Cloe's face he added. "Yes, we got you one too!" he chuckled. "Tell our visitor it'll take ten minutes to get this soap off. I don't want him in there with you for too long, so right at ten minutes send him out."

"Send him out?"

"Send him out." He gave her a nod and they both turned and continued with the deception. He reached into the bucket, grabbed the waterlogged sponge and gave the tail boom another wipe as he walked around the craft. When he was out of sight, he slid open the door enough to reach his phone, pulled up Ziggy's name and sent him a text. *We were seen/followed, Bad guy on deck, wash rack and you better not eat my fries!* He hit send and then tossed his phone back onto the seat. When he looked under the fuselage, a menacing figure was headed his way.

The killer was not waiting for an invitation. When the woman had left the building, he walked over, locked the entry, pulled the shades, then moved and stood next to the tall plant that had flanked the right side of the flight line door. Then he removed his gun.

# 32

He watched as the unsuspecting woman opened the door and walked into the office, knowing the drawn blinds would cause her to hesitate. Stepping from behind the plant, he slammed her on the head with the side of his gun. While she staggered, he quickly slid the trash can into the door frame stopping it from closing, seeing she didn't go down, he hit her again. This time, her knees folded and she fell hard onto the floor. A wicked grin spread across his face. He pulled from the shelf a roll of clear shipping tape and wrapped it around her wrists, ankles and mouth. Squatting down he studied the woman, picked up a few strands of her hair and brought them close to his nose taking in her scent. Once he smelled her hair, he rubbed the strands on his cheek then let them fall between his fingers, then ran the back of his hand over her hip and down the side of her leg while whispering. "Don't worry, when I'm done with the old man, I'll be back for you." Still smiling, he stood-up, returned his gun to its holster then turned, pushed open the door, and walked directly towards the helicopter.

Teddy walked around the chopper and asked. "Can I help you?"

"I'm looking for whoever flew this about three hours ago."

"Can I ask what this is all about?" Teddy asked acting puzzled.

"When this piece of shit went over my house something fell on my car!"

"I'm the pilot! What fell?"

"This." The killer pulled back his jacket displaying a forty-five caliber, semi-automatic Beretta handgun.

Ziggy parked his black Jeep Wrangler and slid out of the seat. He walked over to the side gate that accessed a small equipment storage area and the flight line. Crouching down allowed him to stay concealed amongst the equipment. Peering through the fence and around the gear he could see his friend's hands slightly raised. While duck walking over to the gates lock, he retrieved his access card and looked up at the sky hoping to see an inbound jet. There, on a half mile final approach was a Delta seven-thirty-seven. Ziggy watched the inbound jet and circled his index finger saying, "come on, come on land already." A few seconds later, the noise of the touchdown provided enough cover for the audible click of the locked gate to go unheard and Ziggy enough distraction to enter the space where the equipment had been stored. A hydraulic bowser's extension handle had been leaned against the support beam used to hold up the cover for the storage area. Ziggy picked it up, flipped it end-over-end in his hand and thought. *Yup, this will do.*

Teddy raised his hands up to shoulder height and said. "Hey, I don't want any trouble."

"Look, old man, I know you flew the agent here. Where is he?"

"Old man!? Your mother should have spent more time with you." Teddy reprimanded the thirtyish year-old killer like he was talking to a nephew and if it wasn't for the murderer's hand gipping his pistol, he would have happily reached over and grabbed him by the throat. However, he would not have to, his partner walked up behind the unwanted visitor and smacked him on the side of his head with a steel pipe, dropping him like a sack of potatoes. Teddy quickly bent down and relieved him of his Beretta and looking back up at Ziggy said, "Check Cloe."

Ziggy nodded his head, turned and jogged over to the flight center. Once inside he found her moaning and squirming on the floor. Grabbing scissors from the counter he bent down and gently cut the tape from her mouth, wrist and ankles then helped her to sit-up.

She rubbed her head and asked. "What happened?"

"Everything's okay." Ziggy said rubbing her wrists. "Do you know where you are?"

Cloe continued to rub her head while she looked around her office. "Yes, yes, my office."

"And you are?" he continued to ask with a warm smile.

It had taken her a few more seconds to straighten things out but she said, "Cloe, Cloe Hansen."

"Do you remember someo—"

"We had a visitor, I was out talking to Teddy." She quickly added.

Ziggy smiled "You'll be just fine." Helping her to stand, he continued. "Okay, let's get you up and in a chair."

Ziggy set her in the chair and retrieved a paper cup full of water from their dispenser. He handed it to her and said, "drink this, I'll be right back, I need to check on our friend."

Outside, Teddy grabbed one of the man's ankles and dragged him across the tarmac, assuring his head had bashed into several of the aircraft tie downs. Once they were behind their maintenance shed, he let go of his foot. He raised the Beretta when someone stepped from around the corner of the building however, he quickly lowered it when he recognized his friend. "How's Cloe?"

"Son of a bitch knocked her out, taped her up and left her on the floor." Ziggy answered kicking the man for good measure. "I'll get a few of the zip ties from the shed."

Teddy nodded and added. "Must have seen us in Bishop while he was looking for the agent. When you're in the shed, think about what we're going to do with him."

"I already know."

The two men tied him and then pulled him into the shack. When he had started to stir, Teddy threateningly said, "Yell and I'll shoot you in the knee cap. Yell again and you'll run out of knee caps." Jabbing him in the ribs with the muzzle of gun he snarled, "Understand?"

The killer was groggy but nodded his head, his eyes flickered open to a double vision world. When his eyesight straightened out, he was staring at two stone faced men. The thought of yelling for help had never crossed his mind.

# 33

*November 2012*
*Eastern shores road*
*North Carolina, the home of*
*Mr. and Mrs. Senator Erasmo Jones*

The room felt like it had gone cold and the senator sensed an abnormal shift in the agent. The two stared at each other until Raz broke the icy silence. "Normally, Lambert's very composed however, when she had asked me for your information, her tone and body language screamed something was wrong."

Raz stood, breaking the dark stare of the agent, and stepped over to the picture of his dad and straightened it. "I doubt very much she is at work," he said stepping back from the framed portrait.

"Then give me both. I want her work and home addresses."

Nodding, he took the few short steps to his desk, sat down and looked over at Mark wondering what he was unleashing. He pulled a note pad from across the desk and from the quill holder he removed a pen and jotted down her information. He stared at the pad and thought, *in for a penny, in for a pound*, then finished by writing down her private cell number. After returning the pen, he tore the sheet of paper from the notepad then stood and moved over to a gun safe that stood in the corner. After working the combination, Raz pulled open the door and turned towards his guest. Mark stood and within a few seconds was standing next to the senator who pointed to a pair of handguns that had been propped-up on wooden dowels and said, "You can't keep carrying that three eighty around, pick one of these two," then watched as the agent's hand instantly went for the forty caliber Glock 27, drifting over the Smith and Wesson. He watched him ease the slide back and check for a round in the chamber then drop the magazine to assure it was fully loaded. When he was satisfied the agent slipped it into his empty holster.

Mark looked at the rows of loaded magazines that lined the door of the safe but, before he could say anything, the senator removed two corresponding magazines and handed them over. He dropped them into his pocket and then took the sheet of paper the senator had handed him. After studying both address and the phone number he handed the paper back. "I'll take my leave now senator. I trust as far as anyone else is concerned, we have never met?"

"Outside of this room there are six people that know you are here, as far as I'm concerned, it'll stay that way." From the top shelf of the safe the senator grabbed a cell phone and handed it to Mark. "Don't turn this on until you are well away from here, and, I would only use it once."

Raz turned and pointed towards the door and added, "My driver Niles will drop you anywhere you'd like to go. He's very capable, if you need anything, ask."

Shaking his head, Mark looked around the office and then walked to the door. After opening it, he stepped outside and firmly said, "I'll find my own way," then pulled the door closed.

Mark hardly acknowledged the driver when he walked past the car. He strode through the gate and then suddenly stopped, turned and said. "On second thought, I will take a ride." Looking south and then east he continued. "We came in on the one-fifty-eight. If I'm not mistaken the ninety-five is what? Forty-five, fifty minutes from here?"

The driver shook his head anticipating the agents need. "Roanoke Rapids is off the ninety-five." Then quickly he opened the back door of the town car and added, "Mr. Springfield, I can have you there in thirty minutes."

"Let's go."

After closing the door, Niles walked around to the driver's door. Once inside he wrapped a thin headset around his neck and adjusted a small microphone than had lain alongside of his cheek. Then he started the car and drove slowly through the gate.

Over hidden speakers Mark had heard, "Mr. Springfield in the center you will find some energy bars and drinks, please, help yourself."

Food or drink had never crossed his mind. The one thing on his mind was finding Lambert, he needed answers, and knew she was the key. Coming to terms with secret societies was one thing, but finding out that his mom and dad had been murdered, was life changing. He tried to tamp down the anger he had felt in the senator's office, to control it until he found the truth, and then a thought occurred, *was he being played?* The senator was well connected with obvious resources at his disposal. Why bring a seasoned operative from the Central Intelligence Agencyto your home and tell them someone had killed members of their family? Was he about to be the biggest patsy in history? Was he the attack dog and Lambert the target? The senator seemed sincere but so did serial killers after eating their neighbor and claiming their innocence.

A slight grin grew across Marksface when it occurred to him how to verify some of what the senator had told him and it would start with his dad's co-worker, Colleen Kennedy. The idea drove his plan. He had one call from the senator's phone but, could he trust it?

Mark watched the countryside go by and with the increase in traffic it was clear they were getting closer to civilization. Over the speakers he heard."Mr. Springfield do you have a particular location in mind?"

His plan was simple, get a car and find Lambert. The closest rental agency is what he almost said but seeing his reflection while looking through the window, he changed his request. "I need a change of clothes."

"Yes, sir." After a few long seconds, Niles added. "The flamingo, she grows on you after a bit."

Mark peered into the rear view mirror and into his driver's eyes. He knew Niles meant well, but he was in no mood for small talk or the god-awful flamingo shirt.

*        *        *

After Mark had disabled the fire exit alarm he quickly walked out of the back of the store and walked across a side street and out into a parking lot. Not trusting the senator's phone, he removed the battery and tossed it into the trashcan in a restroom he had recently used to change his clothes. The only things he had had in his hands were two newly purchased cell phones and a small bag from a drug store containing two bottles of hydrogen peroxide, bandages, medical tape, Neosporin, large gauze pads, Tylenol and Motrin. He slipped one of the phones into his pocket and turned on the other, dialed his number and when it went to voicemail, he typed in his code. Mark pressed the phone to his ear when Cameron's message started to play. Although somewhat prepared to hear the news about Veronica, his heart sank when he had heard it from Cameron and his anger grew knowing his friend was standing vigil over the battered young woman. "Damnit!" As soon as the message had ended, he dialed Cameron only to have the call go to voice mail. Mark thought better of leaving something detailed and only said. "God speed." His next call was to Mike Hollister.

Mike, seeing the incoming call was from an unknown number, waited and hoped the caller was Mark and would leave a message. Sixty seconds after the call, the message icon appeared on his phone. He dialed his number punched in his code and heard Mark's familiar voice.

"New phone, call me." Mark let his arm drop to his side and waited for Mike to call. Still unsure of the senator, he scanned the parking lot and looked for Niles. When he felt his phone vibrate, he quickly answered it. "Good evening."

"How are you?"

"Let's just say I've had an interesting day." Not wanting to be long on the phone, Mark went right to the point. "I need you to get Colleen Kennedys deceased record, print the report out in black and white then copy the report onto a yellow sheet of paper, hold it up to the light. Compare it to the black and white copy and tell me what you see."

"You want me to what?" Mike asked inquisitively.

"Let me know what you find." Seconds before he ended the call, he was struck with another thought. "One more thing, do the same for an air force officer, Colonial Kirby. He was killed in the Columbia shuttle accident." Mark ended the call and then peeked at his watch, twenty-six seconds, well below the threshold he had known to be traceable. However, he hoped he wasn't wrong.

# 34

Mike Hollister's normal drive from his home in Clarks Crossing, Virginia to his office in the Central Intelligence building in Langley, Virginia was forty minutes but, after checking his watch, he knew this time of night would afford him a quick twenty-five-minute trip. He grabbed his keys, jumped in his car and headed east.

Sitting at his desk, he had easily pulled-up the file he had been looking at earlier. While he waited for his printer to warmup and the selected page to print, he retrieved the bio of Erasmo Jones on his additional screen. As the agent flipped through the file, he sat back and sipped a cup of coffee. Nothing stood out except his military career so he decided to dig a little deeper and pull up the army intelligence site. He searched randomly on his name and key words. After typing in Intelligence and Cyber together he had a return. Mike stared at a top-secret file marked, IGER UNIT. Attempting to open the file was fruitless. The word *restricted* flashed in a message box. "Restricted, what the hell?" he mumbled. He heard the printer spool-up and seconds later the sound of paper making its way through the device jogged his thoughts. Before removing it from the tray he tried once again to open the file, but had no luck so he turned his attention to the black and white copy laying on the tray. Mike pulled it from the tray and looked it over. "Hmm, looks right," he muttered to himself. Then he held it up to the light and gave it the same inspection and produced the same results, nothing unusual. Pulling open the tray of the copier, he placed a sheet of yellow paper he had gotten from the secretary while on the way to his office. Then he took the black and white sheet he had just printed and put in under the lid and pressed 'Copy' seconds later the yellow sheet appeared and after looking it over, he held it up to the light. It had taken him a few seconds to find it but a T1 was visible next to Colleen's name. Mike munched his eyebrow and turned back to his keyboard and typed in *Colombia shuttle, Colonial Kirby* and pressed enter. The screen filled with several options. Mike moved the cursor over and selected, Colombia Shuttle Crew. Moments later, pictures filled the screen of seven smiling astronauts with accompanying biographies. Within minutes, he had, Mathew Kirby's death certificate in his hand and holding it up to the light. Then he made a yellow copy. The code T4 was clearly visible on the yellow copy next to Kirby's name. "Where the hell is that coming from?" Mike pulled-up the records of several colleagues and a few high school friends who were deceased. After performing the same test, he found that none of them had anything unusual next to their names.

In the spirit of Marks request, Our Eyes Only, he stood, walked across his office to a shredder in the corner, and dropped every sheet of paper through the small slot in the top. A low growl from the device indicated that the copies would never be read again.

"To answer your first question, T1. To answer your follow-on question, T4 and to answer my question, I found nothing on additional personnel." Mike had placed the call to Mark fifteen miles from Langley. He was well aware of the ten-mile zone for cell phone monitoring. However, he added an additional five miles for good measure.

"The senator might be one of the good guys after all." Mark offered. "One more thing, look into his wife's endangered bird project. Her name is Margaret but she goes by Maggie. Her mascot is a pink flamingo. See if it's legit or a cover for something."

"Got it."

"I met a few of her people," Mark said thinking of his helicopter ride. "They are not your average employee." Keeping track of the time he added, "we're at twenty-seven seconds."

"Okay, one more thing. While he was in the army, he was part of a top-secret group called the IGER UNIT. Unfortunately, I can't access the file."

"Now that is interesting." Mark paused and ended the call with. "Let me know when you have something on his wife." Mark pulled the phone away from his ear and ended the call.

A thin smile spread across Marks face, he was well aware of the IGER unit. They had supplied the CIA with information about the Iraqi resistance during the first Gulf War. The way they had received and passed information was no less impressive than his dealings with the Navy Seals. His friend and colleague, Mike was not privy to the operation. However, Mark was starting to warm-up to the senator. If he was part of the IGER unit he had been one of the most trusted in the armed forces. Looking around the near vacant parking lot, he considered stealing a car however, what he had seen when he had looked east seemed more inviting. The last two days had been hard both physically and mentally. *Sleep*, he thought. As he moved closer to the front of the building the words Best Western came into view.

Mark checked in and then immediately left the building and walked out into the parking lot listening for clicks or pings from the engines of the cars. The ones he had walked in front of, he swept his hand by their grills feeling for heat. Satisfied that the cars in the lot had not been recently driven, he quickly made his way over to the hotel's fire escape and swiped his keycard to access the door. Mark quickly ascended the three floors, he slowly opened the fire exit door and looked to the left and right, not seeing anyone and sensing the hotel was quiet he walked to his room, swiped his card and cautiously went inside. Turing back to the door he rotated the thumb turn, locked the dead bolt, and then slid the security safety chain into its solid brass slotted track.

Mark walked into the bathroom and removed the Glock and holster and sat them beside the sink. After unbuttoning his shirt, he attempted to slide his arm out of its sleeve. A scowl grew across his face when he discovered that the back of his shirt had stuck to the blood that had leaked from under the bandages that Ziggy had applied to the back of his shoulder. He winced when he tugged the stuck shirt away from the wound. The mirror's reflection reminded him of a time he had trekked across Russia on a motorcycle, the Ducati Monster 821, trying in vain to reach a colleague. Mark shook the memory and carefully reached over with his left hand and pulled the tape from his skin, removing the gauze from his shoulder. Pulling a washcloth from the rack he dropped it in the sink and soaked it with hydrogen peroxide then laid it over his shoulder and gave it a light squeeze. The normally mild antiseptic burned when it hit the injury, but nonetheless, he laid the rag soaked with antiseptic over the repair and waited five minutes for it to kill any potential infection and stop small exposed vessels from bleeding and oozing. When Mark removed the dressings from the front of his shoulder and side, he was able to get a good look at Ziggy's handiwork and was impressed with his ability to stitch him up while bouncing around in the helicopter.

After inspecting the damage, he repeated the procedure he had learned so many years ago.

When Mark was finished cleaning the gunshot wounds, he applied the antibiotic ointment to the gauze pads and carefully laid them on the wounds. Using a small mirror mounted to the bathroom wall and the larger one that was hanging in front of him, along with two wooden hangers retrieved from the closet, he slowly applied a dressing to the exit wound on the back of his shoulder, using the hangers to place the ointment laden bandage and set the tape. Mark soaked another washcloth in a fifty-fifty concoction of hydrogen peroxide and hot water, then he used the warm rag to wipe over his face, arms and torso. After toweling off, he slowly slid his arms back into his shirt and buttoned it. Then, taking slow deep breaths, he sat on the closed toilet seat, leaned back, closed his eyes and tried to rest.

The buzzing of Mark's phone brought him back from the edges of sleep. The call back from Mike came quicker than he had expected. He stood, turned on the shower and answered his phone. "What did you find?"

"You sound tired." Mike offered

"A little. What did you find?"

"She's been a busy girl, double-majored in Business and Zoology. Her business degree was earned before she had left the navy. The zoology came three years later, and to her credit, she's known for hiring veterans." Mike shuffled thru his notes and added "I have a list of them if you need it."

"Not now." Mark added quickly reflecting on his recent experience with four of them.

"From what I was able to dig up, her endangered bird project looks legit."

"Actually, I'm glad to hear it. I think the senator has built quite the team under his wife's name." Mark hesitated and added, "to do what, I'm not quite sure. I'm going to make a call after we hang up. I want you to track the number I connect to." Mark relayed the number and added, "It belongs to retired Admiral Shannon Lambert. I would really like to know where she is this very moment. After the call my phone will no longer be available. However, when I do call, it will be from a different number." Mark paused and asked, "How long to set up?"

With a slight hesitation, Mike answered. "Give me fifteen minutes, I'll ring your phone once when I'm ready."

"Got it, and Mike, Oscar Eco Oscar."

"Give me fifteen." Mike ended the call… worried for his friend.

Mark reached into the shower and turned it off.

The tired CIA agent walked out of the bathroom and across the room to the left side of the window. Slowly he pulled back the curtain, carefully moving them only enough to look around the front entrance and up the street. Moving to the other side he repeated his action. While Mark was looking down the street, his phone vibrated. *That was fast Michael*, he thought, then dialed

Shannon Lamberts number, pressed the phone to his ear and waited. When the phone connected, he listened intently for anything telling in the background. After several, quiet seconds ticked by, he harshly spoke into the phone, breaking the deafening silence. "Next time send a more capable team." And to twist the verbal knife he added, "and Admiral, don't send a woman to do a man's job." Then he ended the call. Shortly after, he again moved to the other side of the window. His phone vibrated and he let it vibrate two additional times before answering it. This time, the silence was filled with an unpleasant voice.

"Fuck you!" Shannon Lambert growled into the phone. "And the highway patrolman's girl, what is her name? Yes, Veronica, Veronica Gibbs."

Mark clenched his teeth at the sound of her name and seethed. "You had my parents killed."

"Apparently, I should've had you killed, too. My mistake." Lambert then added. "Who do you think you are? You won't live to see tomorrow you son-of-a-bitch. We easily found you once and we'll easily find you again."

Mark's solid grip on his phone caused its screen to crack. Relaxing his grip, he spit. "I'll save you the trouble... I'll find you." Pulling the phone away from his ear and holding it out in front of him, he crushed it, removed the SIM card and ripped the battery from the frame. Walking back into the bathroom he flushed the SIM card and tossed the rest of it into the trash, returned to the living space, sat on the bed and waited. Fifteen minutes later, he picked up the extra phone, turned it on, dialed Mike and left a message. Minutes later, after Mike returned his call, he asked, "What did you find?" After an unusually long pause, he said. "Mike!?"

"Mark, she's in the Smokies."

"Jesus Christ!"

# 35

"Erasmo, I need one of your jets at Dulles. I need to get to Asheville with a few colleagues."

"And what do I owe the pleasure, Admiral?" He asked suppressing his concern.

"This is not a social call. I have business that needs attending to."

"Anything I can help you with?"

"Not unless you have one of your helicopters close by."

Raz chuckled and said. "Sorry, no helicopters, however, I do have a jet in Charlotte. I can have my crew in Dulles within the next two hours."

"Have the pilot call me when they are thirty minutes out."

"Will there be anything else?" Raz sarcastically asked.

"Not at the moment." With that, Shannon Lambert hung up.

Raz pulled the phone away from his ear and looked at it, shaking his head he said. "Shit, Springfield, you just left."

Across from Shannon Lambert sat Jon Miller, a man in his mid-thirties. His close-cropped red hair, solid frame and undeniable presence screamed military. The eight-inch scar down the left side of the army rangers back was his constant reminder of being ambushed in Mosul, Iraq during the 2003 invasion.

He was part of the memberships lower tier however, his hired mercenaries were not. They murdered for two things, money and the thrill. He assembled a team for a quick kill, two men whom he had used before. Spread out on top of a manila folder that had been laying on his lap were four colored pictures and one black and white. A family portrait consisting of Mary, Cole and their two girls, Christina and Ashley. A split photograph depicting a rendering of the cabins front and back. An overhead view showing the road leading up to the property. And an eight and a half by eleven picture of Mark Springfield in a suit, sitting for his official CIA identification. The black and white picture on top of the stack was a more recent photo of the agent. It was a facial recognition of him walking through the terminal at Los Angeles International Airport in California.

"When will your team be ready?" Lambert asked while studying the map that Miller had laid across her desk.

After a quick look at the clock that hung on the admiral's wall he answered. "Equipped in twenty minutes, Admiral." He shuffled through the pictures and pulled out the family portrait. "It will be a home invasion robbery and I will see to the home invasion part personally." He grinned while rubbing his fingers over Mary's face.

"There can be no more mistakes. They must be dealt with and when Springfield returns, kill him."

"More mistakes?" he asked.

"I should have disposed of them long ago. Not doing so has come back to haunt me." Lambert looked up from the map and added, "I will be making the trip with you." Tapping the Asheville Regional Airport depicted on the map she concluded. "This will put us at the foot of the Smokies, the cabin is here," she continued pointing below a mountain ridge on the map.

Miller nodded his head and offered. "I'll arrange the transportation to Asheville."

"No, that won't be necessary." Lambert interjected. "I can get us there, you only have to worry about getting us up to the cabin. Plan on departing Dulles in an hour."

Miller nodded but, he was not ready for what was said next.

"Your team." Lambert paused, then sternly continued. "They cannot leave the mountain."

"Admiral, a million dollars buys both loyalty and silence. These men can be trusted." He pushed, but knowing the power that Lambert yielded he quickly relented after her next statement.

"Are you not up for the task?"

Hiding his regret with a grin he answered. "Understood, they will not leave the mountain."

When their Gulfstream glided onto the runway, Jacklyn's approach and near perfect landing drew a wink and a question from Diane. "Any idea what's going on?"

Jacklyn coaxed the jet off the runway and once she turned left onto the blue lit lined taxiway she answered, "no, but a run for the Assistant Secretary of Defense for Global Strategic Affairs?!" After a slight pause she added, "doesn't smell right." Rolling towards an outlying building they had seen the headlights of two vehicles pointed out onto the ramp. In their glow, four shadows stretched across the ground.

"Gulfstream zero-fifty-eight bravo, your clients are ready for immediate departure."

"Zero-fifty-eight bravo." Jacklyn acknowledged she had understood to the unseen radio operator. Minutes later she took directions from line personnel and stopped her jet when two red handheld lights came together over the lineman's head. Once she had received notification that her wheels had been chocked, she shut down the engines, unlatched her harness, twisted in her seat and said. "If you would finish up and then file with Flight Service our flight to Asheville, I'll greet the guests and look the plane over."

Diane nodded her head and went to work. But after her friend stood and put on her jacket she quipped, "good luck!"

Jacklyn lowered the Golfstream's ladder and trotted down the steps only to be met by one of the men accompanying Shannon Lambert. He stepped onto the ladder in a rush to board the aircraft. However, he was met by a defiant pilot who sternly said. "Step aside, please." The two locked eyes in an awkward pause until the red-headed man yielded and stepped back onto the tarmac with a grin. With an outstretched arm, Jacklyn greeted Lambert with a handshake. "Admiral, so very nice to meet you!"

Lambert cocked her head and said "Thank you miss…"

"Please, it's Jacklyn." Tilting her head up towards the cockpit she continued. "Both Diane and I flew F-18s in the navy and have certainly heard your name."

Lambert nodded her head and asked. "How's our trip to Asheville shaping up?"

Jacklyn pulled up her jacket sleeve and studied her watch. "We should be airborne in no more than…thirty minutes," she smiled. Motioning towards the stairs she offered to the small group. "If everyone would board the jet, we can finish up our preparations and be on our way." In her periphery she noticed the man whom she had met on the ladder staring at her, lingering until the rest were in line for the stairs. Jacklyn turned towards him as he stepped past her, she said. "No one boards the aircraft uninvited. Now you have been invited."

He ignored her, and continued up the ladder.

Once she completed her preflight, she too walked up the stairs and stepped in through the doorway, turned, retracted and locked the door. Then pointing to the bar and refrigerator, she said, "Please help yourselves. We will be airborne shortly." After she slid into the left seat, Jacklyn placed her head phones over her ears, seconds later she heard Diane.

"How's the admiral?"

"The personality of a bent shit-can," Jacklyn offered.

"And her 'team'?"

"You saw it too?"

"I watched them come up the ladder, special forces, every one of them."

"I'll deny I said it but, I kinda wish Teddy and Ziggy were here."

"Well, let's get going, the sooner we dump them off in Asheville, the better."

Diane trimmed the Gulfstream and set her cruise at three hundred miles an hour. The one-hour trip to North Carolina through a clear sky and smooth air made it feel as if they had never left the ground. Thirty minutes into the flight, Jacklyn pushed herself out of the pilot's seat and walked aft to check on her passengers. Noticing that the three men were huddled around a table and speaking in hushed whispers, she approached Shannon who was slowly swirling the drink she held in her hand while staring out of the window.

She walked up to her, slightly bent at the waist and asked. "Admiral, is there anything I can get you?"

Lambert tilted her head and stared up at Jacklyn. After several, uncomfortable, long seconds she finally said, "no."

Jacklyn stood, turned, smiled and said. "Gentlemen, we will be landing in approximately twenty minutes." After a few steps back towards the cockpit, she heard."Thanks honey."

Not missing a beat, she replied without looking at the men, "not hardly!" and continued into the cockpit and directly into her seat. After adjusting her headset, she murmured, "jackass!"

✳     ✳     ✳

After the smooth approach and landing into the Asheville airport the Gulfstream taxied to its assigned spot and the attendant chocked the wheels. Jacklyn pushed herself out of her chair and walked over and addressed Lambert. "Admiral, we hope you enjoyed your flight this evening."

"Yes, thank you," she replied.

Jacklyn turned, unlatched and pushed open the door then turned to the table of men, she noticed the redhead was busy with a phone call, but still offered in an even tone while pointing to the exit, "Gentlemen." When no one moved she said again, "gentlemen!"

The red head held up a finger while continuing his call.

It took Jacklyn all she had to hold her tongue, there was something about him that she despised. She returned to the cockpit and checked on Diane. Minutes later, Miller walked up and stood inches behind her and said, "We are on hold for roughly thirty minutes."

A startled Jacklyn backed out of the cockpit and into Miller. He grabbed her hips and said, "There'll be time for this later."

She raised her hand to slap him but he caught her wrist and quipped, "feisty!"

Diane quickly twisted out of her chair and pushed herself between her friend and Miller. She grabbed Jacklyn by the shoulder and said. "Come with me, they want us outside." Giving her a twisted looked she led her off the plane. Once they were on the tarmac, both women walked into the flight center and remained there for forty minutes until a white Ford Escape followed by a gray Range Rover drove up to the fence line. Both women stood at the window and watched the four of them trot off the plane carrying their large bags.

"A wounded fed and now these characters." Jacklyn offered with her arms folded across her chest.

Diane nudged Jacklyn with her right shoulder and said, "but a cute fed."

Jacklyn stared at the men and watched them walk through the gate. After they ducked into the Ford, she turned to Diane and then tilting her head towards the departing cars she added, "You know, the senator never said anything about waiting for them."

"You don't have to tell me twice, I'll take care of the pre-flight if you do the paperwork," Diane retorted.

"Deal! I want to be airborne in fifteen."

"I can already feel the wind in my face," Diane said with a smile. Walking towards the door she heard Jacklyn say. "And yes. He is kind of cute."

Diane stopped and turned towards her friend who had a shy smile spread across her face. With a smirk, she turned and walked thru the doorway out towards the jet.

# 36

"We got a hit in Asheville, North Carolina. I just looked at a map. She has to be headed to your cabin."

The exhaustion and pain vaporized and Mark wanted to scream. He was hours away from his family. He ended the call to Mike and then quickly stood, ran into the bathroom and grabbed his gun. Stepping out of his hotel room, he walked directly over to the fire alarm and pulled it then ducked into the fire escape, quickly descended it and walked out into the parking lot. After scanning the lot, he slowly walked over to a 2009 silver Dodge Challenger that had been backed into its parking spot on the outside edge of the hotel's grounds. He stepped into the thick shrubbery that lined the property, crouched down and waited.

A line of guests funneled through the main entrance and from the emergency exits. The blaring alarm could be heard for blocks. Mark gambled that the cold November night would drive guests to wait inside their cars, and it paid off. A man in his early forties hurriedly walked to the Challenger, opened the door and sat inside, seconds later the engine was running. Mark waited until the earsplitting sirens of two fire engines filled the night air. The owner slid out of his car to watch the engines arrive and when he did, Mark struck. He emerged from the bushes and like a cobra he struck hard and fast, he wrapped his thick arm around his neck and applied a choke hold and cut off his vocal cords while instantaneously driving the inside of his foot into the back of his victim's knee. He folded and Mark dragged him back into the shrubbery. Seven seconds was all it took for Mark to cut off his jugular veins blood supply and have him lying unconscious on the ground.

After peeking out over the tops of the bushes and seeing that everyone was still involved with the approaching fire engines, he stood and walked over to the car, slipped inside and slowly drove out of the parking lot. He judiciously drove through the small town and then sped up when he found the on-ramp for 85 South.

The trip would be long, he mentally calculated that if he could maintain ninety-five miles an hour, he could reach the foothills in under three hours. The Challenger ran strong and smooth, it had easily maintained the high speeds. And on some straight a ways, Mark had reached one hundred and ten miles an hour. He had kept a sharp eye for animals, hitting a deer at that speed would not only kill the deer, it would kill him as well. The transition for 85 South to the 40 West was seamless but, he relentlessly pushed the car, gripping the wheel as if he were choking the life out of Lambert. His only thought was getting to the cabin first. He picked up his phone and dialed Cole's number and when there was no answer, he called Mary, nothing, the phone was silent. When he glanced at the screen, he noticed that there was no reception, irritated, he tossed the phone onto the seat. It was a spotty area and in the Smokies it was hit or miss. In the early hours, he had only passed a handful of cars and was hopeful that the police where asleep in their cruisers on this cold night. He looked at his watch. It was the third day of the longest three days of his life.

The gash in Marks shoulder had started to throb so he relaxed his grip on the wheel however, when he felt, what he assumed, was blood running down his back he retightened his grip, gritted his teeth and mashed the gas pedal to the floor.

When the lights of the Challenger lit up the Asheville sign, a slight grin spread across his face. A quick check of his watch indicated he had made the trip in less than two and a half hours. However, the high speeds of the Challenger sucked the gas from a tank that wasn't full to begin with. A quick trip thru a gas station was in order. After a smooth deceleration, Mark exited the 40 West at the first station he had seen while passing through Asheville. A CITGO gas station fit the bill. It sat outside of town and the small store was closed, but the pumps were open. Mark swiped the Daniel Ricci credit card through the reader, pressed the 87-octane button and stuck the nozzle in the tank. He pulled and locked the pump handle and considered a nearby restroom. After finding that the doors located on the outside of the building marked Men – Women were locked, he relieved himself behind a set of dumpsters and then walked back to the car. Looking in the direction of his cabin, he mentally drove the route. From the time he had received the call from Mike he was two and three quarters of an hour behind Lambert. He didn't think for one moment she was alone.

This time of night it would be slow going for anyone unfamiliar with the mountain but, he had been driving it extensively and was very familiar with the old abandoned logging routes that he had driven many times in his nineteen-ninety-four, Ford F-150 pick-up, occasionally being accompanied by his nieces hanging off his arm, howling with laughter at every bump. The routes did not show-up on any map and would cut crucial time off the trip. The Challenger served him well but he would destroy it to get to his family.

The disengagement snap of the pump's handle shifted Marks attention back to the Dodge. Quickly he removed the nozzle, hung it up, slid back into the car and within minutes he was back on the 40 headed west. Fifteen minutes later, he made his first cut into the wooded area. The small road was visible during the day, but in order to find it at this time in the morning would take someone familiar with the mountain. He worked the gas pedal, accelerating and decelerating at the most opportune times, occasionally bouncing off low-cut tree stumps while speeding through the curves. Twenty minutes later, Mark was dumped out onto the main road, and knowing his next cut-through was only five minutes away, he accelerated until it took all of his skill to keep the car on the road.

Knowing the next leg of his trip had a drop at the transition to the logging road, he slowed the Challenger enough to roll through the deep, wet trench, then sped up when his back tires found solid ground. Eighteen minutes into the drive, Mark stopped the car in a turn that positioned him in the general direction of his cabin. He peered through the trees, looking for anything that caught his attention. He studied the road that ran for several miles. Not seeing any signs of movement he eased the Dodge around the turn hearing the loud shrill scraping of tree limbs along the doors and quarter panels. Suddenly, through a small clearing, he could see headlights along the main road that appeared to be stationary. He quickly stopped the car. Hurriedly he switched his headlights off and slowly drove the car, straining his eyes in the dark and trying not to hit anything that would stop his forward momentum.

"Son of a bitch." Jon Miller lowered his Night Vision Goggles and turned to Lambert. "That's Springfield!"

She shook her head and said in disbelief. "No! Can't be. He's in California."

"No," he replied looking through the goggles again. "He's a quarter mile from us." Lowering the device, he handed them to Lambert, then pointing to the car in the distance, he uttered, "If that's not the same guy in the photo, I don't know who is." He turned to Lambert and added, "when he came around the last corner, I noticed the lights, then all of a sudden they stopped."

Lambert lowered the goggles and handed them back to Jon. "I don't see anything," she said with a question in her voice.

Miller took the NVGs and looked through them intently and said, "and now," he paused, "they've been turned off."

"He's knows we are here," came a voice from the back seat.

"But he can't know who we are," Lambert offered.

"He's being cautious. It's what I would do." Then Jon turned around and said to the hired guns. "Get the ARs. We'll stop him here."

Mark saw the faint interior light come on and seconds later, it was off. He slowed the car and tried to discern if the group was Lamberts or someone who had broken down. Another light had illuminated from the rear of the car when the rear hatch was opened, "Flat tire." He uttered to himself. Then one of the passengers pulled something from the rear and even though the image wasn't clear there was enough light for Mark to determine the dark outline was a rifle.

Mark knew he had been seen and quickly made a plan. With his right hand, he reached up and repeatedly beat the interior light console with his fist until the plastic lens covers and pieces of glass bulbs rained down from the roof. Suddenly the Dodge hit a deep rut in the road that caused him to ram the left side of his forehead into the window post hard enough to crack the plastic cover.

As Mark bounced around, he hit a second rut that caused the side of his face to bash into the steering wheel. Gripping the wheel with both hand she looked for the clearing he knew was coming. He strained to see it and just as he thought he may have passed the spot, it was almost upon him. He sped up and quickly pushed open the door and waited. In that instant a bullet smashed through the windshield and the second bullet caused the windshield to explode. The bouncing front of the Challenger took several more rounds from the AR-15s. Mark held the door open as far as his arm would allow. His body was hanging halfway out of the car. He turned the car to the right and jumped from the open door. He hit the ground hard. His leg slid across a cut tree that tore a chunk of flesh from his thigh. He rolled for several feet while feeling the stitches in his back popping as the wound ripped open. The Challenger traveled an additional thirty yards and slammed into a tree. Mark stayed prone and buried his face in the dirt, gritting his teeth but not letting out a sound even though every part of his body screamed in pain. Slowly, he lifted his head just enough to watch the muzzle flash from the rifles as they continued to pummel the car. After several minutes, the only remaining sound was hissing from several holes in the blown-out radiator.

Mark waited and listened. He knew the group would assure that whoever had been driving the car had been killed. While waiting, he checked the mobility of each limb, assuring he still had control over his body. When he was certain that everything still worked, he raised his head until his eyes were above the scattered branches and debris on the ground. Suddenly the AR-15s spit additional rounds into the car. The muzzle flashes were several yards away as two men peppered the car. Mark listened to the snapping of scattered branches when they slowly walked towards the Challenger, now, only firing occasionally. He judiciously reached down, withdrew his Glock, and laid it flat next to his shoulder keeping a light grip on the stock while he waited. The shooter closest to the car fired and the bolt of the AR locked back. Quickly, he ejected the magazine, inserted another and continued to fire. Mark knew the shooter's magazine closest to him had to be low. Both men were to his right and slightly in front of him. When the shooters bolt locked back, Mark slowly pushed himself up to one knee and took careful aim at the shooter further away. He covered his torso with the front sight and pressed the trigger.

# 37

Mark sent three rounds into the shooter's body then quickly transitioned to his head and gave him two more. It happened before the second shooter knew why his partner had fallen to the ground. The tree next to Mark exploded. It caused him to flinch as he fired at the second shooter. The shooter fired again and his slide locked back. Mark heard anther round whiz by his head while he watched the shooter eject his magazine. Mark knew, he only had seconds. He hunched over to avoid being shot and rushed him. As he ran towards him, he ejected his magazine and inserted a fresh one, thumbed his slide lock and pointed the Glock to the left at his enemy.

Jon Miller smiled as his men fired on the car, he was happy to have the agent out of the picture, the rest would be easy. A home invasion on an unsuspecting family would be a cake walk. Unexpectedly one of the men seemed to stumble and then fall. Simultaneously, he heard gunfire from his right. Jon watched as someone shot at the men. *Springfield* flashed in his mind. He raised his gun and fired. The agent rose from the ground and ran towards his remaining man.

Mark twisted his body and fired at his unknown assailant. He continued to charge in the direction of the man with the AR while pressing the trigger of his Glock several more times.

Miller saw the muzzle flash and knew he was being shot at and the sound of the car behind him being struck by rounds verified it. He felt a bullet fly between his arm and body and a third round struck his handgun. The impact jarred the gun from his grip and the bullet fragments cut his hand.

Mark turned back towards the shooter and charged him as hard as his legs would allow. Every pounding step sent lightning bolts of pain throughout his body. He watched the shooter fumble with his magazine and then toss the AR onto the ground and reach for a pistol from inside his waist band. Mark brought up his Glock and fired, but he stepped into an unseen rut that caused him to stumble. The shot went wild and gave the shooter time to withdraw his pistol. Mark let out a blood-curling shriek and was now close enough to see the shooter's eyes, he never had time to take aim. Mark was on him, jamming his body into the fender of the car knocking the gun from his hand. The shooter threw a wild punch but, Mark easily deflected it with the only arm that wasn't hurt. But the block came with a price, the wound in his side felt like someone had jabbed it with a red-hot poker. The adversary pushed back hard getting some space between him and his attacker. Very aware of the other foe, Mark swung his Glock to his rear and fired several more shots towards the dark shadows in the distance. While he was looking in the opposite direction, the shooter punched him hard in the gut causing Mark to let out a loud grunt. He staggered but lunged towards his enemy and grabbed him by the neck with his bear-like hand, gritted his teeth and pulled him to the ground. He tried to knee Mark but it landed in his inner thigh. Mark stuck the Glock in the man's side and pressed the trigger. The shot was muffled and Mark felt the bullet punch into the man's body who let out a load groan and started to violently convulse. Seconds later, Mark felt him exhale his last breath.

Mark rolled off the dead man and into a kneeling position with his gun raised, but it was futile; the two shadows were gone.

During their struggle, Lambert crept behind the men, she tried to achieve a concealed vantage point. She had never shot anyone but the idea excited her. She had carried a small 9mm Beretta which she had shot many times while on the range, but now outside in the low light, she felt the firearm wasn't big enough. But it didn't matter, she would shoot the agent, then walk up, and finish him. She watched Springfield turn back towards the dead men. She stepped from the shadows with an outstretched arm and said, "Don't move."

Mark turned back to check the dead men. When he did, he heard a woman voice and stopped.

"I would shoot you in the back, but I want to see the look on your face when I kill you."

Limping on one leg, Mark slowly turned around and faced his new aggressor as he took a step towards her.

"You hurt the women I sent for you." Lambert hissed. "I told her, I would watch you die. And you can drop that gun of yours."

Mark opened his hand and the Glock fell to the ground. He titled his head and said, "Shannon Lambert, I presume."

"You presumed correctly."

Feigning shifting his weight off his bleeding leg, he took another step towards her and offered a snide remark. "This isn't very Admiral-like of you."

Lambert pulled her gun back slightly while a satisfied smile spread across her face. Then she pressed the trigger.

Mark watched the gun's muzzle slightly dip and returned her smile. Quickly, he moved towards her, watching the gun's muzzle move repeatedly as she backed up with a look of disbelief on her face. However, he reached in, stripped the gun from her hand, drew his hand up and smacked her to the ground. Mark stepped in close to Lambert and showed her the side of the gun, and offered an evil grin. With his thumb, he flipped the safety off, then flipped it on. He repeated the action three more times, shook his head and added. "Leave the killing to the professionals."

Lambert, still spinning from the agent's hard slap, watched him walk away and retrieve his dropped pistol.

But she felt anger more than fear, and knowing he would not kill, embolden her.

The pain, Mark had felt in his body vaporized. He no longer felt the chill in the air when he walked over to Lambert and stared into the face of defiance. He watched as she rubbed her jaw. In an even tone he finally said, "you killed my parents, and you were on your way to kill the rest of my family."

Lambert laughed and said, "and a god damn safety kept me from killing you."

Her flippancy had no effect on Mark, he knew what he was going to do when he left the senators office. Shaking his head, he said. "I don't think you understand." He narrowed his dark eyes and added, "you're not leaving this mountain alive."

Lambert pursed her lips and offered, "you're a government agent, you're not a murderer," she said with a brazen tilt of her head.

Mark stepped in close and stood over Lambert, not thinking or caring about anything except for the one thought that filled his mind, *I'm going to kill you.* Consequences meant nothing. He had a firm grip on the stock of his Glock seventeen, which had hung by his side. While he pressed his index finger onto the slide of his pistol another thought had emerged. *What am I going to do with the body?* However, it was fleeting, he didn't care. He would leave her to rot.

Lambert looked up into the face of Mark Springfield, his eyes were soulless and they said it all, her life was over. In her periphery, she detected movement from his side. Seconds later she was looking down the barrel of the semi-automatic handgun. She tried to stay defiant but the opening in the barrel looked like a cannon and as the horror and reality set in, the past came rushing back, men she had been with flashed by in a blur. As a consequence of her childless womb, there was no laughter echoing from the corners of her mind. In that instant, she tried to make sense of her life. The power she had yielded was only known by a few and had only benefited her and the membership. Her lower lip started to quiver, she felt the corners of her eyes fill with tears. Suddenly, she felt empty. She started to cry out, but then… Blackness.

Mark did not hear the loud crack nor feel the recoil of the Glock. For the first time, he had taken a human life for the simple fact of taking a life. It was an act of revenge. When he laid his finger on the trigger, there was no going back. The woman lying on the ground was pure evil, a psychopath that had caused the death of untold innocent people, but most importantly, she had caused the death of his parents. He had accepted their deaths when he had believed they had been in an accident, an inexplicable twist of fate. However, he could not accept this new reality, the pain he felt inside would never end. Knowing she would never see the inside of a courtroom, he decided, he alone would be her judge, jury and executioner.

Feeling unsteady with the pain slowly returning, Mark sat down and rested. The cuts in his leg and gash on the top of his head throbbed and was now bleeding. The gunshot wounds were too much for his body to endure. Twisting his wrist, he checked his watch. It was a habit he'd gotten into years ago, one he had picked up from a now retired agent. Tracking time and watching its consistent movement kept him grounded during high-stress situations. It had helped him to focus. Closing his eyes, he thought of his sister Mary. He loved her and her family beyond words but, she would never know the truth about their parents or the fate of the person responsible for their deaths.

Before he opened his eyes, Mark used the back of his right hand to wipe the blood and sweat from his brow. When finished, he looked down at the Glock and then over at the woman. Then ejecting the magazine, he performed a quick count of his remaining rounds. *Six,* he said to himself, knowing the two additional magazines he had acquired from the senator had been depleted. He refocused on the red head. He needed to find him and, he needed to kill him.

The solid whack from the tree branch on Mark's right arm dislodged the gun from his unsuspecting grip. The assailant pulled the branch back and then jammed it into Marks side with such force it had knocked him over. The pain from his ripped open wounds caused stars to dance in front of his eyes, the pain so great it almost rendered him unconscious. He blinked trying to clear his vision while searching for his attacker. He tried to stand but lost his balance and tripped over a large rock, ending up flat on his back. His body cried out for relief. Mark patted his pocket and found his knife. He quickly pulled it out and thumbed it open. When the dancing stars faded, it was clear he would not have to look far for the red head. The man was searching for the gun that had been knocked from his hand.

Mark clawed his way to his feet with gritted teeth, his jaws locked from not only pain but anger. He charged the red head and stumbled before his attack, but he was able to stretch out his arm enough to jam the knife's tanto blade deep into the back of his enemy's thigh causing him to cry out. With his other hand, he grabbed the back of the red heads shirt but the man twisted to the right ripping his shirt in Marks vice-like grip. Mark fell to the ground but still held onto the knife while cutting a gash in his opponent's leg. The red head turned far enough away from Mark to shake him loose. Scrambling to his feet, he charged and was met with a fist he was able to deflect with his left arm however, the red head landed a kick to Marks inner right thigh which caused him to twist and fall to the ground. The red head raised his foot high and brought it down hard on Marks shoulder. The wounded agent let out a deep moan but grabbed his attacker's ankle with his left hand

and pulled the foot tight into his body then swung his feet around, trapping both of the red heads knees with his powerful legs. Mark rolled his torso, collapsing the killer's body onto the ground.

Jon Miller could not believe the strength left in the agent. His leg burned, but the blood-soaked shirt of the agent told him that he had been severely injured and wouldn't last long. He was surprised when the agent trapped his legs and brought him to the ground so quickly, but it was of no use; there in front of him, to his left, was the gun that the agent had dropped. Miller easily reached the pistol, but suddenly, he felt a hard tug on his right arm and then blinding pain shot like a lightning bolt throughout his body. His vision flashed from black to white and then.... darkness.

Mark grabbed his assailant's arm and pulled himself up and with all the strength he had left, jammed the blade of his knife deep into the middle of the red heads back, severing his spine, and killing him instantly.

When Mark did not feel any movement from the killer, he let go of his knife, laid back and let out a long groan. The cold, light rain that had started to fall on his face temporarily went unnoticed while taking long, slow, deep breaths through the almost unbearable pain. He lay there for several long minutes letting the rain cool his burning body.

Mark rolled over, pushed himself up to all fours and rested for a few seconds while the rain soaked his back.

Opening his eyes, he could see pink water dripping from his soaked shirt and the reflection of red in the drops that had formed and dripped from the tip of his nose. He brought up one leg, stretched out his upper body so he was on one knee and rested, then pushed himself up and leaned against a nearby tree. He looked around for his gun and was surprised to see it at the tips of the red heads fingers. He stared at it and wondered for a second if it was worth bending over for. He grinned, stooped down, picked it up and slipped it back into its holster. Mark begrudgingly returned to one knee, patted the man's jeans and located a wallet in his left back pocket. He reached over and with some force, pulled his knife from the killers back and wiped both sides of the blade on the dead man's pants. After cutting a large square from his shirt, he folded the blade back into the handle and returned it to his pocket. Using the fabric, he pulled the wallet from the jeans in such a way to avoid getting fingerprints on it. After opening it, he used a corner of the square and thumbed through the cards and pulled out and read his driver's license. Jon Miller, Hesperus, Colorado had been written next to the photo of the all too familiar face. Mark studied the license, then returned it to the wallet and tossed it on the ground. He stood, looked through the trees and out into the distance, wondering how long it would take for the black bears or the vultures to find the bodies.

Limping away from the corpses, he pressed his left arm to his side, trying to stop the bleeding from the wound that had had the stitches ripped from it. He knew that if he wasn't careful, he would end up as bear food, too. Finding a grove of trees that provided some cover from the light rain, he sat down and rested. He tilted his head back and stuck out his tongue, trying to catch any water that had made it through the trees' branches. Mark looked in the direction of their car. *The sun would be up soon*, he thought, and their car would attract attention, however the Dodge and carnage might go unnoticed long enough for the bodies to be carried away by mother nature.

Mark pushed himself up and took one last look around. Seeing that the hood of the Dodge had sprung open from the impact with the trees, he walked over and closed it with his elbow making it less noticeable from the main road. Then, he retrieved the fabric he had stuffed in his pocket, reached inside the car and wiped down everything he thought he had touched. Satisfied that he had cleaned it thoroughly, he turned, and walked past Lambert without giving her another look.

The car felt like it was ten miles away and when he was revisited by the dancing stars he stopped and took long deep breaths.

Sitting in the car Mark knew he was in bad shape, he couldn't remember a time in his career when he fought so hard to keep his head from spinning. He looked over towards the carnage and although he struggled with his vision, he could not see the Dodge.

A quick U-turn and he was headed back down the mountain and fighting to keep the car in his lane. He had to put distance between him and his aggressors. They could not be discovered. The glare from the rising sun, dusty windshield and his spinning head made it even harder for him to drive and when he could not feel his wounds anymore, he knew he should pull over, but he pressed on and when he saw a sign for interstate 40, he felt relieved. Five minutes later, Mark Springfield slumped over the wheel and the white Ford Escape ran off the road and over an embankment.

Mark drifted in and out consciousness. The muffled voices, flashing lights and the sound of a helicopters spinning rotor was like a dream. He heard himself mumble while slipping into a murky blackness. Occasionally, he was visited by apparitions.

# 38

Two days later, Marks eyes fluttered open to an empty hospital room. He looked around blurry eyed, trying to regain his senses. A television hung on the wall in front of him. To his right in the corner of the room, was an open door leading into a bathroom and on the same wall was the door leading out of the room. A plastic cup of water sat next to him on a silver table. A small couch was positioned under a large window to his left. In the left corner of the room a chair stood next to a low table that had items scattered around the top. With his vision still blurry he could not make out what had been strewn on the table and chair. A small beige controller connected to a cord which had stretched to the floor, had been laid over his extended bed rail, *Nurses Station* had been printed on an adhesive sticker.

After looking around the room, he finally reached for the water and downed the entire contents. Several minutes later, when he remembered who he was and why his body was so sore, he reached for the control and pressed the red button.

Mark laid back, closed his eyes and waited for a nurse. In those few minutes before the door swung open, he started to remember the details of the past few days. Suddenly he heard and felt the door bash into its rubber stop.

"Uncle Mark, Uncle Mark!" His niece Ashley bolted into the room and directly to the side of his bed.

Seconds later, Mary trailed in behind her daughter. While shaking her head at her battered brother she said. "Don't jump on your uncle! Heaven forbid she not want to jump on you." Mary walked over to the decanter on the counter and refilled her brother's cup. "And you." She said sounding concerned. "Gave us a scare." She finished filling the cup and returned the decanter to the counter. "You're gone for three days then we get a call saying that you're in route to the hospital, in a helicopter needless to say." Mary leaned in, kissed Mark on the cheek and added with a chuckle "And sleeping for two days? So unlike you."

The nurse entered the room and walked over to Mark and checked his vitals. She recorded the information displayed on some of the equipment onto a chart and asked, "How are you feeling?" She continued after watching Mark nod his head, "you know, your sister has been here every day with those very cute girls of hers." She said waving to Ashley. With a smile she added, "The doctor will be in shortly."

Mary stopped the nurse before she left the room. "Thank you, Bethany, for checking on our guy." Mary turned towards Mark and mouthed *she's been great!* Then she followed her out of the room.

Mark looked around and licked his lips. With his mouth as dry as the Sahara Desert he reached over, grabbed his water cup and once again downed the entire contents then looked up, shook the cup at Mary when she returned, and set it back down. Then looking over and smiling at Ashley, he said, "tell your mom I'd like to have some more water."

"Yeah, yeah, yeah, I got it." Mary huffed jokingly.

Mark rubbed Ashley's head and in a raspy voice whispered, "I need to talk to your mom. Will you give us a minute?"

She slapped the top of her uncle's hand, turned and bounced over to the table were her toys had been laid.

Once she was involved with her things, Mark asked "So, Cole and Christina are here somewhere?"

Nodding her head, she replied. "Out getting some lunch."

"Want to fill me in on how I got here?" He remembered Lambert and her men but was foggy on how he ended up in the hospital.

"Well, I received a call from the police. They very nicely explained that my brother had been involved in an automobile accident and was in route to the hospital by way of an air ambulance. I know, it freaked me out. You were driving a white Ford Escape and crashed. The car rolled down the side of a steep precipice, hitting several trees before it crashed into a boulder field where it finally came to rest, thank God."

"Thank God?" He questioned. "It sounds like I took quite the tumble."

"Oh, you did, but according to the police, if you would have been two hundred feet further on the curve, they may have never found you."

Mark gave his sister a questioning look. "By the way, where am I?"

"Charlotte, North Carolina." Mary answered with a warm smile.

"There was another thing." Mary offered hesitantly.

"Go on."

"When I was on the phone with the police, he asked if you had recently been involved in another...event, as he called it. He told me that you had some recent repairs done to your shoulder and side." Mary questionably looked her brother over, started to say something but stopped herself.

"It's unlike you not to speak your mind." Mark offered. "What else is there?"

Mary glanced over at her daughter and seeing she was still preoccupied with her toys moved in close and whispered. "Said that it looked like you had been shot about three times." Mary moved back while dabbing the corners of her eyes with the palm of her hands.

Mark returned a soft stare, smiled and held up two fingers. "No, it was only two." He assured her.

It had taken her a few minutes to regain her composure. Reaching across the bed, she grabbed the cup of water and drank it. "That's not funny!" She chastised.

Mark reached up and took Mary's hand. "Hazards of the job," he smiled. "What did you tell him?"

"I told him I didn't know much about your job." Mary started to tear up again but quickly composed herself when she had heard her daughter, Christina talking in the hall. Through a few sniffles she added, "Mike was here yesterday. He had asked me to call him when you finished resting." She watched her brother smile and shake his head, then blurted, "I love you, you know."

"I know," he grinned. A little more seriously he added, "Mary, what happened over the last few days, we can't talk about."

Mary shook her head, turned towards Cole and Christina who had just walked into the room and said. "Ok, let's give your uncle some privacy, gather-up your things."

Cole moved close to Mark and inquired, "need anything?"

With a slight smile Mark answered, "I'm fine." Mark turned and observed his nieces gather their toys and slip them onto their pink and purple back packs. He also looked around the room wondering where his clothes might be stashed.

Fifteen minutes after his family left, the doctor walked in and talked to him about his injuries and the time required for them to heal completely and, if they were somehow torn open again, short of a skin graft, they would be unrepairable. Mark nodded his understanding and when the doctor told him they were holding him for an additional two days due the condition of his body, he again nodded, thanked him and asked. "Hey doc will you lower this rail so I can use the bathroom? We can have the nurse pull it up at bed time."

"Oh sure," he said while unlocking and lowering the rail. "Be careful getting out of the bed."

Mark slowly swung his feet over the side of the bed and stood up. After checking his balance, he pushed the stand that had held two bags, both with tubes running into his arm, across the room and into the bathroom. Once finished, he returned to his bed and continued his conversation with the doctor.

One hour later, a nurse appeared and took his vitals. As soon as she had walked out of the room, Mark threw his feet over the edge of the bed and sat up. He looked at the two needles that had been taped to his right arm. Both ran into clear bags that were hanging from the rack standing next to the bed. He was instantly brought back to the last time he had been in a hospital. It was while he was on assignment in Germany, but instead of a pleasant conversation with family and staff, he was getting shot at and the IV that had been taped to his arm had been ripped out. Without further thought, he pulled the adhesive strips that had been securing the hypodermic hub to his arm and the back of his hand, then he withdrew the needles from his veins and let them drop onto the bed. Mark pushed himself up and stood, walked over to the counter and checked the drawers. He stopped when he found what he had been looking for, band aids. After he applied one to the crook of his elbow, he slapped one on the back of his hand. Mark went through the closet and quickly found a brown bag containing his clothes. He shook out his pants, shirt, socks and underwear thinking that everything looked as if they had been jammed into the bag when they brought him in. Minutes later, Mark was tucking in his torn shirt when he heard. "And where do you think you are going?"

Mark turned to the familiar voice and answered. "With you."

Mike Hollister had been leaning against the door frame but then stepped into the room. "You know the funny thing is, I called the hospital and they told me you were to be discharged in two days. And it didn't take two days to drive down here from Virginia." Mike kidded.

"If they think I'm staying here another minute, they have another thing coming. Let's go."

Both men turned and walked out of the room and past the nurse's station. Mark stuck his hand in his pocket and his fingers brushed against a hard slip of paper. He removed a business card and in the right-hand corner was a sunglass wearing, pink flamingo dressed in a yellow Hawaiian shirt. Underneath, in an arch, was typed Endangered Species. To the left side of the card was written, Jacklyn Phelan. Underneath her name written in silver was the word, pilot. Mark smiled when he read it. When the doors of the elevator closed, Mike broke his concentration. "So, Mary tells me you may have been shot a few times."

Mark gave his friend a sideways look and smiled. "You know little sisters; they tend to blow everything out of proportion."

Mike returned a knowing grin and when the elevator doors opened, the men walked across the lobby and out into the cold night air where Mike continued his query. "Is there anything you can tell me?"

Shaking his head Mark answered, "no, my friend, it was just another trip to the Smokies and an unfortunate car crash." Mark looked at his liberator and quietly added, "forget everything else."

Mike started the car and slowly drove through the near empty parking lot.

"Are we headed home?"

"Not a chance." Mike answered, "I'll come rescue you from the hospital but you're not driving any distance tonight. I have a hotel not far from here."

"But...!"

"But nothing." Mike retorted. "I know you're pretty banged-up and another night's sleep before a long drive won't hurt ya."

Shaking his head Mark said, "by the way, thanks for coming to get me. Hospitals are not my thing."

Mike returned a concerned grin and continued their drive in silence and then offered. "You know one day this may all come back to haunt us."

"It was just a trip to the smokies with an unfortunate car accident," Mark repeated, then added, "and, I hear I'm lucky to be alive." Turning somber and lowering his voice he stated. "Michael, the less you know on this one, the better."

"I just don't like being out of the loop and not very helpful." After a few reflective minutes, he continued. "Mark, we have been friends along time. If there's someone I feel I can trust, it's you. I hope after all this time, you feel the same."

Mark gave his friend a slight grin and replied. "You're not getting soft on me, are ya?" Then after a short chuckle quietly added. "You were helpful beyond words."

"If you say so." Mike paused for a minute and looking over at Marks hands asked. "Now tell me, whose card do you keep flicking between your fingers?"

Mark looked down at the business card and laughed quietly. After rubbing his finger over Jacklyn's name, he asked. "Can I borrow your phone?"

# 39

Mike Hollister, Mark Springfield, and Erasmo Jones walked into Marks office. Raz stepped over to a window that overlooked the courtyard. A small gathering in the corner of the quad had attracted his attention. Raz tilted his head toward the event and asked. "A lunch-in?"

"Probably," Mike answered while joining Raz at the window. "Departments occasionally use the quad to have little gatherings for some reason or another."

"Water?" Mark asked. He watched both men nod their heads then he opened his small refrigerator, retrieved three bottles of water and handed one to Mike and one to Raz, he then pointed to the two additional chairs sitting on the other side of his desk. The men drank from the plastic bottles and then slowly walked over to the chairs.

Raz smiled a question. "Aren't you supposed to be in the hospital?"

"I left." Mark said with a wave of his hand. "Believe me, two days were enough."

Mike munched his eyebrows and offered Mark a heartfelt smile. "You looked like shit when I picked you up. We all thought your office was going to be vacant for at least two weeks and what has it been, hmm, two days?"

"They just needed to redo some of those stitches the senator's medic put in me." Mark said dismissively. "Director House put me on bed rest for ten days, so I was thinking about using that time back up at my lodge. And besides, I knew the senator here was meeting with him today." Mark chuckled and added, "I wasn't missing a meeting with the Director."

"I do have a question," Raz added and then whimsically asked while looking at Mark "Why did you get into my helicopter? You had just been shot, on the run and here's this helicopter out of the blue sporting, of all things, a pink flamingo. What was it about Ziggy that convinced you?"

"Medics, helicopters, and pink flamingos. You might be right, I may not want to know." Mike stated while looking at Mark.

A smile grew quickly on Marks face as he shook his head, then addressing Raz he explained. "Your team seemed trustworthy." Then pointing at his fellow agent quipped, "but it was Mike here, I trust him and he had already told me that he trusted you because of his damn water bottle test. So, when your crewman Ziggy mentioned your name, I figured, what the hell." He watched Mike display a broad smile, chuckle and take the last few steps to his chair. Once he had sat down, he said, "Michael, care to enlighten the senator."

Mike looked at Raz and said, "When you came into my office, you seemed sincere but no one gets out without the test."

Mark laughed and said, "you got lucky."

"Wait, I don't get it!" Raz interjected. "What the hell is the water bottle test?"

"It's better than a lie detector," Mike kidded.

With a smirk, Mark pointed his bottle at Mike and explained, "Mike here opens a bottle of water and sets it in front of whoever during a tense conversation and if that person drinks it right away, he's not sincere. However, if they continue their exchange and stay focused and ignore the water, then…"

"Their hearts are in the right place." Mike concluded.

Raz sat down hard in the chair and exclaimed. "You trusted me and bet your friends life based on when I drank from a bottle of water!?"

Holding up his bottle of water Mike kidded. "It works every time!"

Raz shook his head and gave a smiling Mike a questioning look. "But you told me where he was and who he was with!"

"True, but it wasn't until after you drank from the bottle that I told you exactly where and gave you Cameron's phone number."

Raz shook his head while a smile grew on his face. He looked at Mark who returned a shrug and said, "I guess it works!"

Raz took another drink from his bottle of water, set it on the desk and asked. "The woman from the hotel, what do we know about her?"

Mike, keeping in mind their, Oscar Echo Oscar, shot Mark a questionable look. After Mark returned an approving nod, Mike offered what he knew to the senator. "We don't know anything. Even with the name Mark had overheard, I can't find anything on her and I have checked multiple security tapes and pulled NSAs overhead videos, nothing." After a slight pause he added, "it's like she doesn't exists, she's a ghost."

"Hmmm… trust me when I tell you she's real." Mark offered while making slow circles with his right arm. "And not only that, I'll never be able to smell a honeysuckle without thinking about her."

Both men gave Mark a curious look. "Honeysuckles?" They probed.

"It was her fragrance. Actually, when I first met her at the airport, I was very taken with her, there was something about her, and the honeysuckles, I kind of liked it." Rubbing his side, he quipped, "now…not so much." Then he frowned at their sympathetic smiles. Suddenly his desk phone rang and on the second ring, he picked it up. "Springfield. Yes, he is," looking over at Mike he continued. "I'll tell him." Mark hung up the phone and said. "Your boss is looking for you."

Mike nodded his head, stood, turned towards the senator and offered him his hand. "Senator, it's been fun."

Raz stood, returned Mikes smile, took his hand in a firm grip and gave it a shake. Then he started to laugh. "Water bottle test…Jesus."

As Mike walked past Mark the two agents gave each other a half wave. "Oh, by the way." Mike said quietly pointing towards Bob Ash's office, "Our friend has an interesting picture of you wearing a very tight bathing suit."

Mark flashed a questionable look.

"Something about you swimming in Bahrain last year." Mike said with a smile. "We'll touch base later," he added while walking towards the door.

"Sounds good." Mark replied shaking his head.

Raz sat back down and pulled his left leg over his right thigh and waited for Mike to close the office door and continued. "And we can only assume that the person that had followed Ziggy and Teddy to San Jose was one of the men that had attacked you."

"Yes," Mark stated, nodding his head. "You briefed that to the director but, you never said what had happened to him." Mark gave Raz a questioning look.

Erasmo reached over and took another long drink of his water. When he was finished, he slyly looked at the agent. "How's your sister Mary? I assume you will never tell her."

Mark nodded and presented a knowing grin. Finally, Mark answered, "She's fine and no, she'll be none the wiser. She only knows what she had found out because of the accident."

"Yes, as I hoped it would be." Raz said quietly and then added. "And your Highway Patrolman's friend, I hear she is doing well."

Mark chuckled, "I give them a year and they'll be married. But yeah, she'll be fine. I'm flying out next week to pay them a visit." After some reflection he said, "They're good kids. It breaks my heart what happened to her."

"That's the thing about revenge, it doesn't change the past but, it certainly changes the future."

The comment from Raz struck Mark as odd.

After several long minutes Raz gave Mark a half grin and quietly offered. "They say that during the Vietnam conflict when someone infiltrated a camp and was captured, they were questioned, it's also rumored that if that enemy combatant decided not to cooperate, he *or* she would be taken by helicopter out over the South China Sea and questioned again. I can only imagine what happened to the people that decided not to talk."

Mark nodded his head and looked over at the American flag that had hung on his wall. He reflected on the longest three days of his life and he was in no position to question the actions of Ziggy and Teddy. However, he understood their motivation. Looking back at Raz he asked. "What now, Senator?"

Raz stood, walked over to the window and said, "For starters, we keep what really happened on the mountains to ourselves." He slowly turned and looked knowingly at Mark.

And now Mark made sense of his revenge comment. Narrowing his eyes, he asked. "And what do you know about the mountains?"

"My pilots delivered a few folks to the Asheville airport several nights ago. Three men and a woman. The woman being retired Admiral Shannon Lambert."

"Your pilots being Jacklyn and Diane?" After he watched Raz nod his head he added, "I had dinner with Jacklyn last night, she didn't mention it."

"I would have been surprised if she had." Raz smiled and added. "More interesting was that the pilots flew my wife's jet back to Charlotte without any passengers."

Mark did not answer Raz's underlying question. The two stared at each other, waiting for the other to speak. Breaking the silence Mark offered, "I'm sure they will show up sooner or later. It is probably just an innocent camping trip."

Raz looked at Mark and shook his head. "I know Lambert. If they find her in the woods, it won't be in a tent."

"Sorry, Senator." Mark said with a shrug, "I have never had the privilege of meeting her." Mark studied the senator wondering what was really going through his mind and whose side he was really on.

Raz returned Marks stare and said. "Well, I should be going and let you get some rest. I still can't believe you're at work today."

Mark smile and inquired, "Before you go, I've been curious about this ever since you shared your parents' story but, how did they meet? How does a navy man end up with a Rothschild?"

Raz returned a big smile. He didn't share the story often but when he did, he enjoyed the retelling. "A little back story first." Raz said settling back into his chair. "Something that really wasn't relevant before. My dad flew airplanes as a hobby, an expensive hobby for a young sailor. To supplement his pay, he had a part-time job and almost never frequented the navy clubs. There was a dance to support the troops and my mom, unlike some of her kin, was very civic minded and wanted to help, actually help and not just donate money."

"I like her already." Mark smiled.

"But can you imagine a Rothschild, the publicity the—"

Mark laughed and added "The attention she apparently didn't appreciate."

"Yes, exactly! So, she went as Liz Emelen and no one was the wiser. At the urging of my dad's cousin, Bobby, he ended up at the club the same night as Liz. The story goes, he was minutes from driving off the base convinced he wasn't going to the club after a long day at work, but at the very last second he made a left, and drove into his future."

"He went in for a beer and left with a wife." Mark kidded.

Raz laughed and continued. "She never expected to meet someone she would eventually marry however, her friends suggested she not reveal her true identity. Later she would say how she regretted not telling him. It was a true love story from the very beginning and lasted until her death." The story seemed to choke Raz up and he stopped to regain his composure then blurted. "Okay, I'm going to get out of your hair." Raz said while standing holding out his hand. He took Marks hand in a firm grip and with a grin added. "I'll talk to my wife. Perhaps she can give Jacklyn a few extra days off."

"That would be nice." Mark nodded with a smile.

Both men walked over to the office door and Mark said, "Senator, it's been fun, and I never thanked you for my rescue." Mark led him through the doorway and they both walked down the hallway.

Raz turned towards the agent and said. "Mark, please, call me Raz." He lowered his voice and added. "And the rescue, those guys live for that kind of action." Both men smiled and continued down the hall in silence, crossed the foyer and out of the front door. "Perhaps I can have you back out to the house soon. Maybe dinner and a cigar."

"Sounds good." They continued to walk towards the fence line and said their goodbyes before Raz exited through the security check point.

# 40

Three hours later, Mark closed, locked his office door and left to start his recovery. Driving home, he thought of his cabin and what he could do with his newfound time off. He flipped up his wrist and checked the time, 2 p. m. He started thinking this recovery could take some time because he was already tired.

Mark grabbed the mail that had collected in the box and picked up a few packages from the corner of his patio. He took everything inside and set it on the edge of his couch. In the kitchen he grabbed his kettle from the stove, filled it with water and returned it to the grate. Two clicks later, the stove's igniter had started a fire that would heat the water for his tea. He walked back into his living room and slowly eased into a worn, dark brown leather recliner. The ten-year-old chair fit his thick frame perfectly. Activating the foot rest allowed him to lie back, relax and close his eyes. The house was quiet and the thought of Lambert looking up at him with hopelessness on her face crept into his mind. However, he felt nothing for the woman. Suddenly an old saying rushed into his mind. He leaned forward, pulled his wallet from his back pocket and retrieved a small laminated card he had carried with him for years. It had been given to him by his mentor and it had a simple phrase. *If all you feel is recoil take your finger off the trigger.* It was a reminder. Shooting someone, taking a human life, is an emotional act. When it stops bothering you, it's time to stop. He read the card again and wondered, *is it time to stop?* Returning the card to its sleeve, he tossed the wallet onto an end table and laid back in his chair. While he rested his tired and aching body, his mind continued to work. *Who did Lambert work for? And if the senator was really a good guy, how did Lambert end up in his jet, how does Jacklyn and Diane figure into all of it, and the Vietnam veterans, Ziggy and Teddy.* An inward smile grew at the thought of the two. Suddenly Mark heard a loud blaring whistle from the kitchen and it pulled him back from the edges of sleep.

As he stood in front of counter next to the stove, Jacklyn entered his thoughts and he smiled when he brought the cup of tea up to his lips. Mark turned with his tea, walked back into the living room, pulled a coaster from the stack of his handgun themed mats and placed it down on the coffee table. He picked up the mountain of mail and went through it, flipping envelops on the table in two different piles. Seeing the pink flamingo on a large vanilla envelope he set it aside. The third envelope he flipped to had brought a smile to his face. He had received a letter without a return address, but he could tell from the handwriting that it had been from his young friend, Alexei Azarov, now fourteen years old and residing in the state of Washington. However, he no longer went by his given name. Without opening the envelope, Mark knew the letter would be signed by Benjamin. Mark had helped the young family escape Russia when Alexi was only seven years old and he had secretly maintained a relationship with the young man. The two had created a bond during their escape and Mark knew that Alexei would need an American uncle. He felt for the young family who had been pulled from their way of life because of their father, Karl, a junior lieutenant in the Russian navy who happened to possess information that cost one agent his life. As a reward for turning over the information, Karl, his wife Dina and their two sons were given both a new life and identities in the United States. The government had relocated them to Washington State, the Puget Sound, and employed Karl with the Washington State ferry system. They were given a healthy compensation paid in yearly increments. The payments would continue as long as secrecy was maintained and until the last family member was deceased.

Mark quickly sliced open the envelope and pulled from it the neatly creased paper. After he had unfolded it, he read the first two words and his smile grew even wider, 'Uncle Mark.' He went on to peruse the letter, learning what the family had been up to during the last five months. Mark concluded that over the years, they had come to enjoy their lives and even his mother, Dina had adapted to their new location. Mark set the letter down in his lap and reflected on the night the five of them swam out into the freezing waters of the Kola Bay with first Alexi and then his brother Alexander wrapped tightly around his neck, the memory had caused him a sudden chill and then a smile. Mark refolded the letter and returned it to its envelope. He would send his own letter but would wait for a month to pass. When he had finished with the mail, he opened the large vanilla envelope and shook his head when he removed the contents, a pink flamingo adored Hawaiian shirt was accompanied by a handwritten note. *Mr. Springfield, thank you for the pleasant dinner conversation. Please take our flamingo shirt as a gift. I hope the size is more appropriate. Maggie.* Mark laughed to himself while he held up the shirt, double X L had been stamped on the tag. *It'll fit,* he thought. *but will I wear it?* After draping it over a chair, he picked up the boxes and sat back in his leather chair. A smile crossed his lips as he opened the first box. He had ordered Mary an ornament, a Red Ryder bb gun, he could hear the all too familiar line, *you'll shoot your eye out,* from the popular movie. The small rifle had a working cocking lever and a piece of leather had hung from the saddle ring. It would look great hanging from her Christmas tree. He carefully returned it to its small, yellow and red Daisy box and carefully set it aside. The next package was for one of his nieces. He picked up the package and set it on his lap, being careful while opening the box. However, when he cut the tape and unwrapped the thin corrugated cardboard, he stared in disbelief. Inside laid his very recognizable Glock 23, a thin leather strap had been looped through and tied to the trigger guard and a green rubber ban secured a folded piece of paper to the stock. He slid the paper from the stock, unfolded it and quickly read the one-line handwritten note. *It's not much of a souvenir if you're still alive. I have included a gift. Until next time, T.*

He pushed his foot rest down, stood, walked directly over to his gun safe and opened it. Mark reached inside and withdrew another Glock 23, a quick check of the round in the chamber assured this one was loaded and operational. Next, he methodically moved through his house looking for any unwanted visitors. He walked over to the window and looked around his street then went outside and repeated his actions, studying the sporadic cars parked along his curb. The neighborhood was quiet and nothing seemed out of place. Once back inside his home, he checked his alarm panel to verify that there had not been any entries while he had been away. Finding none, he returned to his living room and looked over the box. Now he had had a conundrum, he could not have the box, firearm, leather strap or note processed. No one knew anything had happened, the details of his longest three days were only known to him. He couldn't think of a way to explain it all away without possibly implementing himself in Lamberts disappearance. He untied the leather strap and held it up. The faint smell of honeysuckles had still lingered and it brought him back to the airport and when he had first noticed it wrapped around the woman's ankle. Mark pursed his lips while thinking about her. Nothing about the woman excited him. There would be no pause, no hesitation, no remorse, he will kill her the very next time they meet.

Mark set his gun down and picked up his retuned Glock and looked it over. He noticed that the loaded chamber indicator was erect as soon as he had unwrapped the firearm and moving the slide back enough to view the brass in the chamber confirmed the gun was indeed loaded. While shaking his head, he ejected the magazine, eased the slide back and removed the round from the chamber. Then he retrieved a pencil from a repurposed, Carolina Blond beer can and dropped it into the barrel, eraser end down, and pointed the gun towards the ceiling and pressed the trigger. To his surprise, the pencil shot out high enough to clear the end of the barrel, he snatched it before it had started to fall. It was clear, the woman had returned the firearm exactly how she had taken it. Thinking about her made his gunshot wounds throb. Mark walked over to his desk and set the gun down and that's when he noticed his blinking answering machine. The device indicated that the single message had been recorded two days ago at seven ten p. m. He pressed play and was greeted with a familiar voice. "Mark, hi, it's Dan Rowe, hey I forgot to mention, probably an age thing," Dan said laughing. "After our conversation, I started thinking about that tragic day and it reminded me of something. Please give me a call, I would be happy to share it with you." Mark stared at the machine wondering if he was up for a sentimental journey. Deciding he was not, he walked back into the room, loaded his firearm and eased himself back into his chair. Setting his Glock in his lap, he pulled his phone out of his pocket and flipped it over in his hand. A slight smile grew on his face as he pondered calling Jacklyn. Suddenly his house phone rang and he pursed his lips when Dan Rowe's name was displayed on the handset sitting on the stand next to his chair. He decided not to take the call but, after the third ring he thought *Uh what the hell*. "Good afternoon, Mr. Rowe."

"Mark, I'm happy I caught you, do you have a minute?" Dan was jovial, too jovial for Mark.

"I sure do, what can I help you with?"

"I left you a message a couple of days ago, I just wanted to make sure you received it."

"Sure did. I have been on a business trip and returned home about an hour ago. I had listened to your message not five minutes ago."

"Great! Well like I said in the message, after we spoke, I started thinking about that tragic day when I remembered getting a call from one of our clients out in California that Monday. I only bring it up to let you know how well liked your dad was all across the country. I remember standing there looking down at a flat tire when I got a call from our clients from Energy out in Fresno. They were desperate to get your dad out there."

Mark leaned forward in his chair, pressed the phone close to his ear and asked. "Monday being February third?"

"Yes, but he never made the trip."

"Never made the trip?" Mark asked scrupulously.

"Well, the accident happened here on the fourth so he had to be in town."

Trying not to sound concerned, Mark asked. "Was it normal for you two not to touch base for a couple of days?"

"It was. If there wasn't a problem, we would simply meet-up for lunch when the jobs were finished and let each other know how it went. And besides, our secretary received notice from the airline that the ticket had never been used. I honestly never gave it another thought because it had only been a one-day difference and you know how plans change."

Mark knew his dad had made the trip out west. In an even tone, he asked. "I sure would like to talk to the person that requested my dad. Do you remember who you spoke with?"

Dan was ready for the question and quickly shot, "Lawrence Williams, Soledad Energy. They have been with us for quite a few years."

"Thank you, Mr. Rowe. I may be giving him a call."

"Great! Make sure you tell him I send my regards. It's been years."

Mark hung up the phone wondering how to get to California undetected. His next call was to the senator.

# 41

"We can have you in Fresno early tomorrow." It had taken Raz a few phone calls but he was able to grant the agents request. "Does this have anything to do with the Smokies?" He prodded.

Mark felt exposed. The senator knew too much about what had happened in the mountains. "Completely unrelated," he countered. "I have personal business I'd rather the agency not know I was on."

There was a long pause before Raz spoke. "You know, Mark, this could work for us, and as you know, our pilots can be very discreet."

Mark stared at the floor for a few seconds before he answered. "I'm sorry, senator, if using your wife's jet sends the wrong signal, I'd be happy to reimburse you for the service."

"No, no, that won't be necessary." Raz laughed. "Use it when you need it." Then slyly added. "If you need directions and a time to meet the jet in Dulles, I'm sure Jacklyn will be happy to take a call from you."

"Thank you." Mark pressed end and then looked at his phone while flipping it over in his hand, a habit he had recently developed. Then muttered, "and who are you Lawrence Williams and how do you fit into all of this? Rest assured, I will find out."

Jacklyn looked over her right shoulder and glanced at her new friend. He was different when they had picked him up in Dulles. Quiet, reserved, lost in his own thoughts were just some ways to describe how he acted when he boarded the jet. It was almost as if he couldn't be bothered with any sort of conversation. *No*, she thought, it was not just conversation; he didn't want any sort of interaction. Whatever was on his mind weighed heavily. Mark Springfield was not the same person as the one who had sat in her jet a few short days ago. She noticed a difference in him at dinner but now whatever *it* was, stood more pronounced and stood directly between the two of them.

Mark stared out of the starboard window watching the country slip by. He decided not to involve Mike. He had helped enough and the last thing he wanted to do was to drag him further into… *Further into what*, he thought. *What else am I getting into? I'm bordering on a textbook rouge agent. If anyone else acted like this, I'd run them in. Jesus.* His mind slipped back to that old laminated paper he had carried in his wallet for years. And he knew, he knew it was time to stop, but not yet.

Jacklyn went unnoticed when she slipped into a chair across the aisle from where Mark was sitting. She stared at him for several long seconds and then stated. "You seem lost in your thoughts."

Mark looked over and returned a half smile while holding her gaze. Jacklyn was a beautiful woman, smart, funny and pleasant to be around. However, Mark was guarded, he had not dated often and when he had become serious with someone, he had to kill her. She had been a fellow agent who had gone rouge, but the vision of a past love lying on the ground with her eyes open in a death stare would haunt him forever.

"A penny for your thoughts." Jacklyn tried again.

He continued to stare. Finally, he had heard himself say in a cold and even tone. "Ms. Phelan, how long until we arrive in Fresno?"

Jacklyn's smile vanished. She wasn't shocked at Marks question but how he had asked it. *Ms. Phelan,* she thought, *you have got to be kidding me?* After several long seconds of cold silence, she replied, "two hours." And then added, "are you sure this is how you want to play this?"

Mark nodded his head and looked away from her, forcing himself to look out of the window.

Jacklyn quietly stood, walked back to the cockpit and closed the door. After she slid back into her seat, she wrapped the headset over her head and a few seconds later, she heard. "Are you okay?" In the low light of the cockpit, Diane could see the hurt in her friends' eyes.

Jacklyn looked over at Diane who offered several tissues. She smiled and said. "I'm fine." Shaking her head, she continued. "I don't know what it is, something is going on with him and he's keeping me at arm's length. I wish I could help."

"Sounds like you may be partial to our G man."

"And that's why it hurts." Jacklyn softly uttered.

"Mr. Springfield, Fresno in thirty minutes, seatbelt." The intercom did nothing to hide the hurt that Mark detected in Jacklyn's voice. He dug out the belt from the corners of the chair and snapped it around his waist. He pushed Jacklyn from his mind and focused on Lawrence Williams.

Mark waited until the ladies opened the door and signaled for him to deplane. Both of them stood on either side of the ladder as he trotted down to the tarmac. Once he had stepped from the bottom of the ladder, he turned to both Jacklyn and Diane, thanked them, turned and walked away. From behind, he heard Jacklyn's soft voice. "Good luck Mark," but it did little to stop him, he continued on his way.

Years ago, when Mark had started with the CIA, it was a fantasy to think that you would be able to carry around, let alone fit in a pocket, your very own personal computer. Even though the Central Intelligence Agency vetted new technology long before the civilian population, Mark had been impressed with the tool. Ten minutes after stepping off the Gulfstream his smartphone listed three locations for Soledad Energy in Fresno. When he placed a call to what was listed as their corporate Fresno headquarters, Mark was greeted by a young female voice.

"Soledad Energy."

"Good morning!" Mark replied jovially. "My name is, Malcom Hooper. I represent Specter Accounting. May I please speak to Mr. Lawrence Williams?"

There was a long pause followed by "Mr. Hooper, I'll need to connect you to his department."

"Thank you!" That was all he needed. Mark ended the call as soon as he had been put on hold. Twenty minutes after hailing a cab from the curb side of the Yosemite International Airport, he stood in front of the Soledad Energy, Fresno headquarters holding the briefcase he had carried from home. Inside the case was an extra change of clothes, six loaded magazines, a box of hollow points and four thousand dollars he had removed from his safe to assure he stayed off the grid.

Mark walked through the main lobby entrance and stopped at the reception desk that was located almost in the center of the room. Sitting in a high back, tan leather swivel chair was a woman who appeared to be in her mid-thirties dressed in a pants suit. Her brown eyes matched her long hair that laid neatly over her shoulders and flowed down her back stopping just above her waist. "Good morning," Mark said while placing his briefcase on the counter. "I'm Malcom Hooper with Specter Accounting, I would like to talk to Mr. Lawrence Williams." As soon as the woman spoke, Mark had recognized her as the one that had answered his earlier call.

"Yes, yes! I think we were disconnected."

With a laugh Mark offered "That's what I thought so I figured I would drop by in person since I was in the area. Would it be possible to talk to Mr. Williams?" he continued pleasantly.

"Please have a seat, I'll have his supervisor meet you."

He turned from the desk but from his periphery, he watched the woman pick up the phone, and speak softly into it. "Is there a problem?" He inquired after she had hung up.

"Mr. Hooper, I really should let his boss talk to you." She said mysteriously.

"Sounds intriguing," he blurted while walking back to her desk. "And Jean, it's Malcom," he offered after glancing down at her name plate.

"Well, and I shouldn't be telling you this, but Lawrence has disappeared."

"No!"

"Yes, and they even called the cops!"

"The cops! Oh my, that is serious. When did this all happen?"

"Five, six days ago. It's all everyone is talking about."

Mark returned a shocked look, however, inwardly, he put Williams' disappearance at about the same time he had met Cameron to explore Mono Lake.

"Jean, do they have…"

"Hi, sorry for the wait, I'm Ken, Lawrence's supervisor." A well-dressed man stated from across the foyer while walking towards the receptionist desk.

Mark turned toward him and offered an outreached arm and a toothy smile. "I'm Malcom Hooper with Spector Accounting, is it possible to talk to Lawrence?" Mark glanced at Jean and gave her a wink.

"Mr. Hooper, please let's go to my office." He turned Mark and walked him towards the door from which he had entered. Inside the office space were a set of four cubicles. Mark had been led to the largest and pointed to a chair. "May I offer you some coffee, Mr. Hooper?"

Mark waved his hand and said. "Please, it's Malcom and no thank you on the coffee."

"What is this about, Malcom? You said you are from an accounting firm."

"Yes, we represent Rowe Integrated Software. We, well, really me." Mark added sheepishly, "are trying to justify some expenditures from two thousand three."

"Two thousand three! Is this a tax issue?" Ken asked inquisitively.

"No, no." Mark laughed. "We had an internal audit." Mark started while assuring his briefcase was turned away from Ken. Then, he opened it and withdrew a note pad and flipped through it as if he were reviewing written information. "It was only for a ten-year period and of course on the ninth year they found something. And of course," Mark laughed, "it was passed to me to find the answers to a few questions."

"How does Lawrence fit into all of this?"

Mark paged through his blank note pad and stopped on an arbitrary page and said. "He set up a meeting with Mr. Jack Springfield. Rowe Integrated bought a first-class ticket for one thousand twelve hundred dollars. Now, one of the ledgers shows it had actually been paid out and one shows it had been cancelled." Mark closed his note pad, sat back, smiled and said, "And that's why I'm here. They either flew Mr. Springfield here or they didn't, it's as simple as that."

"And shall I assume Mr. Springfield has been contacted." Ken asked.

Mark pursed his lips and offered. "Well, Mr. Springfield met with an unfortunate accident and has passed."

"I'm so sorry to hear that. But I personally don't remember the meeting or know anything about it." Ken lowered his voice and added, "and unfortunately, Lawrence is hmm… missing."

# 42

"Missing!?" Mark asked excitedly, feigning just hearing the information. Leaning forward in his chair he asked eagerly. "How long?"

"It's been about six days. We even called the police."

"And his family?" Mark inquired.

"Lawrence has no family."

Mark sat back again and quipped, "Now this is a predicament." He thought of his next move and stalled with "I was hoping to help him go through the records." Then suddenly he heard a voice from the adjacent cubicle.

"It was ever since the woman!"

The comment came from one of Lawrence's co-workers from the next cubicle over and it was one that had caused Mark's very being to go on alert. He laughed and calmly asked. "There's a woman involved?"

"Well, we don't know for sure." Ken added, "and I'm quite sure that Malcom here has no interest in our problems." He concluded, directing his voice over the dividing wall.

"Yeah, but if he saw the pictures I took, I bet he would feel differently." The voice laughed back.

*A picture* Mark screamed to himself. The next thing he knew, a man was peering over their dividing wall. "It does sound intriguing, like a spy novel." Mark jested, and then, he played a card. "I assume you took her picture because she wasn't hard to look at." Mark said with a sly grin.

"Wasn't hard to look at!" shot an enthusiastic reply. "Just a minute." The visitor disappeared then suddenly reappeared holding a phone. After a few seconds, he turned the phone towards Mark and said. "I think the whole place went bonkers when she strutted in."

Mark viewed the picture and let out a low whistle. "Wow! She's smoking hot." Instantly, Mark recognized the woman that had tried to kill him.

"Here, swipe right. The first picture I took, as you can see is from behind." He shot Mark an evil grin, laughed and continued with. "This one she was looking right at us but more so at a loud bang caused by maintenance dropping a tool box. I don't think she even knew we took it," he laughed.

*It's a damn good thing, or you'd be dead,* Mark thought.

"Oh, and this one is a good one of Lawrence." Studying the picture, he added, "Man, she was hot!"

"Anyway, I might talk you into sending that to me?" Mark snickered, flashing his own evil grin.

"See, Ken, Malcom here is just like us." Turning to Mark he offered, "I'll airdrop it to ya."

A few seconds later, Mark accepted the string of pictures. "I can't wait to share these with a few of the guys back home." He quipped rubbing the phone with his hand.

"Well, careful with that, you wouldn't want to start any fires." Both men laughed but it was Ken who broke up their fun.

"Malcom, I'm sorry for the interruption," he said while giving his employee a crossed look. "I can take a look at Lawrence's records and give you a call if I find anything. But if we scheduled a meeting it should be on our office calendar." Ken stood, prompting Mark to follow suit and then pointed him to the door which they had both walked towards. Mark glanced over at the adjacent cubicle intending to offer a quick wave but the admonished employee stayed tucked away.

"Give me until the end of the day and I'll have this figured out." Ken offered.

"Sounds great!" Mark replied as they walked through the door and out into the lobby. "I'll stop back and pick up copies of whatever you find. Let's say, four thirty?"

"Four thirty it is."

"Thanks, Ken, and I'll see myself out." Mark stated then he turned and slowly walked towards the door crossing in front of Jeans desk. As he passed, he turned and said, "Thanks Jean."

"You're welcome Malcom." She replied with a shy grin.

Seeing that Ken had walked back into his office Mark turned back towards Jeans desk and in a hushed voice asked, "Hey, Jean, what's this about a woman?"

Jean shot forward and leaned in on her elbows close to Mark and exclaimed excitedly. "Oh, the woman!"

Mark returned the flirtation with a big smile, leaned in close and offered. "I hear she was very attractive."

"Well, every guy in the place suddenly came out to ask Lawrence a question while the two talked."

"What happened? Do you know if the two of them had met later?"

"No, they left together." Jean pointed towards the front door and continued. "The two of them got into a large black SUV."

"Well, you may have solved the Lawrence problem. He just ran off with a girl." Mark laughed.

After a slight pause, Jean inquired. "How long are in town for, Malcom?"

Mark returned her warm smile. "I guess as long as it takes to settle this little matter, but I'll be back around four. Are you free for dinner?"

With a school girl giggle, she said. "Yes, I'd be happy to join you for dinner. Then maybe dessert back at my place." Her eyes flashed a seductive smile.

"Sounds inviting." Mark beamed while reaching over and squeezing her hand. "I'll see you around four." Then he turned and walked towards the door. As he exited, he glanced over his shoulder and gave her a final smile. Once outside, Mark reached into his pocket and gripped his phone. "I got you!"

\*　　\*　　\*

Mark walked around the corner and located a coffee shop. Once inside he ordered a hot tea and found a table along their back wall. He pulled from his pocket the phone and touched on his photo app and reviewed the pictures that had been sent to him, included were an additional three pictures he had not seen while viewing the earlier set. Although her face had been burned into his memory, he slowly looked at every single picture. Then, suddenly something had seemed familiar, returning to the first picture he studied the surrounding images in the photograph. The picture had been taken from across the lobby with her turned away from the camera. The focus of the picture was her rear-end however, what Mark was interested in was what he had seen through the lobby doors, the black SUV had been sitting alongside the curb. With some obscurity, Mark could tell someone was sitting in the front seat.

With his thumb and forefinger touching the screen, he increased the size of the photo. At the time the photo was taken, the person had been looking away from the building and Mark could only ascertain that it was a male, short in stature or sitting low in the seat. But there was something familiar with whomever it was. He quickly passed to the next picture and with the ability to increase its size studied everything concerning the SUV. This picture had been taken quickly with a slight blur to the image. Mark could see that the woman was looking to her left, off to the right from where the picture had been taken, unaware she was being photographed and he was sure it was the only thing that had saved the photographers life. Unfortunately, the front of the SUV was not visible.

Picture number three told another tale, and he noticed it the first time he had seen it. The photographer was obsessed with her ass. She was turned around and the picture was zoomed in from her waist down. Picture number four was from a side quartering perspective only it was not zoomed in. In this photo, Lawrence Williams appeared to be in mid dialogue with the woman, his finger raised. If a picture spoke volumes, this one had told Mark that Williams appeared upset and since no one was looking at them, he seemed to be in a quiet but heated exchange, however the woman, Tia, seemed unfazed. Mark set his phone down, picked up his cup of tea and while thinking of the front seat passenger wondered, *how do I know you?*

Mark looked up away from his cup and table. And after looking around the establishment to confirm he was not being regarded, he picked up the phone and once again went back to picture number one. As much as he tried, he could not make a mental connection with the front seat passenger so, he moved onto the new set of pictures.

The next photo was taken of the woman's side, from behind Jeans desk. It showed the back of Jean, but cutoff almost everything of the woman except from her chest up, and all of Williams was visible along with a few random people walking across the lobby. The next of the added pictures was from the outside looking into the building. Mark surmised that whoever took the picture had been too embarrassed to do it from inside the building. Then a simple fact occurred to him; her beauty would grant her access almost anywhere, however it was also a weakness. He had been looking at pictures of her for one simple reason, men fantasized about beautiful women. The picture was of her front and Lawrence's back, it was more of the same.

He swept right and viewed the last picture, but what Mark had missed the first time rose to a conscious level. He narrowed his eyes and quickly returned to the previous photo. Clearly visible in the reflection of the lobby door was the front seat passenger and he stared in disbelief at the person he knew and knew well. In that instant, he felt emotionally drained. He started to question his career, people he had trusted over the years. None of it made sense, *how can this be*, he thought. He looked back at his phone and used his fingers to increase the size of the photo, hoping he was mistaken. But he was not. The person he knew came into view even clearer. Mark had started to feel sick.

# 43

Mark thought back to the question he had asked the senator, "Who do you work for?" It was a question he had never gotten a real answer to. Now Mark was looking at someone he had grown to respect. It was painfully clear that if he was with the woman he must be working with Lambert or he was running the show. Mark closed his eyes and shook his head. He felt lost and if he had been given a sheet of paper and told to write down his next move, the page would be blank. For the first time in his career, he felt truly bewildered. Information is power and the person he saw in the glass reflection had most of the power at the disposal of the United States Government. The terse back and forth between him and the senator replayed in his mind. *'That is why I have been trying for the past ten years to figure this out and somehow put a stop to it!'*

*'To what, put a stop to what? More than one secret society, something outside of your Freemasons?'*

*'I - don't - know! I have the notion there's more than one.'*

Mark stared into his cup of tea for a few long minutes. He took a sip and once again looked around the coffee shop studying the patrons to assure he was not being watched. As he did, he thought, *more than one, more than one.* The map that the senator had talked about had started to make sense. He had been tracking historical disasters as if they had been man-made. *Just how crowded was his map,* he wondered. The conversation with Raz was fresh in his mind and his comment, *I can't help but wonder if there are some hidden forces at play. Someone, or perhaps, some entity driving the whole damn thing.* Mark flipped his phone over in his hand and mumbled, "and attacking the Vatican with something that could have been played as a biblical event?" *For what purpose?* He wondered. *Perhaps as if to say, Christianity is evil and blame God, set one religious belief on another.* After taking another sip of his tea he asked himself. *Is this really an attack on a belief or… is it an attack for the sake of an attack? What were they, whoever 'they' are really trying to achieve?* After several long minutes he said aloud "Control!" Mark could now fill in his blank sheet of paper. He sat back and thought about the last handful of days and it all became clear. If the hidden forces were willing to attack a religious institution, they would do anything, kill anyone. It was up to him to find out and stop whatever was coming next. He stood, took the last drink of his tea and tossed the cup into the trash. Lambert was dead, the woman, Tia was a problem. He had hurt her, but he had also underestimated her, he would not do it again.

Mark Springfield was going back to Langley. He needed to confront the person he had seen in the glass reflection.

Mark walked out of the coffee shop with a new purpose. After a quick look around, he had seen a store where he could purchase a prepaid phone. Continuing his scan of the street he had also found a department store that he would visit first.

When Mark walked out of the department store, he held in his hand two hats, one stacked on top of the other. The visible hat was a wide-brimmed, white fedora with a black band, the unseen hat was also a wide-brimmed fedora, the unseen hat was dark green. While he was choosing a hat, he discreetly covered the one he would wear with the white diversionary hat. He would pay for both knowing he would pitch the white one. He knew a hat pulled down low was needed to conceal his identity thwarting any facial recognition software. Next the agent strode directly towards a gas station and walked behind the establishment. Once out of sight he slid the green hat out from under the white fedora then he pinched the white hat's brim like a Frisbee, flung into a dumpster and dropped the dark green hat on his head and pulled it down low over his brow. Mark jogged across the street sporting his new hat with one hand keeping it in place. When he reached the sidewalk, he slowed and nonchalantly scanned the parking lot and across the street looking back at the gas station. Stopping short of the entrance, he fumbled with the carts feigning making a selection while he again took another look around. Once inside Mark located the area that sold prepaid phones and made his purchase, picking up a compliment on his hat while doing so. When he had finished at the counter, he slowly walked thru a number of departments taking time to assume interest in several different items. He worked his way to the front of the store which afforded him a quick exit.

Once outside and away from the store, Mark dialed a number he had used many times before. Only this time, the call would not be friendly. But since his phone had been destroyed over the last few days, he wasn't so sure his newly issued phone would show him as the owner. However, the procedure was routine. He would call and identify himself in a message and the recipient would return the call. On the third ring, surprisingly, the owner of the number answered and Mark started the timer on his watch and braced himself for a verbal confrontation.

"Good morning, Mr. Springfield."

"We need to meet." Mark returned tersely.

After a long pause, "No, I don't think that is a good idea. In fact, if you turn yourself into the local law enforcement, we will get you home."

The comment took Mark by surprise and he thought *turn myself in, get me home, what the hell!* After a few long seconds, he offered, "I know you are involved. With whatever is going on, you are involved."

"And what is it you think you know?"

"I know that you were seated in a black SUV outside of Soledad Energy six days ago. You were with the woman who had attacked me and if you were with her it can only mean one thing."

"And that is," the calm voice asked.

"That you are working with Lambert." Mark shot.

"Speaking of the admiral, there's something you may be able to help us with. She seems to have fallen off the face of the earth. Know anything about that?"

The entire exchange struck Mark as odd. The recipient of the call seemed aloof. It felt as if he were being recorded. He pulled the phone away from his ear and ended the call and checked his watch, *forty-three seconds*, he thought, easily under the two minutes the CIA needed to locate his phone. Looking around the parking lot he thought. *What the hell is going on?* He dropped the cell in the pocket of his overcoat and retrieved his newly purchased phone. Mark had had a knack for numbers and committing them to memory had never been a difficult task. However, the number he had dialed with his newly acquired phone had been used more than he had ever imagined.

"You have reached Senator Erasmo Jones. He is currently unavailable. Please leave your number and a brief message and he will return your call."

"Senator, I have some information for you." Mark ended the call and waited. Thirty seconds later his company phone momentarily buzzed, then buzzed for a second time. He quickly pulled it from his pocket, dropped it on the ground and smashed it with the heel of his shoe. Mark repeatedly brought his foot down on the phone until it was lying in small pieces, assuring that whoever was trying to locate him would hit a brick wall. *Move* he said to himself. Pulling his hat down low he walked briskly across the lot and continued back towards Soledad Energy where he had noticed a hotel two blocks away. When he entered the hotel, he nodded to the front desk clerk and walked across the lobby like he owned the place. He set his briefcase down next to a red chair that was facing the entrance, then strode over to a water container, pulled a paper cup from the stack, filled it with water and returned to the chair. Being inside and away from people afforded him more time to collect his thoughts, but as he thought about his last conversation, his prepaid phone rang. When he looked at the number that appeared on the screen, he pursed his lips and hesitantly answered and then started the timer on his watch. "Hello."

"Sorry it took a few minutes to return your call. I was, let's say, indisposed." Raz laughed.

"I'll cut right to the chase first, no names over this line. Second this number needs to be called at random times, but I need to verify it's you. You told me a story about your mom and dad, convert the months she ended up telling him who she really was into minutes and call this number."

Raz picked up a pencil and jotted the number eight down on a piece of note paper.

"Convert the number of years after your dad had died…"

Raz was quick to the game and said. "I got it." and wrote the number five next to the eight.

"Start now." Mark ended the call and looked at his watch, twenty-nine seconds was displayed.

Eight minutes later, the phone rang. Mark checked the number and answered it.

"What do you have?" Raz asked.

"I'm going to give you a name and I'm only giving it to you in case I get myself killed."

"This means you must trust me."

Mark thought for a second and offered, "I suppose it does. I hope it is not misplaced."

"Go"

"Clifford House." Mark stated solemnly, fighting an unsuspected lump in his throat.

"Jesus Christ, Mark. The director of the CIA? You have got to be shitting me!"

Mark let out a long sigh. "I wish I were. Check your time, start now." Mark ended the call with only twenty seconds on the clock. After ending the call, he looked around the lobby and spied a fruit bowl in the center and considered helping himself to some of its contents, but sitting down felt good. He was mindful of his battered body and tried to stay still when he could.

# 44

The director of the Central Intelligence Agency, Clifford House, had methodically hung up his office phone while tapping on the keys of his cell. The impeccably dressed, short, wiry, bespectacled man, whose hair line was rapidly receding had served two presidents. However, he was one of the Memberships thirteen and had been placed in a position of unprecedented unique knowledge, which for the other global members had meant power. It had taken the Membership since the inception of the CIA to finally sit one of their own as the director. Cliff House had immediately set his roots through the corridors of several agencies as he recruited for the nine compartmental tiers of the pyramid known to the unwitting members as secret societies. Now he had to deal with what he considered a blip on his radar, something or someone that needed attending to. He knew Mark Springfield would not be as easy to control as most since he often worked outside the boundaries of rules and regulations. But the agent was no longer a blip; Cliff knew he was collecting information and had to be stopped.

Sitting on the other side of his desk was one of his agents and he had been giving him a hard stare. Finally, he offered. "I'm sorry, Michael. We have to bring Springfield in."

Mike Hollister sat across from the director of the Central Intelligence Agency with his left leg crossed over his right thigh. He tried to read Cliffs face knowing he had been talking to Mark but, from what he had heard, the conversation seemed cryptic. It didn't sit right but he still returned an even gaze. "Director, Cliff, I'm sure there is an explanation for all of this. Mark's been a loyal agent. I can't imagine he's involved in anything nefarious. I'm sure when he returns, we will get to the bottom of… whatever this is."

The last thing Cliff wanted was for Mark to return. He pointed to the folder that lay on the desk in front of Mike and said, "and that's not enough to convince you? He is not supposed to be working on anything. He is supposed to be home resting."

Mike once again picked up the packet and thumbed through the pages. He pursed his lips, shook his head and uttered. "I've known Mark for a long time. None of this makes sense." Mike went through the folder again and offered, "I know the facial recognition pictures, his phone and the use of the alias credit card is somewhat concerning; however, I don't believe Mark is rouge." Pausing, he added, "Not Mark!" Because of their cryptic communications over the past week, Mike knew his friend had been up to something but he also thought that after Marks hospital ordeal, the meeting with Cliff and the senator it was a thing of the past. But the photos of Mark at the Washington Dulles International Airport were unmistakable and the two from California were concerning. A few long seconds passed when Mike suddenly asked, "Why not take him when he was here? He was just here!"

"We needed him to continue to contact whomever it is he has been working with." Cliff answered.

Mike shook his head, stood and walked over to a large window that overlooked the quad. *This is exactly why Mark wanted to keep me out of it. The less I knew, the better protected I would be. Or he would be.* Mike dismissed his last thought as fast as it had crossed his mind. He would bet his life that Mark Springfield had not gone off the reservation.

Cliff suddenly asked. "Had you been in contact with him before all of this? I'm mean while he was in the Smokies?"

Mike half-expected the question from Cliff. He continued to gaze out of the window knowing he had only seconds to decide whether he should keep what he knew to himself. Looking back at the director, he walked over to his chair, gripped the back with both hands and nodded his head. "As a matter of fact, he did contact me," smiling he continued, "asked if I'd help with some work around his lodge... as he calls it." Mike waved his hand dismissing the call.

Cliff pressed and his seemingly innocent question turned serious. "But nothing regarding his disappearance?" Cliff glanced down at some papers he shuffled around his desk and continued. "I see you made a few calls to him."

Mike recognized what his boss was not only doing but what he had done. A soft interrogation was nothing new, but Cliff went as far as having his call records looked at. Mike had given soft interrogations plenty of times and had been trained to lie his way through them. But what if the director knew what they had talked about. Mike threw the dice and offered. "I guess if you consider plumbing international espionage," he laughed and then continued. "Cliff, I do not know why Mark is in California. Yes, he is supposed to be home resting, but we both know Mark and resting is not one of his strong points."

"But staying hidden is."

"You think he is hiding?"

"We don't have anything on him after he left this coffee shop." Cliff picked up a picture and tossed it to the other side of his desk. Then he added. "And then before that, there's this one from Soledad Energy."

Mike picked up both pictures and studied them. There was no mistaking Mark in the photographs. His image was clear as he approached the front doors of the building carrying his briefcase. He was glad Cliff couldn't read his mind. "I just don't know," he retorted.

Cliff nodded his head, stood and pointed Mike towards the door. A few feet from the door, Cliff stopped and looked at Mike. "If you hear anything," Cliff paused and then continued, "and I mean anything, be sure to let me know. Call me directly."

Mike nodded, reached out and shook Cliffs hand. "If Mark calls me, you'll be the first to know." With a dip of his head he concluded. "Director, it's always a pleasure."

Patting Mike on the back, he ended with. "Thank you, Michael. We just need to put this to bed."

Mike walked away from Cliffs office hoping his friend would not call. He too wanted to know what the hell was going on but not in a million years would he believe Mark was up to no good.

Cliff settled back into his desk and slid open his top desk drawer. Lying inside was a phone that indicated a message was waiting. After removing it from the drawer, he typed in a code that allowed the message to be revealed. *He's flying back to Langley. Take-off approx. 1400.* With a smirk, he thought, *"so, you are coming back for me."* Cliff then looked at the series of clocks on the wall. Pacific Time displayed as 1310. He walked over to one of the safes that stood in the corner of his office and after working the dial, he opened the heavy door and removed a map. He unrolled it across the six-foot conference table and studied it. After jotting down a few notes, he returned the map to the safe.

Cliff picked the phone off his desk, entered his pass code and typed instructions. Then while walking over to his window, he swung his arms behind his back while still holding the phone. He considered what he was about to do and wondered if it would stop Springfield. *It's just another life* he thought, *it was worth the risk*. He pressed send.

# 45

Five minutes later Marks cell buzzed. After glancing at the number, he started the timer and pressed his phone icon.

"What else?" Raz quickly asked.

"Have the ladies pick me up where they dropped me off. I need to get back to my office." After a few seconds, Mark asked. "Can that be arranged?"

"Not only arranged, they never left. I had them hang out for a bit."

"We'll talk." Mark ended the call, flipped up his wrist and looked at his watch. A thin grin grew when he read the time, thirteen seconds.

Jacklyn and Diane flanked the boarding ladder of their Gulfstream as was routine when they greeted guests of Maggie or the Senator. However, Jacklyn felt uncomfortable as she watched Mark approached. When he was close, she turned towards him. "Welcome back, Mr. Springfield."

He stopped short of the ladder and offered. "Thank you for waiting."

Diane pointed up the ladder and said. "Ready when you are!"

Mark nodded and strode briskly up and into the Gulfstream taking a seat and removing his hat. Tossing his briefcase on the couch reminded him of using it not long ago. A few minutes went by and he watched Jacklyn enter the aircraft shortly followed by Diane. Both had given him a friendly nod, turned and walked into the cockpit.

Diane pulled the door closed and locked it. When Jacklyn had given her a raised eyebrow she said. "Let him sit by himself for a while."

Jacklyn returned her smile and pulled out the checklist. Fifteen minutes later, they had received clearance to taxi to the active runway. After the engine run-up, flight control check and clearance from the tower Jacklyn nudged the jet onto the active runway and waited. Four minutes later, they were airborne.

After leveling off at twenty thousand feet, Jacklyn stated with a nod "I have us all set for Dulles."

"Great!" Diane said while reaching into her side pocket.

Jacklyn looked out of the left side of the aircraft and started a scan but as she turned to the right, something odd caught her attention in her periphery. She quickly looked over, only to see Diane pointing a gun at her. Her face instantly twisted into a horrified question. "Dia—"

Diane mouthed the words "I'm sorry." Before Jacklyn had finished her name, she pressed the trigger.

The nine-millimeter slug ripped through Jacklyn's chest and lodged into her seat back. The force of the bullet slammed her back into the chair then pitched her forward into the harness. Looking at Diane she tried to speak, but words would never pass over her lips again. She tried raising her arm only to have it fall to her side. The shock on her face lingered until the life in her eyes faded away.

Because of Diane's headset, the noise was muffed, however, Mark had heard the loud pop and instantly thought *gunshot.* "Mr. Springfield, we have a slight problem and need to make a deviation. Our pilot is looking for a place to put us down." Diane announced seconds later over an unseen speaker.

Mark looked out of the left window wondering what had made the popping sound. The calmness in Diane's voice reassured him that the two former F-18 pilots had it under control. He watched the wing rise into the clear blue sky and the jet make a slow turn to the right. When the wings leveled-off Mark had noticed the aircraft in a slight descent, leveling off minutes later. Calmly sitting back, he looked out of the window at the passing countryside. A short time later, an odor had caught his attention. He turned his head into the aisle and again caught a whiff of a familiar smell. It was faint and hardly recognizable and then, circulating in the ventilation system a more aromatic odor tickled his senses. Gunpowder flashed in his mind. Mark looked up and sniffed the vent above his head. There was no mistake that what he had smelled was gunpowder and what he had heard was indeed a gunshot. He feared for Jacklyn.

He stood and walked towards the cockpit. When he arrived, he reached out and tried to open the door. Not having any luck, he sharply tapped on it with his knuckle and offered. "Do you ladies need any help?" Not getting an answer Mark stepped back and looked the door over. It appeared to be designed to slide into the pilot side bulkhead, with a single heavy duty, flush-mounted latch. Mark leaned against the door and gave it a hard nudge with his shoulder only to verify what he had thought. It was solid. As Mark walked back through the galley, he noticed a black phone hanging on the wall. After picking up the receiver he punched the button marked cockpit and waited. After it had buzzed five times, he pulled the phone from his ear, looked at it, pursed his lips and hung it up.

Mark set his briefcase on a small table in front of the chair he had been sitting in and thought, *who the hell can I trust?* Removing three of the six magazines, he slipped them into his pockets, including the two that had already hung on his left waistband in a leather carrier. He had seventy-nine rounds at his disposal. Mark sat down, removed his Glock, checked it, laid it in his lap and waited.

Thirty minutes later when Mark had felt the jet start to descend, he looked out of the window and studied the terrain. It was clear, he was being abducted. When he was sure they were under ten thousand feet he pointed the pistol at a window across the aisle and pressed the trigger. The first jacketed hollow point smashed into the plexiglas causing it to shatter, the following four rounds had cause it to completely blow out. Mark hunched down, took careful aim and sent four additional rounds into the engine that was mounted to the right side of the tail. Seconds later, a loud bang followed by a powerful vibration shook the plane. It felt like someone was pounding on the outside with a sledgehammer. Mark tried to make it to his seat but was knocked to the floor when the turbofan came apart. Moments later, the inside of the Gulfstream lit up when a fire ball engulfed the rear of the plane. A sharp dive to the right caused Mark to grab the base of the seat with both hands. While fighting the g-force, he ran his thick arm through and around the main aluminum support while his feet floated freely above the chair. With gritted teeth and locked hands, the agent waited for the pilot to regain control. No sooner had the thought occurred that he fought to turn his head towards an unusual sound and when he did, bellowing white smoke was seen streaking from the destroyed engine. Mark was relieved to also see chunks of white fire retardant mixed in with the smoke.

Diane had just ended her radio call when all hell broke loose. Immediately following what had sounded like an explosion, her instrument panel lit up like a Christmas tree. Every warning light for her starboard engine flashed red. The secondary hydraulic pressure and electrical system gauges both dropped to zero while amber warning lights flashed below them. An unseen voice repeated, *fire, starboard engine, activate fire suppression system.* Diane quickly reached over her head, grabbed the red fire suppressions lever and pulled it forward then quickly killed the fuel flow and electrical power. The stricken jet lurched over to the right and started a slow descent. She pushed the nose over to build airspeed while tuning her radio to the emergency frequency. "Mayday, mayday, Mayday this is Gulfstream zero five eight Kilo, altitude going through nine'r thousand feet, heading two seven zero, approximately thirty miles north of Palm Springs. I have experienced an engine failure and I am declaring an emergency."

"Gulfstream zero fifty-eight Kilo, this is center, squawk seven seven zero zero and ident. Are you able to maintain altitude?"

Diane leveled her jet at eight thousand feet, trimmed the aircraft to fly on one engine, and as instructed tuned her transponder and pushed the identification button so she was seen on radar as having an emergency. Then she pulled out the emergency checklist to assure she had not missed anything.

"Center, this is Delta Heavy. We see that business jet trailing white smoke passing underneath us. The aircraft appears to be holding straight and level."

"Roger Delta Heavy."

Diane had heard the exchange between the airliner and Center and once she had her jet under control, chimed in. "Center this is Gulfstream zero fifty-eight Kilo that's affirmative, I am able to maintain altitude. What do you have for me?"

"Fifty-eight Kilo, stand-by."

Diane quickly switched her radio over and buzzed the phone Mark had used earlier.

The noise from the blown out window did not stop Mark from seeing the flashing red light on the base of the phone, he unlatched his seatbelt, and took the few steps needed to reach the handset. He picked it up and pressed it to his ear.

"What have you done?" Diane spat.

In a deep, even tone Mark answered. "Take control."

# 46

The plan was to bring the jet down on his own terms. Outside of that, he was going to wing it. He returned the handset to its cradle and walked to the rear of the fuselage, looking for an emergency exit. Knowing that wherever they would land, rescue vehicles would swarm the aircraft. It would provide the perfect opportunity to escape whatever fate he would have been flown into. He walked into the aft stateroom. Not finding an exit he opened the door to the restroom, and pushed on panels looking for a hidden door. Not finding one he realized the only way out was through the emergency exit windows he had already located over the wings. Suddenly, Mark felt a sharp decrease in the jets air speed and held tight to the back of a seat while it banked left. Quickly he returned to the mid cabin and peered through the windows. There was no mistaking where they were being diverted to; Las Vegas, Nevada spread out before him. The pulsating whine from the port engine told him that Diane was preoccupied working the throttle to keep the jet from falling out from under them.

Another quick glance out of the window and Mark surmised that with the speed and descent rate they would be on the ground in roughly twenty minutes. Looking over at the airport, he could see flashing lights lining what he assumed was the runway, but as the jet crossed onto the center line, he lost sight of the rescue vehicles.

Mark grabbed one of the remaining magazines from his briefcase and swapped it with the partially depleted one in his Glock, then he returned to his seat, wrapped the seat belt around himself, latched it, and pulled it tight.

\*     \*     \*

Diane France entered the naval academy soon after she had graduated high school. The 4.2 grade point average, high SAT scores, and a glowing recommendation from her state senator had all guaranteed her a spot in the naval academy. Her focus was to become a Naval aviator. Since the first time she had flown in an airplane, she had dreamed of becoming a pilot. The flight in the Cessna 172 had been a birthday gift from her dad in which she had sat on his lap in the front seat. The instruments, controls, switches and knobs fascinated her and the passion solidified when the pilot turned the airplane over for her to 'drive it around the sky' as her dad would retell the story to his friends.

Diane had worked during her high school years to pay for flight lessons. She soloed at only ten hours of instruction and passed her flight test to achieve her license at exactly the required forty-hour mark. At the encouragement of her parents, she had set herself up to enter the naval academy and excelled in every aspect of her schooling, which had caught the attention of the school's Commandant, Vice Admiral Calkins. Of the few military persons of the Membership, Calkins was the most senior. He, as well as the previous forty-four school Commandants, starting from Lincolns assassination in 1865, had been part of the Membership. They had been placed perfectly to watch students from not only the United States but from around the world. Setting the roots throughout the pyramid and watching them grow had been well established by the Membership and Diane had been easy to turn. She had earned her wings and had flown in several conflicts. However, she had started to feel despondent with the ever-growing rules, regulation and political correctness that had started to plague the armed forces.

Eight years into her commission and using a training flight as a cover, she had borrowed an F-18 and flew to a military base located close to her family to attend her mother's birthday celebration. It had been a ruse that was uncovered by her commanding officer. Watching her career closely, Vice Admiral Calkins secretly intervened and the incident was quietly dismissed. Until what appeared to be a chance meeting, Diane had no idea why the incident had suddenly disappeared. However, when she had pulled into a gas station, her guardian angel was revealed. She had been followed by a black 1966 convertible Mustang that had slowly rolled to a stop next to the pump she had been using. Instantly the car had caught her attention and she was happy to offer her appreciation. "Very nice! she said.

Calkins finished carefully inserting the fuel nozzle and replied with a grin. "This old thing!"

"This old thing?" she laughed. "Looks like it just rolled off the showroom floor."

"Thanks!"

After looking it over she asked, "sixty-five?"

"Pretty close young lady, she's a sixty-six. Hi, I'm Brian Calkins." He said with an outstretched arm.

Diane retuned a big smile. "Diane France."

Calkins retuned her smile and said, "You're Eiffel."

Diane shot him a guarded look. "You know my call sign?" He was easily twenty years her senior, but there was a familiarity about him.

"Maybe I should tell you who I am. Vice Admiral Calkins at your service. You might remember me as the commandant at the academy."

Diane studied him for a moment and nodded her head then asked. "Have we met, Admiral?"

"No, we have not, but I know of you," moving in close he offered, "I also know you had gotten into a little trouble a couple of months back."

"Admiral, I—"

Calkins raised his hand and stopped her. "Diane, there's a steakhouse about two miles from here. I'd like to buy you dinner."

After a long pause she started. "I don't thi—"

"It's a very public place," he smiled.

"I was going to say," she quipped pointing at the mustang, "I don't think you should drive that beauty without me."

The dinner Diane had had with the Admiral seemed like so long ago. And it was fortunate for the Membership that she had found employment with Maggie's endangered bird organization. The Membership used it as a way to keep an eye on the Senator. And killing came with huge bonuses.

Now, Diane fought the stricken jet, and even though the jet had been designed to fly on one engine, it had taken all of her concentration to bring it in. She was not worried about the dead body next to her. She knew that too would be taken care of. Her saving grace was that Las Vegas was only a one-and-a-half-hour flight west of the intended airport in Crownpoint, New Mexico. Cliff House's text had instructed Diane to fly the agent to the facility know as *Navajo*. The top secret government facility consists of a landing strip, and three windowless buildings that were both fenced and guarded. Shortly after receiving the divert instruction from flight service, she radioed Cliff's pilot and informed him of the change. Then she throttled back and flew the jet dangerously close to its stall speed, giving them time to meet her in Vegas.

In Marks mind's eye he had already planned his escape. As soon as the wheels touched down, he would remove the emergency exit window on the right side of the plane. When the plane slowed, he would exit and slide off the wing onto the ground. The second the wheels hit the runway his plan came to life. However, since the Gulfstream was still moving when Mark had slid from the wing, he hit the ground hard, lost his footing and fell hard on his butt jarring his bruised body. He rolled to his knees and pushed himself up to a standing position.

The instant Mark had removed the window exit the indication illuminated on the instrument panel and Diane knew Mark had left the aircraft. She quickly radioed Cliffs pilot so he could relay that the agent was on the run.

But Cliff did not require a call from Diane. From his vantage point he had seen clearly that Springfield had left the aircraft. He watched him drop down from the wing and sprint across the runway towards the terminal. He turned to the two men who were standing next to him and ordered. "Kill him." Cliff slightly raised his hand and pointed at the jet and uttered to the third man. "Kill her."

Cliff had boarded a C-21 twin engine Learjet out of Andrews Air Force Base shortly after Mike had left his office. With him were three men contracted to support special ops. All three sported black 511 pants, matching shirts, tactical drop leg holsters, M4 carbines with extra thirty-round magazines and Velcroed across their chests in three-inch letters were the words US Marshal. They knew little of the circumstances that had led them to the desert. They had a job to do and were happy to do it. The group had landed in Vegas fifteen minutes before the stricken jet and Cliff watched as the Gulfstream trailed a thin stream of white smoke and touched down between a sea of rescue vehicles.

Both men quickly walked after Mark keeping their M4 rifles held low and pulled tight on the slings that had hung over their shoulders. The fourteen-and-one-half-inch-longbarrels made it easy to maneuver in and around the employees who had gathered to witness the smoldering jet. The two black clad men dressed in US Marshals uniforms moved easily through the parting crowds.

Mark had tried several doors trying to gain access to the terminal. Every one of them were locked and required a key card to open the cyber latch. In his peripheral while looking back at the jet he noticed movement within the crowd. He studied the commotion and noticed two armed men headed straight towards him. Pursing his lips, he withdrew his Glock, held his arm over his eyes and blasted the lock including the surrounding wall. He changed the magazine when his slide locked back and although his ears were ringing, he heard people screaming. Thumbing the slide lock, he continued to shoot the mechanism until the power had been cut to the magnetic locks and the door opened. Mark pulled open the door and started to step through when suddenly the top glass and side wall exploded. Both men fired over top of the crowd with their M4s peppering the door and the surrounding wall with 5.56 x 45 mm rounds. Mark was hit twice and forced forward stumbling into a set a red plastic chairs and the opposing wall. He turned and his large frame slid down so hard onto a chair that he cracked one of its legs. He raised his Glock and waited.

Both men, after exhausting their thirty-round magazines, yelled to the crowd, "US Marshals," while dropping their empties to the ground, inserting loaded ones and running the charging lever. Working as a team, one approached the door while the other studied the crowd, both listening to the sirens headed in their direction.

Marks body burned, and through gritted teeth took in deep breaths. He pulled a magazine from his pouch and held it in his left hand while he waited for them to come through the door, counting on their training to bring them through in a certain way.

Seconds felt like hours, then creeping into view was the muzzle of the M4, it was pointing at the ground then snapped up to a firing position. Mark held his fire until more of the rifle came into view. Then he let loose a volley of forty-caliber rounds into the rifle's frame, ejected the depleted magazine, inserted the one he had held in his hand, and continued to fire. The volley worked. The M4 was pounded into an inoperable state and so were two fingers of the shooters left hand.

The shooter let his rifle drop and quickly withdrew his handgun and rushed the doorway. Mark had been in the middle of swapping out magazines when his adversary stepped through the door.

There were only feet between them, so he threw the empty magazine at him causing him to instinctively bat it away, which had given Mark time to insert a new one and fire. Forgoing any body armor, he concentrated his rounds at the shooter's head. The first round missed; however, the ensuing three rounds found their mark and the one through the eye stopped the fight. The impact from the rounds pushed the shooter back, causing him to slump down into the door frame. Mark raised his Glock, stepped over the body, walked outside, and fired. Within seconds, the next shooter had met the same fate. Kneeling down, Mark relieved the shooter of his M4 and a spare magazine. However, when he stood, he let the carbine fall to his side. Then he reached into his pocket and removed his identification. Raising and opening his left hand, he flipped his billfold open and waited. Minutes later, the sirens he had heard earlier descended on him. Mark quickly counted the officers and made a mental note of the ones with the AR-15s.

"Drop your weapon!" Came a shouted command.

"Not happening." Mark countered. "I'm CIA. I need to talk to your commander."

"I said, 'drop your weapon!'"

"Listen, don't fuck with me. I don't have time for this shit!" He shook his ID and said, "Here, take this."

The officer pulled his gun in close to his body, approached Mark and took his ID. After he had stepped back, he raised the billfold and compared the picture to the man standing in front of him. Then lifted his radio and spoke into it.

Over the sea of patrol cars, Mark had seen an unmarked car slowly lurch to a stop. A woman driver, accompanied by a male passenger, walked towards the officer holding the ID.

The officer handed it to her and, even though the word CIA had been printed in bold letters, he commented, "CIA."

Mark watched the male passenger give the officer a raised eyebrow.

She looked at the ID and then handed it the male passenger who withdrew a small flashlight, tilted the ID and flashed it over Marks picture and said. "Looks legit." Then turned off his light and returned it to its pouch.

Handing the ID back to Mark he said. "Agent Springfield, I'm Gene Winchester. This is Aileen McKinney." He offered pointing to the driver.

"Before we go any further," Mark started, "there are eleven officers pointing guns at me, three are holding

ARs. Would you turn around and verify you know every one of them."

Gene turned and scanned his men. Turning back to Mark he nodded his head, "They all belong to me." Looking down at the body Mark was standing over he asked, "and what do we have here?"

"Gene, we need to get on that jet and detain the pilot."

Winchester looked back at the jet then over at McKinney, and said. "We were just on the jet. We have two dead female pilots."

"Shit. That means there's another one. By the way, your men are still holding me at gunpoint."

Winchester nodded his head and confirmed, "Yes, they are, but let's figure this out, so we don't get ahead of ourselves." He said pointing at the two dead bodies.

"They look the part, but my guess is you won't find any real identification on them." Mark said in a suggestive tone.

Gene pointed to the dead man and said to Aileen, "Check'em."

While Aileen checked the pockets, Gene focused on Mark's bloody arm and side and inquired. "Agent, I'm sure you're aware that you've been shot." Pausing, he asked, "Do you need an ambulance?"

Mark offered a thin grin and said, "Yeah, I'm afraid to look, but since I'm still standing, I thought I'd wait."

Gene returned a painful look.

Aileen finished her pat down and walked over to her boss and showed him what she had found, two silver-colored, blue eagle-topped metal shields, and their wallets. It was what she didn't find that had caused Winchester to turn towards his men and wave their guns down. He looked at Mark and said, "The badges?"

"The current Marshal badge is gold, a five-point star set inside a circle." Mark answered.

"These are Patty Hearst badges." Gene offered.

Aileen shot her boss a questioning look.

He laughed and said. "In the mid-seventies, Patty Hearst was front page news. The deputies were photographed with her so often that their badges had won their own nickname." He paused, and then continued, "problem is, they are outdated." He turned towards his men and ordered, "Get these guys out of here." Motioning toward Mark he continued, "Mr. Springfield, walk with me."

After walking away from the group Mark asked. "How did you know?"

"Know?"

Mark shot Gene a raised eyebrow and said, "My ID, you knew how to check it."

Glancing over his shoulder and then back at Mark he answered "The reversed picture, two layers down. I'm a retired navy master chief. I worked intel. Over my thirty-two-year career I've learned a few things." He put his hand on Marks shoulder and asked, "now, do you mind telling me what the hell is going on at my airport?"

Mark shook his head and said sincerely. "I can't, but I'm guessing you have at least one more US Marshal running around here. And Gene." Mark said nodding towards the smoldering plane. "I need to get back on that jet."

"Back on the jet?" Gene asked inquisitively.

"That's a story for another time. May I?"

"Like my officer said, you're CIA." Gene kidded.

Nodding, Mark turned towards the jet and started the walk that he knew would break his heart.

Mark approached the cordoned-off gulfstream and was met by two airport police. "Agent Springfield?" one of the men asked.

Mark held up his ID, showing it to both men.

"Boss radioed you were headed this way. He wanted us to warn you that it's not pretty in there."

Mark nodded and pointed to the ladder he was all too familiar with. After receiving a nod from the officers, he slowly climbed the steps stopping after the second one to catch his breath. However, before going any higher, he pulled up his M4, clicked off the safety, turned to the guards and said. "Don't let anyone else on." After stepping through the door, he looked right, left and then took the torturous steps towards the cockpit. Diane was first to come into view. Her body was slumped to the right, resting in her harness. Blood, bone and brain matter had been splattered over the entire right side of the cockpit, including on the windshield. Mark slowly looked to his left knowing what he would find. Jacklyn had been shot in the chest and leaned back into her seat. Mark knelt down, picked up her ashen hand and held it.

After a few minutes, he reached up with two fingers and closed her eyes.

Mark walked back to the mid cabin and sat down. Suddenly, with mounting frustration, he leaned forward and slammed the table with his thick fist, stood and walked down the jet's stairs. One of the guards broke his concentration.

"Are they with you?" One said pointing at a non-descript jet. "The tower is trying to get them to stop but they keep harping about the US Marshal service."

Mark looked in the direction of the pointed finger and instantly recognized the C-21 Learjet taxiing at an accelerated pace about two hundred feet in front of him. "Shit, no, you don't," he said more to himself. Then jumped down the remaining three steps, stumbling as he landed. His body was hurt and exhausted, but his adrenaline picked him up and pulled him in the direction of the airplane. Mark ran across the tarmac and down a taxi-way in an all-out pursuit of the jet dodging light aircraft and support equipment. He watched the jet turn onto another taxiway and he ran at an angle that would put him ahead of the plane. Five minutes later and exhausted, he stood in front of the plane and raised his M4. The jet lurched to a stop Then moments later, Mark heard the whine of its engines. Looking at the pilot, he shook his head. Suddenly, Cliff House forced his way between the pilots and pointed at Mark who, unfazed by Cliff's appearance, continued to shake his head. The C-21 jolted forward as the engines spun up to full power.

Mark stepped to the right and waited. When the jet passed, he opened fire and concentrated on the engine.

Nothing seemed to happen at first, but then sparks burst into the air followed by a loud shriek. Black smoke engulfed the Lear while hydraulic fluid, oil, and gas poured onto the taxiway.

Thirty rounds later, the M4 fell silent, smoke poured from its short barrel. The silence only lasted seconds. Mark ejected the spent magazine, inserted his spare, ran the charging lever, and took full advantage of the leaking gas. He continued to fire until the first explosion.

The heat from the engine coming apart blasted his face like a furnace. He twisted away from the flash and covered his face and head with his arms. The second explosion knocked him to the ground. He pushed himself up to a sitting position and continued to fire until pressing the trigger had no effect. Suddenly from under the belly of the plane, Mark had seen fire falling to the ground. "Shit, the fuel tanks." He stood, ditched the M4 and ran from the plane as hard as his broken body would allow.

The force from the jet's fuel tank explosion blew Mark to the ground. Crawling for a few feet, he covered his head with his arms as another explosion ripped through the plane, throwing burning debris all around him. Mark pushed himself up, found his balance, and continued to run.

When Mark was far enough away, he slowed to a walk and turned back towards the burning jet and stopped.

The putrid smell of fuel and oil filled the air. He watched it burn until the rescue vehicles descended on the doomed plane.

Fishing around in his pocket, he retrieved his phone and placed a call. After two rings, Raz answered, sounding concerned. "Mark!"

"Your pilots are dead. Diane was turned; she killed Jacklyn in route."

"Jesus Christ!" Raz blurted, trying to process what he had just been told. "Mark, I...I."

"Senator...I'm in." Mark paused, looked back at the Gulfstream, and fighting the lump in his throat, added, "Let's stop the son of a bitches."

THE END

9 781733 977210